THE BLINDSIDE

Ann Evans

To Lynette
I hope you enjoy this.
Best wishes
Ann Evans

Copyright Ann Evans 2024

Ann Evans has asserted her right to be
identified as the author of this work in
accordance with the
Copyright, Designs and Patents Act 1988.

All characters and events in this publication
are fictitious,
and any resemblance to real persons,
living or dead,
is purely coincidental.

All Rights Reserved.

No part of this publication may be used
or reproduced, stored in a retrieval system, or
transmitted, in any form or by any means
electronic, mechanical, photocopying,
recording or otherwise
without the prior permission of the author.

This is my third novel. It has been seven years in the
making because I had writer's block.
It is set in a fictional town, Chesbury,
Somewhere in the North East of England.
It is also partly set in my childhood stamping-ground along
the Mawddach Estuary in North West Wales.

When Netty is the victim of rape at the
age of seventeen, she finds herself
the mother of a mixed-race child.
At the behest of her elder sister Pauline, she invents a
husband who has been killed in an accident,
and raises her son in the belief that his father is dead.
However, a chance encounter over thirty years later
between Pauline and the child's father, opens his eyes
to the deception that has cost him his only son.

Tony immediately abandons his life, and sets out to find
his son, and the woman who concealed
his very existence, with revenge on his mind.

The novel includes a cameo appearance
by Michael and Rachel Fenton,
the parents of Mickey
in The Foundling.

Also by Ann Evans

The Foundling.

When Mariana discovers a tiny baby boy abandoned in the park, she believes him to be
the answer to all her prayers.
However, something is wrong with Danny,
and her actions will have far-reaching
and tragic consequences, as a
tangled web of secrets and lies unravels.

The Legacy

When artist Adam and his wife Maggie move into the big white house on the hill overlooking the bay, they can scarcely believe their luck.
A drawing of a mystery girl, however, is about to change their lives forever, and those of many other people.
Who is she, and what does she want from them?

An intriguing tale of mystery, romance,
and the supernatural.

ONE: LAUREN. (December 8ᵗʰ 2005)

Lauren shivered, drawing her oversized cashmere coat around her and tugging her cloche hat firmly down over her ears as she set off on the short walk home. The wind snatched the heavy swing door with its brass handle from her hand and slammed it back behind her, where it rocked violently to and fro on its hinges, the warm convivial sounds of the King's Head bar ebbing and flowing with its motion. Lauren's black silk trousers clung to her legs in an icy grip and she wished she had thought of wearing woolen tights underneath. Perhaps, she thought ruefully, she should have accepted Mark's offer of a lift after all, but she had worried that there may be strings attached, at least in his mind. Mark was ok, she thought grudgingly, but not really her type, and he could really do with losing some of his arrogance along with a couple of stone. *How can you be practically obese, yet still think you're God's gift?* she wondered. She had never understood it, but it seemed to be a man thing; women are much more self-deprecating. Lauren was tall and slender - rather too slender in her opinion. She had a heart-shaped face, with prominent cheekbones and an aquiline nose. Her mouth was a thin line with a high cupid's bow drawn down sharply at the corners giving her a permanently melancholy look emphasized by her large pale emerald eyes. Her hair was a distinct shade of light auburn that she herself described irreverently as 'ginger tom'. It was collar length, with a wispy fringe that reached her eyebrows. She once thought of dyeing it, but a hairdresser friend told her that ginger hair was unpredictable when dyed, and anyway, she was fortunate in that it was unlikely to turn grey for a few more years at least. She would have dearly loved to lose a couple of inches in height, gain a few pounds in weight, and have the sort of skin that tanned nicely in the summer, instead of breaking out in freckles on her face and arms while her legs remained permanently milk-bottle white.

Leaving the sounds of music and laughter behind her she hastened along the deserted street. By now the rain had stopped, and shimmering puddles of water lay on the lamp-lit pavements, stirred into rippled molten gold by the wind. Deep shadows draped themselves seductively within doorways and around the tall brick pillars hung with heavy wrought-iron gates, as she passed down the rather grandly named Madison Avenue. The wind lashed the trees that lined the far side of the road and they swayed and susurrated eerily, their naked arms festooned in coloured lights reaching out towards her in a grotesque invitation to dance. Beyond the trees, the river was swollen and slick behind iron railings to which in summer traders would attach wooden boards displaying their wares to tempt the passing tourists. Badges and fridge magnets depicting local landmarks, key rings, ballpoint pens, and stuffed toys wearing t-shirts bearing the slogan 'I love Chesbury', with the word love superseded by a red heart. Artists would offer to paint or sketch your portrait while you waited. Wearing smocks and berets to fulfil the expectations of the tourists, they imagined themselves on the Paris embankment instead of a small northern cathedral city in England. For seven months of the year this approach to the town was a vibrant eclectic mix of fine art and tourist tat, and even at this late hour would be populated by couples strolling hand in hand or groups of friends returning home from a night out. Tonight, however, in deepest December, the benches that lined the pavement were damp and unoccupied, and the tall elegant guest-houses were shrouded in darkness, their rectangular white 'vacancies' notices in the bay windows illuminated by the streetlights, their Bed and Breakfast signs swinging and complaining with every gust of wind, and only the occasional brightly lit Christmas tree in a window punctuating the gloomy facades.

    The seemingly endless avenue seemed to retreat before her. It never looked this far in daylight. She was tired, her feet ached and she longed for home and a nice cup of tea. At last the bus station came into view, its stands silent and empty of buses. She crossed the road and headed away from the river, slowing down as she began to climb the hill that led to the cobbled street of semi-terraced houses where she lived. Built of mellow brick, they stood in pairs separated by alleyways that were fronted by tall arched wrought-iron gates. Sheltered now from the wind; her footsteps echoed between the houses – click-clack went her heels, and were answered by a softer echo that kept time with them unfailingly. With a slight sense of unease, she glanced over her shoulder. Did something move into the shadow of a doorway lower down the hill? She couldn't be sure, but quickened her pace again. With her breath rasping in her throat now, a sharp pain in her side, and her feet stinging from the effort of climbing the hill in high heels, she tried to walk on the balls of her feet eliminating the clatter of her heels so that she could listen for the sounds behind her. The sound of her own heavy breathing and the pounding of her heart in her ears would have masked an elephant's approach as the gradient and the adrenalin did battle, and the gradient gradually prevailed. Another glance over her shoulder; the shadow seemed closer now. Unease was rapidly escalating towards terror, her throat constricted and her legs now threatening to give way. She fumbled in her pocket and withdrew her mobile phone. Keying in 999, she kept her finger poised over the call button as she half walked, half ran towards home. The road began to swing round to the left and in a few more moments Castle Row would be in sight.

She began to rummage frantically in her handbag for her keys, panic washing over her as they eluded her searching fingers. At last she felt the reassuring tangle of steel that lurked in the corner of her bag, and withdrew the keys, singling out the one that would open her front door. As she approached the house a security light clicked on above her door, its large owl's eyes illuminating the steps and the pavement below them. The gate into the alleyway between her house and the next was ajar. She frowned and peered into the gloom beyond, where neither the wan street light nor the carefully positioned security light penetrated, the latter casting only dark bars of shadow on the wall from the open gate. Suddenly something rose from the shadows and Lauren gave an involuntary startled yelp!

"Charlie! You scared the life out of me," she cried, bending down and scooping up the bundle of fur as she pushed her key into the lock and turned it, throwing a last glance over her shoulder as the door swung open. Further down the street the shadow in another doorway deepened, and she caught a slight movement. The cat struggled free from her grasp as Lauren slammed the door shut, dropped the snick and put the security chain on. Relief washed over her as she leaned against the door to catch her breath while her long-haired tabby friend rubbed ecstatically around her trembling legs, purring loudly. The streetlight outside illuminated the hallway through a window at the side of the door, casting an eerie shadow on the wall from the pot plant on the windowsill. Still uneasy, she pulled down the blind before turning on the hall light. Charlie ran ahead of her to the kitchen at the back of the house where Lauren checked that the back door was also locked. She turned on the outside light and peered through the kitchen window at the back garden. The tall wooden gate that led into the alleyway was closed and bolted, and everything looked normal. The cat peered through the window also, turning anxious amber eyes on Lauren.

"It's ok Charlie, I'm just being a scaredy-cat," laughed Lauren wryly as with slightly trembling fingers she tore the top off a pouch of cat food from a box on the counter and squeezed the contents into a fish-shaped bowl, setting it down on the floor next to the back door. Charlie tucked into his meal with gusto as Lauren took off her coat and hat and hung them on one of the ornamental cast-iron pegs that lined the wall between the kitchen and the lounge. Entering the lounge, she moved quickly over to the bay window and drew the heavy curtains across, shutting out the night before turning the dimmer switch that illuminated the alcoves on either side of the rather grand and original fireplace. Its graceful arched grate contained a gas fire that sprung into life at the touch of a button and was almost indistinguishable from the real thing except for the sound it made. The gas fire was so much more practical than an open fire but the designer in Lauren wondered idly whether anyone would ever invent one that also crackled, spat and sang. When her grandmother lived there, there was always a fire roaring in the grate, and she had happy memories of toasting bread or crumpets over the glowing coals and slathering them with melted butter from a china dish on the hearth. The room was simply furnished, with two matching sofas in soft grey twill, draped with faux-fur throws and strewn with brightly coloured kilim cushions. A large rather battered wooden chest bound with metal served as a coffee table, and in the corner behind one of the sofas stood a small octagonal table made from ebony on which stood an enormous ceramic table lamp with an elaborate art deco style fringed and beaded shade. The wooden chest, the table and the lamp had all belonged to her grandmother. The alcoves still had the original built-in cupboards that used to be painted but now were stripped and waxed. They housed her television and DVD player on one side, and her stereo on the other. Above them was shelving containing books, photographs, and ornaments. Lauren turned on the stereo and kicked off her shoes, curling her long legs under her on the sofa, drawing the throw over them and tucking it around her feet as the gentle tones of Dido filled the room. Charlie climbed up and settled in the crook of her arm, purring fiercely and kneading ecstatically. Lauren closed her eyes, lay back against the cushions and relaxed.

Almost an hour later she came to with a start. The CD had finished, and Charlie had moved to sleep in his customary place on the opposite sofa. She glanced at her watch. It was one-thirty in the morning.

"Damn!" she muttered. She must get to bed, but it would be hard to sleep now, and she had an early start in the morning. Her legs were stiff and she winced as she rose and turned off the gas fire and the stereo. Rain was lashing against the window now and the thought of her warm bed with its downy duvet was inviting. Wearily, she climbed the narrow stairway using the handrail to pull herself up. At the top of the stairs the landing on the right led to her bedroom at the front of the house. To the left, it doubled back to a second smaller bedroom that overlooked the back garden, and a small but well-appointed bathroom that lay above the kitchen. In her grandmother's day the bathroom had been cold and draughty, split in two with the toilet separate, but now it was warm and elegant with a roll-top bath with shower over, a low-level toilet and a large basin set into an antique stripped pine cupboard with an enormous extravagantly ornate mirror surrounded by lights above. Beside the basin was a tall heated chrome towel rail hung with an array of pristine white towels. Lauren took a bottle of cleanser from the shelf above the washbasin, and a cotton wool pad from a glass jar and carefully removed her makeup. Afterwards, she splashed her face with toner and cleaned her teeth before making her way to the bedroom.

Passing the spare bedroom, she noticed a draught coming from under the door. She opened the door and peered around it into the room. To her surprise, the sash window was slightly raised, accounting for the draught. The curtains were moving gently in the wind and rain had spattered the windowsill. *Strange,* she thought, *I don't remember opening it.* She moved across the room and pushed it firmly shut, sliding the crescent-shaped lock into place. She peered down into the garden, but could see nothing in the darkness. She wiped the windowsill with her sleeve absently. She must have opened the window a couple of days ago when she was dusting. She remembered that it had been a fine sunny day, the rays of sunlight reflecting off the dancing dust motes that rose and filled the air. She must have forgotten to close it. Satisfied with her own reasoning, she turned away, closing the door softly behind her as she left the room.

Her bedroom sported two tall windows overlooking the street. The streetlights illuminated the king-sized bed with the grey velvet throw at the foot that Charlie liked to burrow under to sleep during the day. This room caught the morning sunlight and Lauren, who had always been an early riser, sometimes left the curtains open in summer so that the sunlight flooded across the bed and woke her gently with its warmth. Tonight, she drew them firmly across after glancing up and down the cobbled street.

Living alone had never really bothered Lauren. At forty-nine, she was self-sufficient and resourceful. She was also quite set in her ways and knew she would find it difficult now to share her world with a partner, making the inevitable compromises that marriage involves. Lauren was an only child and quite at home in her own company. She would have liked more pets, but had decided they would be too much of a tie, so Charlie reigned supreme and was spoiled rotten. Lauren didn't have any particularly close friends, although she was never short of someone to go out for a meal or a drink with, and her comfortable guest bedroom was always available to anyone who wished to stay the night. The dining room at the back of the house hadn't seen any social or family gatherings since her grandmother's day. Now, it housed her computer and her sewing machines, the walls were lined with shelves loaded with boxes of the fabric, thread, and notions that were the tools of her trade, and she took her meals at the kitchen table, or in front of the fire on a cushioned lap tray.

Lauren was a seamstress, and for the past seven years had owned a small shop in the local indoor market where she sold the children's clothes she made, and where she took orders for her bespoke couture range that sold for several hundred pounds apiece. She had built a reputation for originality and reliability. Her clothes looked classy, fitted well, and lasted; they were worth the money. Nowadays she had outworkers who made up her designs from the patterns and fabric she supplied, leaving her free to concentrate on the designing and the final fitting. Many of her designs were based on the fashions of the twenties; beaded Flapper dresses in exquisite flimsy fabrics; elaborate evening gowns in rich devoré, crisp moiré and extravagant dupion silks, and lightweight cashmere and linen Duster coats. She made head-dresses too; extravagant creations embellished with feathers and gemstones. The internet had made things easier of late, allowing her to source her materials and ideas without having to leave the house, although she declined to sell through a website, preferring the personal approach. Lauren worked hard, but it was a labour of love and she considered herself to be lucky to be so gifted. She had no formal training and had learned most of her sewing skills from her mother, but with an added natural flair for colour, texture, and style that cannot be taught.

Lauren considered herself a strong, self-sufficient woman. To others, she sometimes seemed aloof.

When she and Ken split up seven years ago, they sold their marital home of twenty years and Lauren returned to live with her parents, investing her share of the proceeds in professional quality sewing equipment, her first consignment of fabric, and her first six months' rent on the shop. Three years later, her grandmother died and left her the house. She and her father, a retired builder, worked together to renovate it to Lauren's specifications, carefully retaining its features and the intimate feel that she loved. She had been living there now for nearly two years.

She turned on her electric blanket and undressed, carefully folding her black silk trousers and placing them on the bed. Her velvet top was soft and darkest green like the heart of a pine forest. Its cowl neck and batwing sleeves draped softly over her slight frame, and a beaded band sat below her hips drawing it in to show off her long slim legs. She smiled with satisfaction as she opened the door of the large French armoire and hung her outfit in place alongside her other creations. As always, her clothes had drawn compliments from her companions. They were different, unique, as indeed was she. She donned the long pale jade satin nightdress from under her pillow and climbed into bed. Within minutes she was fast asleep.

Dawn broke the next day dark, damp, and dreary, but the wind had dropped and the rain had ceased, albeit temporarily. Lauren reluctantly slid out of bed, showered, and dressed in jeans and a warm Aran sweater. Checking out the bread bin, she found only a stale crust. She wrinkled her nose and decided to head down to town to get some fresh bread from the artisan baker's on the corner near the railway station. Charlie was sitting by the back door. He turned enquiring eyes on Lauren, who opened the door and watched him amble sinuously down the garden to stretch and sharpen his claws on the apple tree in the corner. Breaking the offending crust into small pieces, she held it under the tap, then threw it out onto the grass for the birds. The garden was long and narrow, bordered by shrubs and flower beds and enclosed by a high red brick wall. Near the kitchen door a tall wooden gate led to the alleyway where Lauren and her neighbour on the opposite side kept their wheelie bins. For most of the week, the wrought iron gate across the entrance to the alley was kept locked, except on Thursdays when it was left open for the bin men. Lately, Lauren had taken to checking it daily since she knew that her neighbour was inclined to forget to lock it behind him. At one time she wouldn't have given it a thought, but she had developed a heightened sense of vulnerability since the murders had begun.

There had been two in the last twelve months, evenly spaced about six months apart. The victims were women of middle age both of whom had two things in common – namely auburn hair, and green eyes. No wonder she felt nervous, since she fitted the brief. The last one had been back in July, and if the pattern was to be maintained, another was due any day now. Lauren had never been inclined to be nervous, but recently she had developed the habit of checking and double-checking the windows and doors, since the women had died in their own homes. It worried her that she could have been so careless as to leave that bedroom window open. She kept ladders in her garden shed, and they had proved useful on several occasions. She wondered now, however, if she should get rid of them altogether, despite the substantial padlock that secured the shed door. She chided herself for her paranoia as she set off down the cobbled street to the town to buy her breakfast.

The town was just beginning to wake. People were drifting to work, and a council road sweeper in a high viz jacket gestured with his broom at the litter of the night before with a marked lack of enthusiasm.

"Mornin' Miss Lauren," he greeted her as she hurried down the street, a broad smile illuminating his somewhat dour features.

"Morning Arty," she replied. She had long since given up trying to get him to drop the 'Miss'. Arty was old school.

"Another one last night Miss, just down from your place. It's all over the Herald this morning." The smile never wavered as he delivered the news of the third murder within a year. "Found by a drunk relieving himself in an alley at two o'clock this morning – gave him the fright of his life I'll bet. Just made the earlies, but no details yet."

So close, thought Lauren with a shudder. "Oh, that's awful, even if we were expecting it! I'll admit we'll all sleep a little easier for a while now though. Who was she Arty, did they say?"

"Not been id-d yet as far as I know. Might be something in the later editions."

"Well, whoever she was, it's a dreadful business. I hope they catch him soon. I think I need a cup of coffee after that." She gave him a parting smile and continued on her way as he returned to his sweeping with renewed vigour, whistling tunelessly through his teeth.

Next to the artisan bakers on the corner was a small independent coffee shop. It was open from seven a.m. and by eight-thirty would be packed out with office workers needing a shot of caffeine before facing the hectic monotony of their day, or people on their way to the station who couldn't face the indeterminate muddy beverage served up in the platform café. The aroma of freshly ground coffee wafted towards Lauren as she passed the door on the way to purchase her croissants.

"Morning Jonny," she greeted the baker.

"Morning Lauren, usual is it?" Without waiting for an answer, he chose two golden croissants from a heap on the counter and loaded them into a large brown paper bag.

"I'll have a small sourdough too please, I'm doing the shop today, Bessie's got a touch of the flu; she had to miss the Christmas do last night. It'll do nicely for my lunch with some cheese and olives." Jonny pushed the dark-crusted sourdough loaf into another bag and handed it over the counter as Lauren fished in her purse for a five-pound note.

"Were you out last night then?" he asked, raising an eyebrow. "There was another one of them murders they're saying."

"Yes, I heard. We had a meal at Giorgio's then went on to the King's Head for a couple of drinks, but I didn't stay out late. It was really windy, and I was a bit jumpy walking home alone, but no one else from work lives over my way. It's an awful thing to say, but it's almost a relief there's been another – I'll feel a bit safer now for a few weeks."

"Well, you take care with that hair of yours, that's all I'm sayin'." Jonny frowned at her with concern.

"Oh, I keep it covered when I'm out at night, don't worry!" Lauren retorted with a grin as she gathered up her purchases. "I have a collection of hats."

Coffee and Compliments was warm and welcoming. She ordered an Americano, and sat in a tub chair by the window to watch the early morning world go by. You can tell a great deal about people just by observing them passing by. It was too early for the office workers and too late for the all-nighters who would now be sleeping it off in readiness for the next session. The train to Birmingham was due in ten minutes, and several passengers hurried by, mobile phones in hand, clutching briefcases or trundling suitcases behind them, glancing anxiously at their watches because they should have allowed a little more time for queuing. Others sauntered by casually, having purchased their tickets in advance online, including the first class passengers with their sharp suits and laptop bags. Lauren observed the cut and style of their suits, mentally assigning them designer names and pondering what the wearer's occupation might be – investment banker, lawyer, high end financier – or these days IT whizz-kid designers of computer games for men who refuse to grow up. *Takes allsorts,* mused Lauren; *but they're all anxious not to miss that train!* Suddenly, she spied Mark, crossing the road, heading straight for Coffee and Compliments. *Oh, no!* It was too late; he had evidently spotted her, and she braced herself as he entered, acknowledged her with a brief nod, then made his way to the counter to order. He reappeared a few minutes later with a large caramel latte – *no wonder he's such a podge,* thought Lauren.

"Hey, Lauren. Where did you get to last night? I was going to run you home. You shouldn't be walking home alone; there was another murder last night you know. By the time I got my coat you were gone. Are you ok?"

"Looks that way," Lauren replied somewhat ungraciously. Mark deposited his latte on the table, slopping it into the saucer as he did so, and settled himself down in the chair opposite. *You're welcome,* thought Lauren.

"What brings you in here at this time of the morning then?" he asked, spooning sugar into his latte enthusiastically. He took a serviette from the dispenser on the table, and folding it in four, placed it in his saucer where it soaked up the spilled coffee and became a brown soggy mess. Lauren grimaced.

"Same as you I guess; fancied a coffee," she replied. "I just came down for some bread really."

"Got a hangover then? I'd have thought you'd have one of those fancy coffee machine things at home for that."

"I don't have a hangover, and I don't have a coffee machine either. I like to sit and people-watch sometimes, and you can't do that at home. How about you? You're a little out of your way, aren't you?" Although Mark had a stall in the same market as Lauren's shop, selling old maps and books, china and bric-a-brac, he lived in the opposite direction.

"I know. I usually go to Costa, but I fancied a change of scenery. Look! There goes Nutty Netty. Quite a gathering of the clans this morning. Didn't see her there last night, did you?"

Lauren glanced out of the window and saw Netty Lipton hurrying by. You couldn't miss her really. She wore a multi-coloured poncho, baggy green and purple paisley trousers and an ancient pair of yellow ankle length rubber boots. She had a long yellow scarf wound several times around her neck and a purple beret perched on top of her unruly mop of curly henna red hair. She was like a bright beacon as she made her way through the growing throng of sombre suited commuters towards the station.

"Not their scene I should think. I wonder where she's off to?" Lauren mused. Netty Lipton and her son Razzy were also market traders. They had a small stall on the same side of the market as Mark, selling new-age paraphernalia – tarot cards, amulets, incense burners, and books on divination, the chakras, meditation and suchlike. Razzy was in his thirties; the colour of the station coffee; a Rastafarian, sporting long matted brown dreadlocks. Lauren hadn't a clue how old Netty was, but she would have guessed somewhere in her late fifties. Last night's Christmas celebration had been somewhat depleted with several market traders absent for one reason or another. *Why do we bother?* Lauren thought. *We none of us really have anything in common except that we work in the same place.*

"What the hell happened to you?" she asked, suddenly noticing that Mark's nose was swollen and discoloured, and there were fresh scratches on his face.

"You should see the other guy," he quipped. "No! I had a few too many last night and I'm afraid I had a bit of an accident. Fell over on the garden path and landed in the shrubbery. Stupid really, but no real damage done, not even to my dignity as nobody saw!"

Lauren screwed up her face in a grimace of distaste. *Typical,* she thought.

"I think we should make that the last Christmas do," she announced on impulse, voicing her thoughts. "I'm sure we all must have better things to do at this time of year,"

"Get you! Bah humbug or what?" Mark retorted. "It comes to something when you can't even spare one evening to spend with the people you work with all year, doesn't it? I thought it went ok, though I'd have preferred Deep Liquid to the King's Head."

"Aren't we all a bit old for nightclubs Mark? Well, I am at any rate, my feet were killing me as it was. I like Christmas as much as the next person, but I quite like to celebrate it how and with whom I choose."

"Ooooooo! cutting! Somebody got out the wrong side this morning. What's eating you then?" *You are,* thought Lauren. Netty had disappeared now through the ornate wrought-iron arch that marked the entrance to the station. Lauren downed the last of her Americano and rose, fastening her coat and gathering her purchases from the table.

"Going already? Hang on, I'll walk with you." Mark leaped up, gulping down the last of his latte, and hurried after her, donning his coat as he went. He caught up with her as they reached the far side of the street, seemingly oblivious to the fact that his presence was definitely unwelcome, and tagging along at her side as she climbed the hill towards home in stony silence.

"Are you ok Lauren?" he asked, stepping ahead of her and turning to walk backwards so that he could look into her face. "You can talk to me you know. I'm a good listener, and it won't go any further, you have my word."

"There's nothing to tell Mark, for goodness sake! I just wanted to sit and enjoy some peace and quiet before work. You kind of put paid to that. But it's ok, only I'll have to hurry now or I'll be late opening up." She dodged around him and quickened her pace towards home, aware of him gradually dropping back as the gradient took its toll on his lack of athletic ability, refusing to glance over her shoulder, knowing that he would have a face like a whipped puppy. A pang of remorse assailed her, and she dismissed it hurriedly – it wouldn't be fair to encourage him, perhaps he had mistaken her customary polite friendliness for something else, and it's sometimes necessary to be cruel to be kind, and not generate false hopes. Nevertheless, her conscience pricking, she turned in the doorway to give him a quick wave goodbye, but there was no sign of him.

TWO: A VISIT TO PAULINE.

Netty hurried along through the town towards the station. Along Bank Street – that wasn't its real name, but the locals had dubbed it thus owing to the large number of financial institutions ranged along its length – and down the hill past the double frontages of W.H. Smith, Marks and Spencer and River Island. Further down the hill, the big names gave way to small independent businesses – a hairdresser, a health food store, souvenir shops and the like. She limped slightly; her sciatica was playing up this morning and the boots didn't help; they were cumbersome and slopped around on her feet uncomfortably, but they had plenty of good wear left in them yet. At the bottom of the hill the station came into sight and she quickened her pace as she passed by Coffee and Compliments and Jonny's Artisan Bakery. The clock on the station wall said five to eight – she would make it by the skin of her teeth. She had waited in for Razzy, and in the end left him a note. There was no time to worry about where he might have been last night. After all, he was a grown man and she preferred not to ask too many questions for fear of what the answers might be. He had a strange way about him did Razzy, and she saw too much of his father in him sometimes. Right now, however, she was more concerned about Pauline, and for the second time that month she was heading for Birmingham to make sure that her sister wasn't properly ill this time. As she entered the station, she delved into her carpet-bag for her purse. The bag was a gift from Pauline on Netty's fiftieth birthday three years ago, and she had found it to be invaluable – you could cram so much in it and it went with everything. Today it contained only her washbag, two spare pairs of knickers and a pair of socks, a box of organic green teabags and a knitted bedjacket that she had just finished making for her sister. She worried whether the wool she had used was really suitable. It was a little rough and might be itchy, but it was all she had and it's the thought that counts after all.

The train was standing at platform three, and she settled herself in a forward-facing seat and hoped nobody would sit opposite. It always made her feel uncomfortable when that happened, as though they were scrutinizing her too closely, and in her turn, she would studiously avoid looking directly at them, but it wasn't always easy and detracted from her enjoyment of the journey. At this time of day the seats soon filled and she found herself with not only someone sitting opposite, but to her dismay, alongside too. A family of three – a man, a woman, and a child of about nine or ten years old. The man sat next to her, the woman and child opposite. The woman sat next to the window, and stared wordlessly out at the scenery rushing by. The child stared brazenly at Netty, blowing enormous bubbles of pink gum, sticking his tongue through them to burst them, then scraping them off his face to start again. In between bubbles he chewed loudly, his eyes fixed on Netty's bright henna-red hair and mismatched clothes in sullen insolence. Netty averted her eyes and concentrated on the view from the window, but couldn't quite obliterate the child from her peripheral vision, or the sucking and popping of the gum bubbles. As they approached Wolverhampton, she was happy to see the father stand and retrieve their bags from the overhead rack as they prepared to disembark amid the hiss of brakes and slamming of doors. To her relief, the seats now remained empty, and she settled down to enjoy the rest of the journey.

At Birmingham New Street, she disembarked and made her way to Lower Bull Street. Here she caught the number 33 bus to Perry Barr where her sister lived. Pauline's house was a sixties semi situated halfway down a pleasant tree-lined street. Netty let herself in with her key, depositing her carpet-bag in the hallway.

"Pauline, are you there?" she called out, opening the door into the lounge as she did so. There was no reply. The lounge was deserted, and bore no signs of recent occupation, the cushions arranged neatly, the antimacassars on the backs of the three-piece suite straight and pristine. Beyond the lounge was the conservatory, also unoccupied, its windows firmly closed and a musty air pervading. Netty opened a couple of the windows. Even on this winter's day it felt stuffy, the radiator on full blast and the wan winter sunlight magnified by the corrugated perspex roof. Back in the hallway, she called out again as she began to climb the stairs that were carpeted in a brown and gold design of autumn leaves, firmly held in place by shining brass stair rods. At the top of the stairs, the landing led to the bathroom and a double bedroom on the left, and the remaining two bedrooms on the right. Her sister's room was the large one overlooking the front garden. The door was ajar, and Netty approached it with apprehension, afraid of what she might find. Pauline's message on the phone had been brief but compelling.

"Netty, you have to come quickly, I don't have much time, and I need to see you before I go." All her subsequent attempts to phone her sister had failed. There was no answer other than the usual curt recorded message 'I'm not here, leave a message'. Netty had left several messages, but had had no response. Pauline had suffered ill health – real or imagined, for the last twenty years. Each time Netty hurried to her aid, she had made a remarkable if not to say miraculous recovery by the time she arrived. She was always pleased to see her however, and Netty was never prepared to take the risk that

perhaps this time her sister might actually be seriously ill. It drove Razzy mad –

"Why the fuck do you go running every time she clicks her fingers?" he would say. "She's just using you; there's nothing wrong with her. She's a lonely old woman and she has no friends, and have you ever wondered why?" Netty, however, would not be shaken in her loyalty to her sister, and always went to her aid.

She tapped softly on the bedroom door, pushing it tentatively until it swung open. She stepped inside the room, dreading what she might find, for there was a particular odour of staleness or even decay about it. The bed was empty, the room was empty, the curtains half closed and the pink satin coverlet folded over neatly to reveal crisp white sheets and pillowcases – Pauline decried the use of duvets, preferring blankets and sheets, with neatly fashioned hospital corners. Trembling with panic, Netty ran from room to room searching for signs of life, but there were none. Each of the three bedrooms was spick and span, and completely deserted with no sign of recent occupation. She stumbled down the stairs and made for the kitchen. The blind was down on the kitchen window, and the kettle was upended on the draining-board. The bin had been emptied and there was not a crumb or a watersplash in sight. There was, however, an envelope propped up against the canister marked TEA that stood next to the fridge. It was inscribed with her name, 'Annette' in her sister's beautiful cursive handwriting. With trembling hands, Netty opened it and withdrew a letter:

'My dear Annette,

I'm sorry you didn't manage to get here in time to see me off. I wish you would pick up your messages more often. I'm sorry I won't see you over Christmas. I have gone away for a little while. I won a competition for a three week holiday in Majorca. I leave from Birmingham International on Wednesday 7th, and I'll be back home in the early hours of Wednesday 28th. I wanted to ask you to keep an eye on the place for me, I don't much like going off and leaving it empty for so long. I'm sure Paul won't mind doing the shop, and of course you must make yourself at home. There's plenty of food in the freezer. If you leave before I get back, please make sure you put the hoover round, empty out the milk and the kitchen bin, and change the sheets on your bed.
Your affectionate sister,
Pauline.'

"Oh Pauline!" sighed Netty, as relief and exasperation washed over her in equal measures, causing her legs to suddenly buckle beneath her. She almost collapsed onto one of the chairs that surrounded the small formica clad kitchen table. The chair was small and uncomfortable, barely accommodating Netty's ample proportions, the little curved backrest sharp against her back, but she didn't notice. This time she'd been stitched up good and proper! She marveled at her sister's capacity for selfishness. She wondered what Razzy would say when she arrived home and he learned of her little game, and decided that she wouldn't tell him. Coming here had been a complete waste of time and money; the train fare was not inconsiderable, and the stall wasn't doing so well these days. How could Pauline even imagine that she could leave Razzy in charge for so long? But then she remembered that, of course, Pauline didn't know that she, Netty, was the owner of the stall, and she probably thought someone else would have to stand in for her. Even so, she would not have wanted to abandon Razzy over Christmas either! She knew he was under pressure and that was why he sometimes stayed out all night – not often, but nevertheless it worried her since he would return home in a bit of a state and never talked about where he had been. She was hoping that the three days off they would have over Christmas would give them a chance to do a bit of bonding. He would not be happy when he returned this morning and found the note she left asking him to open up the stall, so she would at least have to invent some valid reason for her trip to Birmingham.

What really saddened her however, was the fact that she wouldn't after all see her sister.

Pauline was her senior by fifteen years. When Netty – Annette – came along unexpectedly in 1952, their mother turned to drink and took no interest whatsoever in her new baby. She was probably a victim of post-natal depression, but in those days it was barely acknowledged and largely left untreated. Fifteen-year-old Pauline, however, was captivated by her little sister and was more than happy to adopt the role of mother, especially as it meant that school became a thing of the past. Their father had left when he discovered the pregnancy – he couldn't be doing with a squalling brat about the house, and even expressed doubt that he was actually her father. He provided for them, however, in the shape of a brown envelope containing a not inconsiderable amount of cash that he shoved through the letterbox on the 28th of every month. Pauline always tried to get to it first, and split its contents before replacing it, making sure that she had enough for their daily needs and some to put by for a rainy day before their mother squandered it all down the off-licence. They never saw their father again, although the brown envelope appeared as regularly as clockwork for the next six years until Pauline reached the age of twenty-one.

Pauline enrolled Netty at school when she was five, and made sure she attended every day. The school was a short walk away and the sisters would walk there hand-in-hand. Pauline would mingle with the other mothers at the gates. Some would ask after their mother, but those who didn't know them would simply assume that they were mother and daughter. She was a stickler when it came to Netty, always ensuring that her clothes were clean and ironed, her hair and teeth brushed until they shone. From the very start, she insisted on calling her by her given name, spurning the abbreviation that everyone else used. After dropping her off, Pauline would return home and make breakfast for their now bed-ridden mother, wash her and sit her up in her chair by the window if the sun was shining. Their mother spoke little, except occasionally to demand a drink and then hurl abuse when it wasn't instantly forthcoming. Pauline allowed her a large whisky last thing at night, into which she slipped her Valium that ensured that she would sleep through the night. Every afternoon, she would read to her from the newspaper or the Woman's Own before settling her back into bed and collecting Netty from school. Pauline was small and dark and as neat as a pin. Netty was inclined to plumpness, she was what old ladies called 'bonny', with bright strawberry blonde curls and an infectious smile. She knew the woman in the front bedroom was her mother, but she rarely ventured in to see her because she was frightened of her. Pauline was the only real mother she had ever known.

Netty's infants' teacher was Paul Stockton. Around thirty years old, he was quietly spoken and inspired confidence in even the most nervous of his pupils, who ranged in ages from five to eight. He wore tweed jackets with leather patches on the elbows, grey flannel trousers and knitted Fair Isle pullovers in varying muted shades, and he smelled of Palmolive soap and Extra Strong Mints. To Netty he was the only father figure she had ever known, and she adored everything about him. Pauline too, it seemed, had more than a passing interest in him, and would blush prettily whenever he addressed her. Sometimes they would chat together for several minutes before the start of class, while the class fidgeted and squirmed in their seats in order to get a better view of them through the glass-panelled door of the classroom. Soon, the whisper was rife throughout the school that Mr. Stockton was sweet on Netty Proctor's sister.

One sunny Sunday in June Paul came calling. Pauline had been up since the crack of dawn, pushing the Ewbank around the floor and polishing the furniture. Netty could hear her rattling around in the kitchen as she lay in bed enjoying the sunshine that streamed through the window. She heard her go into their mother's room, and the low grumbling that meant she was busy with the morning routine of bedpan, bed bath and the transfer to the chair by the window whilst she threw back the covers to air the bed. She heard the window opening, and the rattle of her mother's breakfast tray, containing cereal, toast, and a cup of lukewarm milky tea.

"Eileen's coming to sit with you this afternoon Mum," she heard her sister saying. "She's bringing the News of the World, and I hope she takes it away with her too – I don't want Annette seeing that scandalous rubbish." Her mother mumbled a reply, but Netty couldn't catch it. Eileen was a neighbour who would babysit their mother on the rare occasions that Pauline left her post. Netty wondered what the occasion was, and with her curiosity aroused, hauled herself out of bed and trotted downstairs to the kitchen. Pauline had been baking – the delicious aroma of Victoria sponge filled the air. The cake was cooling on a wire tray on the kitchen table. Scones were the usual Sunday teatime treat but Victoria sponge was reserved for very special occasions. There was a jar of raspberry jam by the sink, and a carton of double cream. Netty's mouth watered in happy anticipation.

"Ah! Annette, there you are!" Pauline bustled in, depositing her mother's tray on the draining board. "Do you want Sunday breakfast?" Sunday breakfast was a long-standing tradition. It meant you got to choose freely what you ate, regardless of suitability. For Pauline, it usually meant a bacon and egg sandwich, for Netty, chocolate biscuits and Ovaltine.

"Can I have some cake?" she asked quickly.

"Nice try sis, that's for this afternoon; but you can help me whisk the cream and then you can lick the bowl if you like." Netty nodded assent eagerly – *whipped cream – yum!* She settled for a breakfast of jammie dodgers and tea so as to save herself for the afternoon feast, and sat at the table munching happily in the sunshine that was streaming through the back door.

"What are we doing this afternoon?" she asked, pushing an errant piece of biscuit back into her mouth.

"Don't talk with your mouth full," her sister chided. "Paul...Mr. Stockton, is taking us out in his car for a picnic on Wendley Hilltop. I want you on your best behaviour mind." Netty squirmed in her chair with excitement. She'd never been in a car before, although last summer Pauline had taken her to the seaside in a charabanc, which would have been wonderful except that on the way home, a little girl named Alice who was sitting behind them was sick, and the smell was dreadful. Netty declared that she never wanted to go to the seaside again.

Paul Stockton's car was green, with shiny chrome bumpers and headlights. Pauline said it was a Morris Minor. There was a boy at school named Maurice who Netty was not very fond of, but nevertheless, she thought the car was lovely. It had red leather seats and windows that wound down with a handle. She sat in the back happily winding them up and down as they drove the fifteen or so miles to Wendley Hilltop, a local beauty spot. At the top of a long winding hill the landscape opened out to windswept moorland covered with heather and dotted with grazing sheep. They pulled off the road onto a grassy patch, and Paul took a plaid blanket out of the boot and laid it on the ground. A large picnic basket followed, and a round biscuit tin containing Pauline's Victoria sponge. They sat on the blanket and munched happily on spam sandwiches and pork pies, followed by custard creams and the delicious cake. There was lemonade for Netty, and cans of shandy for Paul and Pauline. Afterwards, they stowed everything back in the boot and went for a stroll across the moorland. Netty picked some heather and chased some butterflies. Paul and Pauline held hands and conversed in low tones, their heads close together.

Netty fell asleep in the car going home, and Paul carried her up to bed without waking her. They sent Eileen on her way with a large piece of sponge cake from Pauline and five shillings from Paul. After that day, Paul became a regular visitor to their home, and there were several other outings, although Netty wasn't always included. Suddenly, their mother found her tongue, and complained bitterly about Pauline's absences. Eileen had to bear the brunt of her disgruntled ramblings, and Netty kept well out of the way.

One evening in late August, events took an unexpected turn. Pauline was excited because Paul was taking her out for a special meal that evening.

"I think he's going to propose," she told Netty excitedly.

"What's that?" asked Netty.

"It means he's going to ask me to marry him," she replied. "Isn't that exciting!" Netty wasn't sure. She had an inkling that married ladies usually went away to live somewhere else, and she wondered what would happen to her and her mother if Pauline went away. Perhaps Eileen would move in with them, but she was pretty sure there was a Mr. Eileen, and there wouldn't be room for him since there would only be the one spare room. She waited anxiously for Pauline's return, but she was asleep long before her sister got home.

She woke in the night to hear crying coming from Pauline's room. She slipped out of bed, and crept into her sister's room. Pauline was lying on the bed still fully dressed, her face buried in her pillow, sobbing as though her heart would break. Netty climbed up beside her and nestled against her back, slipping her arms around her waist. This made Pauline cry all the more, so Netty withdrew and lay back waiting for her to stop.

"Why are you crying?" she ventured at last. "Aren't you going to marry Paul?" Pauline stopped crying and turned to face her. "No Annette, I can't," she said sadly. "Come on, I'll make some cocoa and tell you all about it."

They sat at the kitchen table with their cocoa.

"Men are not always what they seem," Pauline told her. "I thought Paul was my knight in shining armour, but he isn't, and I won't be seeing him anymore."

"Why not?" Netty asked. She was a little puzzled, as she had never seen Paul wearing anything other than his tweed jacket and flannel trousers. She wasn't sure whether to be sad or relieved, but decided that as Pauline was sad, she must be too. "Didn't he pro…ask you to marry him?"

"He did," replied Pauline sadly, "but he said Mother would have to go into a home. Offered to pay and everything, but he said he couldn't have her living with us. I told him I couldn't do that to her, and he said that in that case, he couldn't marry me. I'm sorry Annette."

"I'm not!" Netty declared. "I'm glad! I didn't want to live with Eileen." Pauline stared at her aghast. "Live with Eileen?" she said.

"Well, I thought when you got married and went away, Eileen would come to live with us instead. I'm glad you're not going away sis, but I'm sorry you're sad."

"Oh! Annette! What would I ever do without you?" exclaimed Pauline, and hugged her little sister.

When school started again in September, there was no sign of Paul Stockton, and a new teacher named Mary Crabtree was there in his place. Pauline never mentioned him again, and neither did Netty.

Three years later, however, a mysterious envelope arrived in the post addressed to Pauline. She glanced at the crest on the envelope, and withdrew wordlessly to her bedroom. Netty crept up the stairs and listened outside her door. After what seemed like an hour, but was probably no more than ten minutes, she heard her sister crying. Quietly, she slipped inside the room and climbed up beside her. The letter lay opened and discarded on the bed. Netty picked it up and read it. It concerned 'The Last Will and Testament of Paul Stockton.' She didn't fully understand it, but it seemed that Pauline was now the owner of a house in Perry Barr, Birmingham, and all its contents, left to her by the late Paul Stockton, who had died of consumption. There was a 'letter within a letter' too. It read:

'My Dearest Pauline,

I'm so sorry that things didn't work out for us. I didn't mean to upset you, and I hope you have been happy. There has never been anyone else for me, and I hope you will accept the gift that I wished to give you three years ago. I knew then that my days were numbered but I didn't want you to marry me just because you felt sorry for me – if I'd told you, I would never have been sure. I'm sorry that I couldn't cope with your mother, I didn't want to share whatever time we had left together with such an ungracious, controlling woman who would have done everything in her power to spoil things for you. I was, however, very fond of Netty and I hope she has fond memories of me, despite not being quite the star pupil. Have a happy life Pauline. My love for you will never die.

Affectionately yours,
Paul X

Netty sighed at the memory, and picking up her carpet-bag, made her way wearily back to the bus stop. She should be able to get a train back to Chesbury within the next hour. She would talk to Pauline when she came back from her little holiday.

THREE: MARK.

Mark was sick to death of women. What was wrong with them? They just didn't know a good thing when they saw one. After all, he was reasonably good-looking, if a tad overweight; he had his own business and his own home, and he was more than willing to share everything with a female companion. He was caring and loyal, and great in bed. He remained, however, unattached, despite all his best efforts. Take Lauren Woods for instance – *stuck up bitch thinks she's too good for me, but she's not, she's no better than I am.* Oh, she was quite happy to let him buy her drinks when their paths occasionally crossed in the King's Head or the Lion on a Saturday night, but then she'd come on all independent and hoity-toity when he offered to give her a lift home. Ok, he shouldn't drink and drive, as she pointed out to him, but he'd be quite willing to walk with her and pick his car up next morning – no skin off his nose.

At the Christmas do, he thought he'd finally cracked it. She was in a good mood, animated and sociable, having a laugh. The meal at Giorgio's had been excellent as always, and afterwards they went on to the King's for a couple of drinks. There was the usual crowd from the market, except for Bessie, and Netty and Razzy – *wonder what happened to those two?* They had congregated around the bar, and Lauren sat on one of the tall stools, crossing her long elegant legs in their black silk trousers. Always looked smart Lauren; like she'd just stepped out of a magazine. He knew she made most of her own clothes, and admired her skill. The clothes flattered her straight up-and-down figure so that she looked streamlined rather than gaunt. She could look a bit miserable with that turned-down mouth and pale eyes, until she smiled – then her whole face softened and lit up and his heart would lurch sickeningly. He had tried every tactic known to man – well, every tactic known to Mark anyway. Nothing made any difference – she remained friendly but distant, and his frustration grew.

He had followed her home that night. It was wet and windy and he had offered her a lift and even curbed his drinking a little, only some wine with his meal and a couple of pints of Guinness with no chasers; he was sober as a judge. She said she was going to 'powder her nose', but she must've collected her coat and slipped out the side door, and by the time he realised, she was out of sight. He hurried along after her and at the end of Madison Avenue he spotted her in the distance, walking quickly along the sheltered left-hand side of the street. The wind whipped at the trees and the river was high and swept along in a dark turgid mass beyond the pavement and the railings. Mark kept close to the wall and ducked into gateways to avoid being seen, but she held onto her hat and coat and didn't turn until she reached the junction at the end of the avenue, where she turned to the left, looking behind her before crossing the road and setting off up the hill. Mark had moved to within fifty yards of her now. She seemed nervous, glancing over her shoulder from time to time, forcing him to dive into an accommodating doorway. He was determined to see her home, and oblivious to anything or anyone else that might also have been moving along the streets that night. Once, he had a strong sense of a presence behind him, and whipped round suddenly, but there was nothing there. *Don't be such a girl's blouse,* he chided himself. *You're supposed to be a knight in shining bloody armour!* For a minute or two Lauren was hidden from view as she turned the corner into her street, where the smooth tarmac gave way to glistening cobbles and the street lights were quaint and inadequate. Mark glanced behind him again as he turned the corner, and distinctly saw the orange glow of a cigarette in a doorway lower down the hill. *It's a good job I saw her home,* he thought. *Silly bitch shouldn't be wandering around by herself at night – specially with that ginger hair!* He slipped in behind some bins as she reached her house and watched her pick up her cat in her arms before unlocking the door and disappearing inside. He heard the door slam, and then a light went on, and minutes later he saw her draw the curtains across the big bay window. Ah well, she was safe now, and he could return to the King's for another pint or two of Guinness. He set off back down the hill. Someone was walking some way ahead of him. Strange he hadn't seen them pass. There was something vaguely familiar about the sauntering stride and he tried to catch up, but when he reached the crossroads the figure had gone, and left only the still-glowing stub of a cast-off cigarette on the pavement.

He returned to the King's Head, where he had left his car. The bar was less busy now; most of the market traders had left, except for Reg the Veg, (not his real name, but nobody really knew what that was) who was always reluctant to go home to his perpetually nagging wife.

"Alright Marky?" The greeting was cheery, and Mark took his place at the bar beside him and ordered a pint of Guinness, "And one for my mate," he instructed the barman, and Reg beamed his thanks thinking, *he's alright that Mark, in spite of what people say.*

"Where d'you get to just mate?" Reg asked, sucking at his glass and emerging with a moustache of creamy white froth.

"Aw! I went to see that Lauren got home alright. Don't like the idea of her walking home alone with that bloody psycho about."

"I'm surprised she let you," remarked Reg, "She's a law unto herself that one, won't take nothin' from nobody."

"Oh, she didn't know, I just followed her to make sure."

"There's a name for blokes like you, you'd better watch yourself," chuckled Reg with a wink, and took another long pull of his pint. "You've a soft spot for her, haven't you? Forget it man, she's out of your league." Draining his glass, he swiped his sleeve across his mouth. "Well, that's me done, I'd better get home before I get locked out. Count yourself lucky you live on your own mate. Take it from me, it's a much better deal." He swung himself down from his bar stool and left with a backward wave. Mark looked around. There was only a handful of people left now as midnight approached, and he didn't know any of them, although he thought he'd seen one guy in there a few times. He ordered a scotch. It slid down his throat like fiery silk, and he swiftly followed it with two more. He slid from his bar stool and stood for a moment contemplating his next move. He should walk home really, but he didn't relish the idea, especially in the rain. He fished in his pocket for his car keys.

"I think I'll head home, get myself a doner on the way," he announced. The barman looked up with a wry expression.

"I'll pretend I didn't see those," he said, inclining his head towards the keys. "You take care now mate." He turned away, shaking his head as he draped the bar cloths over the pumps and began switching off the lights.

There was a late-night kiosk selling the glutinous chunks of indeterminate meat stuffed into half a hollowed-out baguette with some lettuce and copious amounts of spicy-flavoured mayonnaise. Mark pulled over to the kerb and put in his order, watching the vendor slice chunks off the rotating 'elephant's leg' at the side of the van and stuff them into the baguette that he then proceeded to wrap in paper to protect the buyer from the grease that was already beginning to seep through the bread. He tucked into it with gusto – there's nothing like a doner after a night on the booze. As he pulled away a few minutes later, he saw a familiar figure approaching the van – Razzy! So he *was* out tonight then after all! Must've had other fish to fry than the works do. *Hmm…h*e mused. *I wonder if Nutty Netty knows he eats the odd doner, they're supposed to be veggies!*

Some time later, he pulled into his driveway. Mark's home was a half-rendered thirties semi with an arched red brick open porchway, squared-off bay window and a garage at the side that like most of the others along the street was never used for its intended purpose. The front garden was small and plain with a neat square of lawn, a low ornamental wall and a concrete apron in front of the garage. Low-growing shrubs lined the pathway to the door. By contrast, the back garden was large and tangled and Mark rarely ventured out there; he had little time and no inclination for gardening – plants were unnecessary in his opinion.

He threw his keys down on the hall table and went through to the kitchen. It was small and cramped, but adequate for a man whose idea of cooking was to throw something in the microwave and press a button. It was, however, spotlessly clean, and now he deposited the greasy paper from the kebab into the plastic swing bin next to the cooker, washed his hands and face, and reached into the fridge for a nightcap. He took his can of lager through to the lounge that was dominated by an oversized television with a surround sound speaker system. On the opposite wall was a large black leather corner seating unit, in front of which was a long mahogany coffee table. A matching sideboard beneath the window housed his DVD collection – mainly action movies, but with a sprinkling of wildlife documentaries featuring David Attenborough, some comedy shows, and a collection of soft porn. The room was stark, the walls bare, and the vertical blinds at the window gave it a vaguely corporate feel. An archway led to the former dining room that Mark had incorporated into the lounge when he first bought the house. The whole of one wall was a home office setup with a large-screen computer, a printer, and box files containing Mark's business invoices and receipts, all arranged methodically in alphabetical order. A leather swivel chair stood in front of the desk, and the window sported more of the vertical blinds. On the opposite wall to the desk was a large map of the Chesbury district and an equally large calendar, plain and functional. Both were dotted with stick-pins in various colours holding strips of paper with names and addresses of auction rooms, junk shops and car boot sale venues.

Throughout the house there was no sign of the bric-a-brac, books and maps from which he made his living. These were consigned to the garage, on shelves and in boxes, all labeled and sorted into categories. It paid to keep things tidy, and saved time in the long-run as Mark well knew. Almost anything a customer asked for could be produced in a matter of hours or even minutes, and often his bits and pieces fetched inflated prices because they were just what someone had spent months searching for. It would be no use if you didn't know exactly what you had stashed away. He once sold a plastic cup for thirty pounds because a woman wanted it for her mother who had dementia and thought she was nine years old, demanding her Minnie mouse cup that she had been given for her birthday in 1956. Was it exploitation? Mark didn't think so and neither did he care – it was simply a case of supply and demand. In his own home, Mark had an intense dislike of clutter and embellishment, and his interest in the items he peddled was strictly non-personal and didn't extend beyond an unfailing instinct for what would sell.

He wondered what Lauren would make of his home. He thought she would be impressed with its cleanliness and order, as well as his impeccable taste. Women generally assume that single men are incurable slobs, and he was a shining example of what every woman secretly desires – a man who is tidy and methodical. He lay back on his corner sofa and sucked at his can of lager. The sofa had cost nearly two grand. It was genuine Italian leather, soft and buttery, not the hard shiny stuff that you couldn't fall asleep on lest you slide off onto the floor. The floor was covered wall to wall in a high quality beige wool twist carpet. Everything was neutral and tasteful. Yes, he was sure Lauren would be impressed, though he'd have to hide the porn he supposed. If only he could just get her to accept one of his many invitations to dinner, courtesy, he supposed, of a Marks and Spencer Dine in for Two. He imagined her lounging elegantly on the sofa, her long legs outstretched, a glass of wine in her elegantly manicured hand. She always wore pale nail polish – none of that strident red, or worse still blue or green stuff that seemed to be popular nowadays. Her voice was soft, low and lilting, and she smelled of summer flowers. Her hair was like fine copper silk and her eyes like glistening pools of pale emerald. On his bedside cabinet, he had a picture of her taken at last year's Christmas party. He had a friend isolate her image from the throng, and blow it up, photoshopping the background away. She was relaxed, smiling, a glass of wine in her hand, just as he imagined her here in his home. Every night he would hold the image to his lips before turning out the light and imagining what it would be like to hold her fragile body, kiss her cupid's bow lips and stroke her silky hair back from her forehead gently before making love to her, and how she would cling to him and moan softly as they climaxed together in a tsunami of ecstasy. And every night, the harsh reality of his cold and empty bed would make him bury his head in his pillow in an agony of unrequited love.

He sighed and rose to his feet. In the kitchen he deposited the now empty lager can in the bin, and gathering his thoughts, prepared himself for the gruelling task ahead of him.

FOUR: POPPY

At five to ten, Lauren turned the key in the door of her little shop. It was one of several enclosed units that ranged along the sides of the market hall, set apart from the stalls that filled the large central space with their canvas covers that rolled up during the day, and at night were zipped or tied into place covering their contents. Concrete steps led past the council offices and the market superintendent's eyrie on the first floor to the second floor where a narrow balcony ran along three sides lined with yet more stalls whose metal blinds pulled down at night and secured to the counter tops. Their tenants were mainly craftspeople or artists who worked away behind the counters at their skills in the relative peace and quiet that two steep flights of steps inevitably created. Lauren herself had started her career in one of these units before moving downstairs to her present location.

She gathered up the post that lay on the formerly splendid, but now somewhat cracked and faded Minton tiles inside the door – a couple of Christmas cards, a hand-delivered official notice from the market superintendent reminding all traders of the Christmas opening hours, and another envelope with handwriting that she didn't recognize. She placed them all on the counter and went through to the tiny cubicle at the back of the shop where she hung up her coat and put her lunch down on the shelf beside her electric kettle and coffee jar. She rifled through the index file next to the kettle. There were three orders for personalised garments that must be filled today. She could see that Bessie had begun cutting out the letters for the first one and laying them on the bib ready for sewing. These appliquéd garments for children were among Lauren's best sellers. Dungarees, skirts, dresses and blouses in bright primary colours with names appliquéd on the front, on the pockets, or around the hemline.

Absently, she flicked the switch on the kettle – already it seemed a long time since that cup of coffee earlier. The day loomed ahead filled with tedium and she wondered, not for the first time, if the market shop was worth keeping on. Perhaps she'd be better off closing and concentrating on her couture designs. She sighed; it wasn't going to happen. Bessie needed her job, and without the shop Lauren would become too much of a recluse if the truth were known. The kettle hissed fiercely and she realised that she had forgotten to fill it. She held it under the cold tap of the sink. *Damn,* she muttered under her breath and cringed as the icy water hit the element with another loud hiss – *not a good idea,* she thought, *no wonder I go through so many kettles!* Returning to the front of the shop, she picked up the post again. One Christmas card was from a friend she hadn't seen in a while. She smiled inwardly. Wendy was the kind who keeps a birthday book and a Christmas card list, so that even years after their friendship had dwindled, the cards continued to come regularly, if mostly unreciprocated. The other was from Netty and Razzy, a hand-made creation from their stall that she remembered admiring a few weeks earlier. *I wish I was more organized or more thoughtful, or both,* she thought to herself. She had purchased a box of assorted Christmas cards from the Cats' Protection shop and tended to keep them under the counter to be dealt with as and when required. She held the third envelope in her hand and gazed at it for some moments. It was addressed in an untidy scrawl to **Mrs Lauren Stevenson, The kids close shop, Chesbury Market.** Lauren recoiled at the use of her married name; she had long since reverted to her maiden name of Woods. There were several other shops and stalls that sold children's clothes. *It's a wonder it found its way to me at all*, she mused. There was no stamp, whoever sent it must have posted it through the letterbox at the entrance themselves.

The envelope clearly contained a letter, and quite a long one at that judging by its thickness, and she was intrigued, yet inexplicably reluctant to open it. She returned to the kitchenette and made herself a cup of instant coffee. She turned the envelope in her hand again. *What's the matter with you?* said a little voice in her head. *Just open the bloody thing!*

With a deep sense of foreboding, she carefully slit open the envelope with the scissors that lay on the counter and extracted the contents. There were three sheets of lined paper, clearly torn from a ring-bound notebook and filled with the same hasty scrawl. There was no return address on the top, the letter opened immediately with the words:

'Dear Mrs. Stevenson,'

'U probly wont remember me, but I remember u.' the letter began. *'Im a friend of ur daughter Ashley.'* Lauren stiffened, with a sharp intake of breath. Her instinct then had not been wrong – this letter spelt trouble. Cringing at the copious grammatical errors, she read on.

'We was at primary school 2gether an a few years ago I bumped into er an she told me she left home at 17 an ad never seen any of er family since apart from once about 9 years ago when she were 20.'

Yes, thought Lauren – *when the police finally tracked her down and informed us of her whereabouts after three long years of heartbreak.*

She had been arrested for shoplifting and possession of drugs, and after hours of intensive questioning had finally admitted who she was and allowed them to send for her parents. On seeing Lauren and Ken, she broke down in tears and they ended up standing her bail to the tune of five hundred pounds. They took her home; she said she was tired and she would talk to them and explain everything in the morning.

The next morning her bed was empty – she had disappeared again with the contents of Ken's wallet. She failed to turn up for her court hearing, and Ken forfeited his bail money.

That was the beginning of the end for Ken and Lauren. He had wanted to leave Ashley in custody while they thought things through, but Lauren, seeing her broken and vulnerable, accused him of being insensitive and insisted that they take her home. To be fair, he never once threw her bad judgement in her face, but for the next twelve months she became obsessed with a renewed search for Ashley. Her efforts, however, were fruitless, and she eventually cleared her mind of her errant daughter. Ken had said she was wasting her time, they should leave her be and she would turn up again one day like a bad penny. The conflict of interest gradually took its toll on their already strained relationship, driving the wedge more firmly between them, and after less than two years they separated.

'Ashley dont no Im writing 2 u,' the letter continued, *'but I dint no wot else 2 do. She left me int lurch, an I need your elp. I seen that bit int paper about ur shop, an reconized ur foto, so I desided 2 write 2 u. I ope u will help. Not 4 Ashleys sake, I cud understand if u refused after wot she did but 4 ur grankid Poppys sake.'*

Oh my God! I have a grandchild? Lauren read the sentence again. With a sick feeling in her stomach, she paused, and placed the letter face down on the desk for a moment. This was too much to take in. She had never really considered the possibility that Ashley might produce a child at some point. With trembling hands, she returned to the letter.

> 'Poppy is 4 years old. Shes a quiet little girl an never bin no truble. Its not that Ashley neglecs her but she just dont seem to get that she needs more than just food and close. She means well but she just dont think things thru. Poppys ok but she dont say much tho you mite think that for a kid thats not such a bad thing. The thing is, Ashley went 2 Amsterdam on holiday for a week an she asked me 2 look after Poppy because she cudnt take er with er. Shes goin thru sum heavy stuff with er boyfrend (not Poppys dad in case ur wondering) an needed 2 sort things out with him. Well that were 3 weeks ago, an I ant eard from er since. She messaged me 2 weeks ago 2 say she were comin back, but she ant showed up an now she int ansering er phone. My boyfrend int appy with the situashun at all an as laid it down its Poppy or im. Im fond of Poppy, but I luv my boyfrend an tho he may sound a bit harsh, he int really being unreesnable - after all Poppys not are kid. Ive racked my brains 4 another way but without Poppy goin in2 care which Ashley wud never 4give me 4 ur my last resort. If you wud just meet up with me an see wot a little cutie she is Im sure ud agree to look after her til Ashley gets back an Im sure shell be back any day now she must of bin delayed at the last minit. Ill bring Poppy 2 the market on Satday afternoon @ 2 an wait 4 you at the Bird in Hand caff. U wont ave no truble reconizing er - shes the livin imij of Ashley. Im sorry 2 put this on u but ur er Granny after all, an if u carnt help poor Poppy

will ave 2 go into care an then Ashley may never get er back. Im sure u wudnt want that for er an nither do I.
I look 4ward 2 meeting u.
Yours sincearly
Trisha Banks.

Lauren racked her brains. Trisha Banks – the name rang a bell, and not in any bad way. She remembered Trisha as a quiet but not over bright girl from a decent background whom she had considered a positive influence on her wayward daughter. Clearly Ashley had a friend who had tried to protect her from herself, and had apparently failed. Saturday afternoon – *good God! That's tomorrow,* she thought, panic washing over her. Not much time to think about it then. Normally, she wouldn't come in on a Saturday, but she might have to work if Bessie wasn't better. She could see the corner of the Bird in Hand café from her shop doorway, and perhaps she could sneak a surreptitious peek at the pair of them before committing herself to the meeting. Even as the thought crossed her mind, she knew that wouldn't happen. She had to meet up with Trisha and Poppy, and take it from there. *Four years old!* She cast her mind back to Ashley at that age – a real little livewire, always up to mischief, always demanding something and throwing a wobbler if the answer was no. But Lauren was in her twenties then, not her forties, and she'd had Ken to help her out, and a home that was geared to the needs of a young child. She thought about her little house, how she had it just the way she wanted it; how she had waited all her life for a little place to call her own, and how she was apparently going to have to share it with a small child? *No! Surely, this was not a good idea.* Ashley had been a handful from the start, and had quite put her and Ken off having any more children. She didn't even particularly like children if the truth be known, and was relieved when Ashley grew from a wilful young child to a sullen teenager – at least she didn't make any further demands on Lauren's time and energy. She and Ken tried to include her in grown-up things, taking her to restaurants and the theatre, but she made it quite clear that these things didn't interest her and weren't considered cool among her contemporaries. Gradually, they grew apart, until one night Ashley went out and never came home. Then came the trauma of a police search, and such intensive interrogation of Ken that Lauren began to wonder if he had indeed had something to do with her disappearance. Two days later, he was released without charge and the flurry of media attention only lasted until the next nine-day wonder. The rift between them, however, never completely healed, because he knew that she had wondered, even though she had never voiced her doubts. Nowadays they had a tacit friendship, and the subject of Ashley was one they studiously avoided on the rare occasions they spoke. Ken remarried three years after the split, and Lauren designed his new wife Janet's wedding gown, and attended the ceremony, so there really were no hard feelings. She wondered what he would think about this latest revelation. She knew that he and Janet, who was some fifteen years his junior, were trying for a baby. He was unlikely to want to sour their relationship with Ashley's cast-offs!

  For the rest of the day, she threw herself into completing the orders and by four o'clock they were neatly packaged and labeled ready for the customers to pick them up the following morning. Just as she was leaving, the phone rang. It was Bessie, fully recovered and ready for work tomorrow. Lauren heaved a sigh of relief – now she would have the whole morning to prepare herself for what was to come. She gathered up her belongings and turned the key in the lock. She decided to swing by Netty's stall to thank her for the card; but it was all shut up, the brightly coloured canvas cover pulled down and secured.

"They've not been in today Miss Lauren," observed Reg the Veg as he heaved his baskets into place under the table so that he could pull his tarpaulin over. "Netty said something about her sister being ill, and I ain't seen Razzy all day."

"Thanks Reg, I'll catch her tomorrow I expect. See you later." *So that was where Netty was going this morning!* Lauren knew she had an elder sister who lived in Birmingham and was a bit of a hypochondriac. Razzy had no patience with her, but every couple of weeks Netty would hare off in answer to a desperate appeal only to find that there was really nothing wrong with her after all.

"Why d'you fuckin' bother?" Razzy would grumble, his nose out of joint after having had to run the stall alone for a day yet again.

Netty was adamant. "Because one day there really will be something wrong, and I'll be glad I went," she insisted, and that was that. Razzy would take over on the stall each time and would soon overcome his pique as he threw some banter around with the customers and the other stallholders. *It's unusual for him not to step up to the plate*, Lauren thought; but then everything about this day was unusual it seemed.

That evening she couldn't settle. She wandered around the house, drinking in the peace and quiet in every room, and trying to visualize what changes might have to be made in order to accommodate a four-year-old, even for a short stay. Charlie wandered around after her, mewing plaintively, sensing her unease. Would this child get on ok with Charlie? Lauren swept her beloved cat up into her arms and buried her face in his fragrant fur.

"Oh Charlie, what are we going to do?" she asked. Charlie purred loudly for a few minutes, then struggled free of her grasp. Lauren poured herself a glass of wine and turned on the stereo, selecting a disc on the 3CD changer – Ocean Drive by the Lighthouse Family – soothing and downbeat. She gazed into the flames of the fire, and came to a decision. Nothing would change. The child would have to fit in with her life, and not the other way around. After all Trisha had said Ashley was on her way back, so it might only be for a day or two. It wouldn't do to pander to her too much and then have to send her back to whatever chaos her life with Ashley consisted of. Her decision made, Lauren felt better able to cope. She would do things her way, and that was that.

The next morning dawned bright and clear, with a light dusting of frost on the leaves and branches of the trees opposite and on the grass patch in the back garden. Lauren woke early, and then remembered why. Making her way along the landing she entered the back bedroom. It was simply furnished with a large double bed, another tall armoire that housed an overspill of Lauren's clothes, a low chest of drawers topped with a mirror, a single bedside cabinet since there wasn't room for two, and a comfortable chair placed by the window. Because this was colder than her room, she had carpeted it in a rustic tweed wool carpet, thick and soft underfoot. The original Victorian fireplace was still in place, with its pretty tiled surround that was the inspiration for the colours in the blue, green and gold soft furnishings. There was an arrangement of giant fir cones and colourful gourds in the hearth, and tall church candles on one corner of the mantelpiece balanced by a leafy green plant in a ceramic pot on the other side. Above the fireplace was a large framed print of Monet's Waterlilies that lent an air of tranquility to the room. As a guest room it was ideal, although rarely used. She tried, and failed, to imagine it strewn with toys. From the window there was a view of the back garden, with its shrubbery, a small patch of lawn flanked by mature borders and a large paved patio area at the bottom, where in summer Lauren would haul the heavy cast-iron table and chairs from the garden shed and set them out along with her sun-loungers and a large parasol. Beyond the garden wall were tall horse chestnut trees that in spring would be laden with their creamy-pink blossom spikes and beyond the trees was the high wall of Chesbury Castle built of mellow sandstone interspersed with mullioned windows, most of which had been bricked in at some point. It was certainly a secure playground for a small child, she decided with some relief. Feeling more positive now, she decided to go down to the corner shop and buy something to welcome her granddaughter to her home, although she wasn't sure what.

Arty was in his usual place, scooping litter, dust and cigarette ends onto his shovel.

"Amazing where it all comes from every bleedin' morning," he remarked drily. "Doesn't anybody take their rubbish home with them these days? Have you heard the latest on the murder? Young woman this time, late twenties, early thirties, though they're not saying who yet until they've tracked down her relatives."

"Red hair again I presume," observed Lauren.

"That's right. Same as ever," mumbled Arty, and spat extravagantly into the gutter. "Probably something to do with 'is mother – usually is with these serial blokes. Bet she's got red hair 'n all – unless he done away with her too of course. Perhaps that's what set 'im off." He spat again. Lauren shuddered, and hastily took her leave. She wasn't in the mood for Arty's gloomy but gleeful hypotheses this morning. At the corner shop she was faced with an array of sweets, small toys and children's comics. With no clear idea of what she wanted, in the end she settled on a rag doll with stripey legs, plaited yellow woolen hair and a bright red mini dress. The label on its matching red felt hat stated *'Authentic Mostly Molly Doll.'* Lauren had never heard of Mostly Molly, but she was sure that Poppy would have, and it was really cute. She remembered that Ashley had liked rag dolls, and had a particular one that she refused to sleep without. She had even taken it with her when she left, and Lauren wondered idly whether she still had it. As an afterthought, she also bought a small bag of dolly mixtures that she popped into her coat pocket. Feeling pleased with herself, she made her way back home. Arty had moved on, so she was spared another bulletin.

    She arrived at the Bird in Hand with ten minutes to spare. The lunchtime rush was over, and she found a seat near the piano that afforded a little privacy, and waited anxiously for her first sight of her granddaughter. When it came, it was like a jolt of electricity. Poppy was, indeed, the living image of Ashley at four years old. Pale and ethereal, with emerald green eyes in a little heart-shaped face peering out from behind a curtain of pale strawberry blonde hair. She was tiny; small-boned and delicate looking, like a fairy who had lost her wings. She clung to Trisha, hiding herself behind her jeans-clad legs, her thumb in her mouth; eyes wide with anxiety. She wore a thin dress made of cotton gingham, totally unsuitable for the cold winter's day, and a somewhat shabby pale pink anorak. Her skinny legs were white and bare, with her slightly less white socks gathered around her ankles in swathes. Lauren's heart melted. She leaned towards this fairy-child and smiled warmly, holding out her hand. Poppy shrunk further behind Trisha's legs and kept her thumb firmly in her mouth.

"Hello Poppy, I'm your Grandma Lauren." Lauren said, undeterred.

"Say hello to your Grandma, Poppy," prompted Trisha, with no response. Lauren gestured to Trisha to sit down, and she did so. Poppy climbed onto her knee and hid her face in the folds of her jacket.

"I'm sorry," said Trisha, "She's just a bit scared, an she don't know what's goin on. She'll be ok once she gets to know you." Lauren took in Trisha's appearance at a glance – the shapeless faded brown woolen jacket frayed at the cuffs, the two-tone hair that was almost white on top, and almost black underneath. The multiple piercings in her ears, nose, lips, and even one of her eyebrows, and a tattoo of some sort that just showed above the neckline of her rather moth-eaten green jumper. She smelled of something vaguely familiar, and Lauren recognized it as the same smell that pervaded Netty and Razzy – cannabis. At the same time she was wondering how this already frightened child was going to react when the time came to leave with a woman she had never before met. She fished in her handbag, and produced Mostly Molly.

"This is for you Poppy," she said gently. "She needs a mummy, and I thought of you."

Poppy's face crumpled. "Mummy," she whispered, and began to cry. Lauren was mortified. *How stupid can I be?* she thought, as Poppy wept uncontrollably against Trisha's shoulder, brushing the doll aside and clinging to Trisha. *What now?* Lauren thought; *I blew it already!* Trisha shook her head.

"Don't worry," she said, "She's doin this a lot right now, it probly wouldn't have made any difference wot you said. You'll ave to give er time, but she'll get used to you."

"Where's her stuff?" asked Lauren. Trisha produced a small, rather scruffy looking pink backpack and placed it on the table between them.

"Is that it?" asked Lauren. *This gets better and better*, she thought.

"I'm afraid so. She only came to me for a week, and this is all Ashley gave me. I can't get in er flat to get anything else, I'm sorry." Trisha gazed anxiously at Lauren, sensing her dismay and disapproval.

"Have you heard from Ashley?" Lauren asked.

"No. I've phoned er several times an left messages but I've eard nothing. Perhaps she's lost er mobile or something. I wanted to tell er I was taking Poppy to you, but it's too bad, she'll just ave to find out whenever she gets back, I've put a note through er door." Trisha shrugged her shoulders. She had been lumbered, and she'd done her best to sort it out. It really wasn't – Poppy really wasn't – her problem. Lauren was family; it was up to her now. Lauren ordered coffees for Trisha and herself, and a hot chocolate for Poppy, who looked so thin and starved in her inadequate clothing. The hot chocolate arrived smothered in squirty cream and festooned with marshmallows, and the ghost of a smile appeared on the little pale face as Poppy sipped at her drink, her searching gecko-like tongue scooping up cream and marshmallows swiftly. Lauren made a mental note to get some in. She watched as the little girl lifted the big heavy mug to her face and drained the contents, emerging with a huge chocolate grin spread across her face, even though her mouth was still turned down and her expression melancholy. Having finished, Poppy placed the mug on the table, wiped her mouth across her sleeve, and began to slide down from her perch on Trisha's knee, all the while fixing her emerald gaze on Lauren. She sidled over towards Mostly Molly, then made a sudden lunge, grabbed her, and retreated once more to safety. Lauren said nothing, but her heart leaped and she knew that the first hurdle was over. Lauren and Trisha chatted over their coffees, deliberately ignoring Poppy, who was sitting on a tall stool now, playing with Mostly Molly, undressing her and dressing her again, altering the angle of her hat, and re-braiding her woolen hair. Trisha told Lauren that she had tried to persuade Ashley to return home, especially when Poppy was born, but that she wouldn't listen. Trisha and Ashley had shared a flat for some years until Ashley's new boyfriend came on the scene. Trisha didn't like him, and she moved out. Now she had met someone herself, and had even got a job stacking shelves in an all-night supermarket. Another reason she couldn't look after Poppy any longer – she had to leave her with her boyfriend when she was working and understandably he was less than happy about it.

"I'm really worried about Ashley. That Jerzy guy she's with is bad news Mrs. Stevenson."

"Lauren, please! You're not in primary school now Trisha," said Lauren. "Jerzy? That's a Polish name isn't it? Does he have a job – does Ashley?"

"Fuck no! Not what you'd call a job anyway. E's a drug dealer, mostly weed n skunk but e andles some pretty eavy stuff too."

"And Ashley? Does she take it?"

Trisha looked uncomfortable. "Well, we both smoke a bit of weed, but to be honest I'm not sure about the other stuff. I wouldn't touch it, but I know what these dealer guys are like, they get their girlfriends onto coke so that they can control em. That's why I weren't appy when e moved in; it weren't right with Poppy being there. I'm sorry; I did try an talk some sense into er, but I'm sure you remember what she's like."

Lauren sighed, "Unfortunately, yes I do. How long has she been with this Jerzy then?" She was horrified at the thought of little Poppy living with a drug dealer. What could Ashley be thinking of!

"Not that long, about a year I suppose, an she's never been away with im before. They went to Amsterdam for obvious reasons, but it were only supposed to be a week. They was staying with some mates of Jerzy's. I can't understand why she said she were on er way ome, and then didn't come. You watch, she'll rock up tomorrow and ave an absolute fit with me for leaving Pops with you!"

"Well, I guess I hope she does. I made myself stop worrying about her years ago. She seemed well able to take care of herself, but you've certainly got me worried now. Still, I suppose she's been up to all sorts over the years and has come through it unscathed; so why should this time be any different?"

"I ope you're right. I thought Poppy ad forced er to keep er feet on the ground, but it didn't last – poor Pops." Trisha drained her coffee. "I ave to go now, I'm meeting Steve at three." Poppy looked up and saw that Trisha was standing. She leapt down from her seat and clung to the jeans again; Mostly Molly lay forgotten on the floor."

"Let's go to the shop. Poppy can meet Bessie; she can choose a new outfit and Bessie will personalise it for her. Would you like that Poppy?" Lauren smiled encouragingly at her granddaughter, who still clung to Trisha's leg, but nodded assent.

"This is my granddaughter Poppy," Lauren announced to a surprised Bessie when they reached the shop. "I think she'd quite like something nice and warm to wear with her name on it. Do you think you could help her choose Bessie?"

"Of course I can Ducks," Bessie beamed at Poppy and shifted her ample frame along the bench behind the sewing machine, patting the place at her side to encourage Poppy to sit. Poppy released her grasp on Trisha's hand and reluctantly sat on the edge of the bench. Bessie got out the big book of designs with its colourful representations of Lauren's work. She turned the pages slowly, revealing the designs one by one.

"What about this one here?" she said, turning to a warm long-sleeved dress in dark green corduroy with multi-coloured felt flowers appliquéd around the hem and large colourful wooden buttons down the front. Poppy studied it closely, then shook her head.

"Oh! Don't you like that one? I thought it would look lovely with your hair and eyes, don't you think so *Grandma*?" Bessie turned to Lauren with a broad wink. Then Poppy spoke, so softly that Lauren could barely make out the words.

"I want one with Poppy on it," she said. Lauren, Trisha and Bessie exchanged glances.

Then Lauren said, "I tell you what. If you like, Bessie will make you a dress just like that one, but with red poppies and red buttons, and your name embroidered on the front. It will be a special one just for you, and nobody else will have one like it. Would you like that Poppy?" Poppy stared at Lauren, and then nodded; the ghost of a smile lit up her emerald eyes, although it didn't quite reach her lips. "If you're a very good girl for Grandma over the weekend, we'll come back on Monday, and Bessie will have it ready for you, then you can show Mummy when she comes home next week."

"Is that ok Pops?" Trisha said, bending to look her in the face.

"Can Trisha come too?" It was barely a whisper. She turned anxious eyes on Lauren, who immediately replied,

"I'm not sure; Trisha has to go to work Poppy, but she'll come and see you soon."

Poppy's face crumpled, and she began to wail. Trisha bent and kissed her swiftly, gave Lauren a look that said *no point in prolonging this*, and left, hastily promising to try and make it on Monday.

"I want my mummy," wailed Poppy, the tears cascading down her face. Lauren tried to comfort her, but she pushed her away. "I don't like you," she sobbed.

Bessie closed the door of the shop and pulled down the blind. "People will think we're child abductors," she muttered dryly. "Come on Ducks, dry your eyes. Look, Aunty Bessie's got a great big box of buttons here. Let's see if we can find some for your frock shall we?" The wailing continued unabated, however, as Poppy climbed onto her knee and buried her head in her comforting bosom. Bessie soothed her gently, stroking her fine hair back from her face, and gradually the wailing turned into long shuddering sobs. Lauren looked on feeling helpless. What use was she to this little girl? She wasn't even built for comfort!

Eventually Poppy stopped crying altogether, and raised her head from Bessie's bosom to look at Lauren. Lauren returned her stare without smiling – what was the point? Nothing she said or did seemed to make any difference. She just wasn't cut out to be a mother substitute.

"Are you really my grandma?" Poppy asked in a tiny voice, her eyes still bright with tears. She pushed her hair back from her face and regarded Lauren directly, taking in every detail of this woman who claimed to be her family.

"I am indeed," replied Lauren with a sigh, "for my sins."

"What are sins?" asked Polly, her brow furrowed and perplexed.

"Nothing you need to worry about Ducks," interjected Bessie. "Now, aren't you a lucky little girl to have a nice grandma like Grandma Lauren. She'll look after you, and when your mummy comes home you can tell her all about it."

Poppy continued to stare at Lauren. "How did you get to be my Grandma?" she asked now. Lauren thought for a moment. She supposed that Ashley had either not known who was the father of her child, or had not cared, so Poppy would have had no previous experience of grandparents.

"I'm your mummy's mummy," she replied. "You have a grandpa too, his name's Ken."

"Where is he?" enquired Poppy, looking around the room as though she expected him to suddenly appear. Her eyes were round and fearful; clearly she was distrustful of men, thought Lauren.

"Oh, he's not here. He doesn't live with me anymore; there's just me and Charlie Cat, and you'll like him I'm sure."

"Charlie... Cat?" Poppy repeated the name slowly, savouring it.

"That's right," said Lauren, sensing some capitulation. "He's soft and fluffy, he purrs a lot, and I'm sure he'd be happy to sleep on your bed." She crossed her fingers as she spoke. Charlie had no experience of young children, and Lauren could only hope and pray that he would take to Poppy. Poppy, however, had made up her mind.

"Can we go and see him now?" she asked, picking up her backpack from the sewing table. She ran to the door, then paused, and ran back to retrieve Mostly Molly and to give Bessie a quick hug.

"Well I'll be!" exclaimed Bessie, beaming from ear to ear, and raising the blind on the door. "Run along now Ducks; you two get on home and get settled in, and I'll see you both on Monday."

FIVE: GLENN

Glenn closed the door behind him, turning the oversized key decisively in the lock. Merlin rubbed against his legs, purring loudly.

"Sorry old boy, you'll have to stay here. Bronwyn will be around to let you in and feed you later." He bent and stroked the gleaming jet-black fur and was rewarded with another flurry of loud sing-song purring. Merlin followed him round to the front of the house and watched him from the shelter of the little front porch as he made his way down the grass track to the garage at the bottom. Rain fell steadily, beating a rhythmic tattoo through the branches of the trees that surrounded the tiny stone cottage that was his home. The dry-stone walls that bordered the track glistened darkly with rain and the ground squelched and sucked at his feet. In the distance, as he descended the path, he could just glimpse the estuary; a winding silver ribbon beyond the pale reed beds. Moss clung to the tops of the walls, bejeweled with shimmering droplets of iridescent rain. In the branches above, the quarrelsome rooks jostled for position, with raucous, discordant cries. The garage stood a short way up a rough dirt track that also led to the next-door property, if you could call it next-door. The two properties were completely secluded and from each one you would never have known that the other existed. Bronwyn was Glenn's neighbour, and could always be relied upon to care for Merlin in his absence, having three cats of her own. Bronwyn was elderly; Glenn had no idea of her actual age, but she must have been well over eighty, small and spry with a mop of snowy hair and bright bird-like eyes that lit up when she smiled. She was like an illustration from the Welsh folk story books that Glenn had read as a kid, sent to him by his Nain in Anglesey, except that the Welsh ladies in them often wore tall black hats and shawls, whereas Bronwyn had a penchant for baggy trousers and even baggier sweaters or tee-shirts that she bought from the local charity shops.

The car was reluctant to start. Glenn didn't use it often, just the odd trip into Barmouth for supplies or a walk along the seashore, especially in winter when the shore was more-or-less deserted and he could suck in great gulps of ozone and restore his wounded soul.

Eventually it coughed into life, and at the bottom of the drive he turned left and headed resolutely toward Chesbury, some sixty miles away. He didn't want to go; it was always hard, but he owed it to the others. Someone had to help them.

At the weekend, another murder had occurred. Someone else had lost a loved one in the most cruel and bizarre circumstances. Glenn knew the pain, the utter devastation, the guilt and the despair of the aftermath of these murders, for his wife, Alison, was the first victim. Almost eleven months had passed, and Glenn's life had changed beyond all recognition. When the second murder, with its idiosyncrasies that pointed inevitably to the dreaded serial killer, occurred, Glenn determined that no one else would suffer as he had with the guilt and recriminations; the 'if onlys' and the 'whys?'. He enlisted the help of a colleague and set up a victim support group that he named 'Second Sight', because we don't possess such a gift otherwise we should be better able to protect our loved ones, and also with reference to the killer's rather gruesome MO. Every victim was someone's wife, mother, daughter or friend, and Glenn was determined that those they were taken from shouldn't suffer alone.

After what seemed a very long time, the winding country roads gave way to dual carriageways and then the modest conurbation of Chesbury, where he and Alison had lived for their twenty-three years of marriage; twenty-three years of happiness marred only by the absence of the children that would have been the icing on the cake.

On the fateful night at the end of January that year, Glenn had gone out alone to their customary quiz night at the King's Head because Alison had a headache. Their team lost miserably, because Alison was always the one with the answers – bright, intelligent, vivacious Alison whose brain was full of the sort of useless information that quizzers love. Glenn set off home at eleven-thirty in happy anticipation of her glee at knowing she was so sorely missed. As he drove up the hill past the castle and headed downward through the deserted streets towards their three-storey home on the banks of the river, he anticipated her lying in their bed, warm from sleep yet welcoming, her fiery red hair setting light to the pillow, her green eyes soft with love as she greeted him. He would climb in beside her and gently push the molten fire from her forehead, running his hands though its silky softness before kissing her lips, and joining her in her slumbers.

Pushing his key into the yale lock, he was surprised when the door swung open before he turned it. The house was in darkness, and there was an eerie silence that screamed in his head *something is wrong!* Hesitantly, he stepped through the door into the hallway. "Al," he called softly, "are you ok?" The silence was tangible, it made his heart stop as he crept along the hallway in the darkness. He should turn on the light, but fear rose in his gorge and gripped his heart with icy fingers. He didn't know why, but he was afraid of what he might see. The stairs creaked, the sound familiar but suddenly louder than gunshots – "Al, are you awake?" He called again, his voice echoing around the stairwell loudly enough to wake the dead, or so it seemed. There was no reply, no rustle of bedclothes or creaking of the wooden slatted bedstead through the bedroom door that stood wide open. A faint light penetrated the darkness through the bedroom curtains, and he could make out the shape of his wife in the bed, sleeping. Relief washed over him and he hurried across the room to the bedside. His relief was short-lived. She lay still and silent across the bed, face down at an un-natural angle. Glenn reached out a trembling hand, and touched her shoulder. It was warm and soft, and felt as it always did. "Al?" He gave a tug and rolled her onto her back, and then he saw....

It was all over the newspapers the following day. A woman, a doctor's wife, had been found murdered in her bed in the genteel town that was Chesbury. Strangled. The police enquiry was extensive. Glenn was questioned, of course, but soon released when it became clear that at the time of her death he was taking part in the weekly quiz at the King's Head. The murderer had gained access through the kitchen window at the back of the house and had left, apparently, by the front door. No significant clues were found; it was a dry night and the ground was hard from several days of frost so there were no footprints, and of course, no fingerprints, since the perpetrator must have worn gloves. Alison, it seemed, had disturbed the killer in whatever his reason for being there was, and had fought bravely, but she had been strangled, and bizarrely, the killer had then removed her eyes. Shock waves rebounded in the local community and spread nationwide. Could this be the handiwork of a potential serial killer? As the weeks passed, however, and no more bodies were discovered, everyone began to relax and women forgot their fear and went about their business as usual.

Glenn, after two months' compassionate leave, decided that he was no longer fit for work. He no longer felt he could face the daily grind of the busy surgeries where fifty percent of the patients were either hypochondriacs who spent too much time on the internet googling their largely imaginary symptoms, or clinically obese and not willing to change the habits of a lifetime. A further twenty-five percent were suffering from depression, anxiety or insomnia. Glenn felt unable to offer them the sympathy and support they deserved. *'Physician heal thyself'*, he thought, but he was finding it more difficult than he would have believed. He decided to take early retirement, put the house on the market, and search for a place in the country; a place where nobody knew him, where he would be simply Glenn Gibson, widower, rather than Glenn Gibson, husband of a murder victim. Having thought long and hard about it, he decided on North Wales. Not too far away from Chesbury – he still had friendships he wanted to preserve, but remote enough to leave behind the horrific circumstances of Alison's death and not become a local tourist attraction. Property was relatively cheap, and last but certainly not least, the wild beauty of the countryside would be the ultimate catharsis for his grief. As a child, he had spent enchanting holidays with his grandmother who lived on the windswept coast of Anglesey, but he decided to search further down the coast where the climate might be kinder and there was no chance of his being recognised. He trawled the internet looking for a suitable retreat, and eventually he found Argoed; set back off the road with its own driveway, within sight of the Mawddach estuary and within ten minutes driving distance of the sea. He booked an appointment to go and view it, and was informed by the estate agent that the house was empty, and the next-door neighbour would oblige with the key and show him around.

He missed the drive to Argoed completely, and only realised that he had gone wrong when he arrived on the outskirts of the little seaside town of Barmouth. *That's good,* he thought as he negotiated the one-way system back the way he came. *If I can't see it, neither will anyone else.* From the other direction it was a little easier to spot and he pulled up in front of 'his' garage, noting that it was the only one. To the right of the garage was a small rickety wooden gate with a sign on it saying 'Argoed', and to the left, another saying 'Ty Gwylan'. Neither property could be seen from here, hidden as they were behind ancient moss-laden trees and rhododendron bushes. He took the left-hand path, and soon a small white cottage came into sight. On the gable end wall was a large painted mural of a seagull in flight, and a weather vane in the shape of a seagull adorned one of the two chimney pots, from which a thin white spiral of smoke rose into the dull damp winter air. Wood smoke; he could smell it quite plainly. The path climbed steeply, winding round to a small covered porch, and along its length various garden ornaments were interspersed with jars containing tea-lights. A wind chime dangled at the side of the porch that was covered in a profusion of intertwined bare stems, probably clematis, thought Glenn, or possibly honeysuckle. A large somewhat rusty metal bell hung inside the porch with a rope that had a large, jolly and rotund ceramic monk dangling at its end. Glenn seized the monk, and gave the rope a good tug. The bell rang loudly but unexpectedly melodiously, and he heard footsteps from within, and a flurry of rather hoarse barking.

"Shush Pero!" The voice was soft, yet commanding, and the barking ceased. "Who is it?" The voice asked, and Glenn answered,

"It's Glenn. Glenn Gibson, I've come about the house next door."

"Oh! Glenn! Glenn Gibson! That's right." The voice was clear with a definite Welsh lilt. The door opened, and a tiny woman with a shock of snowy white hair stood beaming at him, her pale blue eyes reminding him of a jackdaw's, her head on one side, studying him. "I'm Bronwyn. Bronwyn Evans." She looked him up and down as she offered him her hand, nodding approval, and Glenn clasped it gently. It was small and appeared gnarled, but felt surprisingly soft.

"I'll fetch you the keys and then leave you to it. When you've finished we'll have a nice cup of tea and a Welsh cake." She hurried away across the flag-stoned hallway and disappeared through a heavy wooden door at the far end. Pero the dog was lying on a pile of sacks in the hallway, his nose on his paws, regarding Glenn balefully. He was large and of indeterminate breed – possibly collie crossed with German shepherd Glenn thought.

"Hello boy," he said, and was rewarded with a slow thump of a plumy tail on the gleaming flagstones as Pero carefully shuffled a little nearer so that Glenn could bend down to pat his head and ruffle his ears. The tail thumped harder and a long pink tongue wrapped itself around Glenn's hand.

"Pero!" Bronwyn admonished cheerfully as she reappeared holding a bunch of keys. "Paid a llyfu! Mr. Gibson doesn't want your old tongue soaking him!"

"Oh, I don't mind, we're just getting acquainted aren't we Pero?" Glenn laughed, and stood upright, reaching for the keys.

"The big shiny one's the shed, and the yale one's the front door. The other big one's the kitchen door at the back, but it's a bit temperamental and you have to fiddle with it to get it to turn. Take your time; I hope you like the place. Mind my cats don't follow you in – they've been known to do it before now."

"Have there been many viewers?" asked Glenn anxiously. He didn't want to be pipped at the post.

"Two before you," replied Bronwyn. "But I think they were put off by the climb and the fact that you can't get a car up to the door. It's part-furnished you know, perhaps for that reason. It's been empty for four years since the lady who lived there went into a home. Her family aren't interested in living there, and I don't want it going for a holiday home. That's what usually happens around here. The young people either can't afford to buy, or it's too far from where they work, or they want something with more mod cons I suppose."

"Well, you have to pay for mod cons," replied Glenn. "As long as it's got the basics it'll do me." He took the keys, and set off to explore his potential new home.

The path was even steeper than the one leading to Ty Gwylan, and quite overgrown, although clearly someone had made some attempt at clearing it to allow viewers access to the house, which nestled into the hillside surrounded by deciduous trees and a tangled overgrown garden. Glenn's present home that he had shared with Alison since the early days of their marriage had a small, manageable front garden enclosed by a low hedge, and a back garden that sloped sharply down towards the river. It was difficult to cultivate, and often flooded in winter, so Glenn and Alison had used pots and urns to bring some colour to the upper reaches. Gardening, he thought, would be a good distraction, would tire him out and induce restful sleep. It would help him to bond with his new home which wasn't going to be easy after living for so long in one place. He noticed there were curtains at the window, and remembered that Bronwyn had said it was partly furnished. The front door swung open a short way and then stuck firmly against the flagstoned floor. Making a mental note that he would have to fix that, he squeezed through into a hallway similar to Bronwyn's, with doors opening on either side, a third one facing him that apparently led to the stairwell, and a fourth at the far end that he surmised probably led to the kitchen. The two rooms at the front were small and square but adequate, with wide slate windowsills and shutters. The one on the left had an old-fashioned range set into a recess in the wall, and the one on the right a rather grand cast-iron fireplace with a tiled surround and oak mantlepiece. He tried the windows, but they wouldn't budge – probably sealed up with paint. There was a large and very old oak Welsh chest in the right hand room, dusty and covered in a film of mould from the damp. He lifted the lid, the chest was empty. The lid was extremely heavy, and he guessed that whoever cleared the house had thought the piece too cumbersome to carry away down the path. In the left hand room was another piece of heavy oak furniture in the shape of a large Welsh dresser. He opened the drawers and found them full of all manner of bits and pieces, including some old photographs and letters. He would have to box those up and return them to the estate agents, he thought, and realised that he had already made up his mind to make this house his home. Although it had been empty for so long, it didn't feel as chilly as he might have expected. It had a welcoming feel; peaceful and tranquil; it was exactly what he needed. At the back of the house you went through the small dark kitchen to access the downstairs bathroom which although dilapidated, contained an ancient but serviceable three piece bathroom suite. It was without doubt the only bathroom in the house; not an ideal arrangement, but Glenn didn't care. He would need something to fill his days, and making this little house into a home would fit the bill nicely. Upstairs there were two decent sized bedrooms and from the front one you could just see glimpses of the estuary through the trees, although in summer the leaves would obscure the view. The back bedroom was dark, its windows completely overgrown with ivy and Glenn realised that was also why the kitchen was like the black hole of Calcutta. Both rooms had small cast-iron fireplaces and contained ancient iron bedsteads that Glenn was sure could be restored and put to use. Outside, a path led alongside a wall to a stone-built outbuilding with a corrugated tin roof. It was empty save for one or two rusted garden implements and a wooden saw-horse, but appeared to be dry and serviceable.

  Glenn stood for some time and surveyed his little kingdom, then returned to Bronwyn's for his tea and Welsh cakes.

SIX: NETTY

Netty pushed her way through the throng of alighting passengers as the doors of the train slammed behind her with a noise like rapid gunfire and the air-brakes hissed and groaned before it began to rumble away again towards its next destination. She glanced at the station clock which read 4.45p.m. It was too late now to get to the market before Razzy closed up the stall. She hoped he wasn't too narked about her sudden departure. She had had to leave him a note because he didn't come home last night. She waited in for him so that they could go to the Christmas do together but as the hours passed she realised that he wasn't going to come home in time, and in the morning his bed hadn't been slept in. Some girl again, she supposed. It wouldn't last; they never did, in spite of the fact that she made them more than welcome in their modest and untidy but comfortable home.

Now she hurried home, her mind working overtime, her stomach turning somersaults. She loved Razzy; he was, after all, her only son; but sometimes she almost buckled under the burden of keeping him on an even keel. She mentally perused the fridge and seeing nothing but a few beers and some margarine, moved on to the freezer. There was a curry in there she was pretty sure. Curry was Netty's speciality. She would get fresh spices from the health foods shop in the market and spend hours concocting the complex aromatic meals that were Razzy's favourite, but which she never ate because she had been a vegetarian for most of her life, and lately a vegan. The freezer was full of meals that Netty cooked, but never ate. Nevertheless, she enjoyed her food and was more than capable of rustling up an equally satisfying vegan dish when she could be bothered. She had raised Razzy as a vegetarian, but in his late teens he had rebelled against her regime and, under pressure from his peers, demanded that she feed him 'normal' food. It had been a challenge for Netty to have to select and prepare meat; she would shudder at the feel of it as her knife sliced through it and the smell of it would nauseate her whilst she tried not to think of the innocent creature that had lost its life in some gruesome fashion in order to satisfy her son's lust for flesh. Afterwards, she would kneel before the small shrine that she created in a corner of her bedroom and pray for forgiveness. Gradually, over the years, the guilt subsided and she became hardened to her task, but she always breathed silent thanks to the provider and prayed at least once a week at her little shrine. She had christened her son Paul, naming him after the man who would have married her sister and was kind to Netty. Her experience of men was limited and brutal, and she clung to the memory of the kind man for whom her sister had grieved for more than forty years.

On her seventeenth birthday, she had gone into Birmingham for a night out with some friends from work. Pauline was not happy, but Netty had ignored her pleas and refused to be discouraged. Somehow, during the evening, she got separated from her friends and found herself alone in the city in the company of the boy she had been dancing with for most of the night who had made her forget all about her girlfriends. His name was Tony. He was tall and handsome with skin the colour of Swiss chocolate and a gleaming white smile. She was fascinated by his long, black, shining dreadlocks. He seemed nice, so she happily accepted his offer of a lift home in his car since she had missed the last bus to Perry Bar. Tony was drunk; he drove erratically and laughed when Netty became fearful, but eventually he pulled up at the end of her road and relief washed over her even as she decided that she didn't want to see him again. He leaned over to kiss her goodnight and she shrunk away. His breath smelled of beer and cigarettes and she struggled as he forced his tongue into her mouth, entwining his hands in her long auburn curls and pulling her to him. She reached for the door handle, but he pushed the lock down and tightened his grip on her.

"Come on Baby," he whispered fiercely, his breath hot and foetid, the brown eyes that had seemed so soft now glittering with lust. "You've been teasin' me all night, so don't pretend you don't want it. Taxi would've cost you a fiver, but you can pay me in kind." Before she knew it he had pulled her knickers and tights down roughly and forced himself on her. The pain was searing, but somewhere in her brain she knew she must endure this or perhaps suffer a worse fate. She closed her eyes and her mind and prayed for it to be over quickly, and it was.

"Get dressed," he muttered through clenched teeth, zipping up his jeans and averting his eyes. He seemed subdued now, the domineering attitude gone. He looked smaller and rather pathetic, his long dreadlocks hiding his face from the streetlights. He unlocked the door and Netty made a dive for freedom, stumbling along the pavement blinded by her tears. Thankfully Pauline was asleep, and Netty crawled into bed and thanked God that she was safe. She would never go against Pauline's wishes again; the memory of her ordeal would fade and nothing like that would ever happen to her again. Pauline must never know; she would be devastated.

One morning a few weeks later, Pauline found her sitting on the bathroom floor with her head down the toilet.

"What's up with you kid?" Netty didn't trust herself to speak, but waved her sister away.

"Can't have been last night's tea, we ate the same thing and I'm ok." Pauline gave her sister a sharp look; she wasn't going to be fobbed off. Since her mother's death three years earlier, she had transferred all her caring instincts to her younger sister. She wore her responsibility like a badge of office, and very little escaped her notice.

"When did you last have the curse Netty?" The tight-lipped query struck terror into Netty who, since she had begun working last year, had insisted on some independence and had taken charge of her own personal requirements, with Pauline reluctantly forced to agree. It didn't, however, deter her from her continued monitoring of every aspect of her sister's life – for her own good, naturally, and not from any particular need to be controlling. Now Netty raised her head from the toilet bowl and although she said nothing, the answer was plain to see in her eyes.

"No! You stupid girl!" Pauline exclaimed, her face contorted with rage. She grabbed her sister roughly by the arm and pulled her to her feet. Placing her hands on her shoulders she shook her and forced her to look her in the face. "How long have you known, and why didn't you tell me?" She shook her again, and Netty began to cry as she had when she was a small child and had angered her sister with some careless misdemeanor; only this time it was, she realised, a far more serious matter.

"Because I knew you'd be like this," she sobbed. "I wanted to tell you, but I was scared. Pauline, I'm sorry, it wasn't my fault; I didn't want to do it. I didn't know this would happen after something that only lasted a minute."

"What do you mean, you didn't want to? Did he force you then? Why didn't you tell me straight away? He should be reported to the police. Who is he? Where does he live? How long have you known him? Are you still seeing him? I don't understand...." She finished lamely; the look on her sister's face was answer enough, and they clung together, both sobbing now as the enormity of Netty's situation hit them.

"It's alright Netty, it'll be alright. I'll look after you, I always have, haven't I?"

Pauline was true to her word, and over the next few months bore the brunt of the whispered comments from the neighbours. She invented a fiancée whom Netty had married secretly, and who was forced to work in another part of the country. She bought Netty a cheap wedding ring from H. Samuels, and even helped her to change her name by deed poll from Proctor to Lipton. The name was chosen at random as they were waiting for the bus and saw an advertisement for Lipton's Tea on a roadside hoarding.

Paul Lipton was born three weeks early in the small hours of a rainy morning in March. At Pauline's insistence, Netty had packed a small suitcase in readiness a week earlier. It contained a nightgown, a housecoat and slippers, all brand new purchases from Kay's Catalogue for Netty, along with a bar of pink Lux soap, some ashes of roses talcum powder and two sets of underwear. Alongside these was an outfit for a newborn baby – a vest and nightgown in white, and a lemon knitted jacket, hat and bootees. These were all wrapped in the lace shawl that had enveloped Netty nearly eighteen years earlier. Pauline had kept it carefully, protected in tissue paper in the airing cupboard, for just this occasion. Pauline's view was that a baby was a blessing, regardless of the circumstances of its conception, and Netty's baby would be welcomed and loved without reservation. She was, therefore, quite unprepared for the shock of seeing her new nephew!

He was a beautiful baby, with skin like a polished hazelnut and a shock of jet-black hair. As he grew the skin and hair both lightened until they were much the same shade of drab brown, at odds with the green eyes inherited from his mother. Pauline came up with a plan, and when he was old enough to ask about his father, Netty told him he was a Jamaican who worked and died on a North Sea oilrig. Pauline had seen a TV documentary about the dangers faced by the rig workers and there was no need for the boy's life to be blighted by the sorry truth. By the time Paul started secondary school, he had become obsessed with the father whom he had never seen. Netty wove a complex fantasy around the man whose full name she didn't know. She sang the praises of her tall, handsome Rastafarian 'husband'. She wasn't exactly sure what a Rastafarian was, but she knew they wore their hair like Tony. Pauline insisted anyway that most men from Jamaica were Rastas, and Netty was easily persuaded to be party to the deception as it seemed many of them were also disinclined to eat meat. Thus rapist Tony of no known surname became Tony Lipton, devoted husband and father, tragically cut down in his prime whilst trying to support his family. Sometimes Netty railed at the unfairness, the irony of it all, and when Paul was being difficult, which was lamentably often, she longed to tell him the truth and knock the man who had ruined her off his pedestal.

At secondary school, in honour of his father and to impress his peers, Paul began to shape his dull, frizzy hair into the dreadlocks that soon earned him his nickname, Razzy, as well as getting him into trouble at school. Pauline was appalled, and she and Netty had countless arguments as Netty leaped to her son's defence. "He didn't ask to be born," she insisted, "and anyway, the whole Rastafarian thing was your idea Pauline!"

Life in the Perry Barr semi became increasingly fraught, and it all came to a head when Pauline found out about the cannabis. For some time, Netty had ignored the suspicion that her son was smoking weed, but his clothes, his school bag, and especially those damn dreadlocks reeked of something that wasn't aftershave and try as she might to reason with him, he would shrug his shoulders and retort "So what? Everyone smokes it, it's no big deal."

She asked him once, "Where does the money come from Paul?" The question drew a blank stare, another shrug of the shoulders and a look that brooked no further enquiries. She tried desperately to disguise the heavy, cloying odour by spraying everything with air freshener, but she knew in the end Pauline would realise what was going on.

"What the hell is this?" Netty had never before heard her sister swear. She glanced at her outstretched hand, and the object in her palm, a thin cigarette with the end twisted into a point.

"I don't know," lied Netty, crossing her fingers behind her back as she would have when she lied as a child. "It looks like a cigarette."

"Well, it doesn't smell like a cigarette!" Pauline thrust it under Netty's nose, and the familiar aroma of cannabis assailed her nostrils. "Right, that's it Netty. I can't cope with that boy any longer!"

"Wh…what d'you mean?" Panic rose in Netty's breast and threatened to overwhelm her. Her sister only ever called her Netty when she was seriously vexed with her.

"I can't cope with him, and I can't have him here any longer. It's time you two got a place of your own."

Netty stared at her sister in numb disbelief. "But he's only sixteen! Where will we live? What about my job?"

"You can get another one, it's not like it requires any special skill to work in a shop Netty. I'm not going to just chuck you out. I'll give you some money to get you started; you can have your share of Mother's inheritance and the money from the trust fund Paul set up for you. I'll help you find a flat somewhere, and then you and …Razzy…will have to look after yourselves. It's for the best Netty; this house just isn't big enough for the three of us anymore."

No amount of pleading would change Pauline's mind. Within three weeks, as good as her word and despite Netty's continuous pleadings, she had found her sister a two-bedroomed flat in Chesbury, some fifty miles away, and helped her apply for jobs although as yet she had been unsuccessful in that endeavour.

The three sat in silence on the train as they set off to view the flat, with Razzy hunched in the corner nearest the window although he never looked out once but kept his eyes closed and moved his head slightly in time to the reggae music that emanated through a pair of earphones from his walkman. The volume must have been high, as Netty could hear the persistent echo of the beat above the low rumble of the train. She sought desperately for some topic of conversation to offer her sister, who stared vacantly out of the opposite window. Netty would have liked to sit and watch the countryside flash by, but had to content herself with observing their fellow passengers instead. She tried to imagine where they were going, and what took them there, and she wondered if, like her, they were unwilling participants in some crisis of their life, or were they going on a jaunt, or a family visit, or just returning home from somewhere. The journey took just over an hour and Netty thought it was probably the longest hour of her life.

Chesbury, however, was a pleasant surprise. They climbed the steep hill from the station. The street was lined with small businesses – a florist, an artisan bakery, a shop selling oriental carpets, and a café from whence wafted a delicious aroma of freshly brewed coffee. Higher up, the independent businesses gave way to high street icons such as Marks and Spencer and W.H. Smith. Netty made a mental note that she should want for nothing should she settle here. At the top of the hill, they turned into a narrow sloping side street lined with tall grey-stone houses. Halfway down the street was Netty and Razzy's potential new home. Steep steps led to the entrance beside which were several doorbell buttons with rectangular labels, most of which displayed the names of their occupants. Pauline resolutely rang the one marked Flat 5. A buzzer sounded, and the heavy wooden door yielded to their pressure, admitting them to a Minton-tiled hallway of broad proportions. They trooped up the seemingly endless staircase that had two flats on each floor – flat five being therefore on the third and topmost floor. Netty observed the mahogany stair-rail that was grubby and neglected, the gloss-painted embossed wallpaper that was faded and stained, and the chipped and discoloured paintwork on the doors to the flats. As they climbed the flights of stairs she became increasingly dismayed. The tall windows that spanned the three stories were almost obscured by grime and cobwebs. The estate agent's blurb had said that the tenants were jointly responsible for the cleaning and maintenance of the communal areas. It was clear that nobody could be bothered and in consequence, the once magnificent building was tired and sad. Pauline wrinkled her nose in distaste. Her little semi was always as neat as a pin. Razzy loped easily up the stairs and arrived at the door of Flat 5 long before his mother and aunt. They reached the end of the seemingly endless staircase to find him leaning against the wall outside the flat, the door of which was slightly ajar.

"Did you knock?" Pauline demanded. Razzy shrugged

"Nope," he replied, and slid down the wall to hunch on the landing, pushing his earphones back into place dismissively.

"Razzy, stand up for goodness sakes!" Netty felt the hot flush of humiliation spread up her neck and face that were already rosy from the effort of climbing the stairs. The door of the flat had opened, and a blonde lady in a neat navy suit and kitten heels stood before them clutching a clipboard. She glanced at the somewhat disheveled trio and deciding that Pauline was clearly the most likely spokeswoman, extended her hand to her with a forced smile.

"You must be Mrs. Proctor," she ventured. "I'm Helen Pugh."

"It's Miss actually," Pauline replied and caught the hand in the lightest of grips before letting it fall. "This is my Sister Annette Lipton and her son Paul. They are the prospective tenants." She studied the woman's expression critically, then added in withering tones, "My sister is a widow."

"I see. Do come in. I'm sorry for the state of the place, it's been empty a while. The lady who owns it was keeping it for her daughter but the daughter has other plans it seems." She smiled apologetically and they trooped into the flat. They found themselves in what was clearly the lounge. The room was dominated by a large fireplace with a magnificent mantlepiece. It had been blocked in and now housed an ancient and disproportionately small gas fire. However, there was also a storage heater on the wall beneath a large window through which the sun was now attempting to penetrate the dirt and cobwebs, casting dancing flecks of dust motes into the room. Netty walked over to it and taking a tissue from her pocket rubbed at the coating of dirt on the glass to clear a window within a window. Her gaze took in the view over the rooftops of smaller buildings with glimpses of narrow backstreets peppered with scurrying shoppers and sleeping cats, and beyond them the leafy green space that was the grounds of Chesbury Castle. She wrestled with the casement catch and flung open the window, leaning out to breathe in the slightly acrid air on which hung the aromas of the nearby station, the bakery and the coffee shop. A nearby tree was crammed with assorted corvids jostling for position with their raucous cries echoing between the buildings. Further down the narrow street, a young road-sweeper in a bright orange jacket was moving his broom to and fro in a leisurely fashion, every now and again raising his head to greet a passer-by as he worked his way down the street and out of sight.

Pauline, meanwhile, was casting her gaze around the room, taking in the shabby curtains, their green velour faded to dip-dye stripes, and the worn floral carpet that also must once have been various shades of green but was now a drab shade of khaki dotted with ominous dark patches. She strode across the room and opened a door on the back wall.

"The kitchen," explained the estate agent somewhat unnecessarily. It was a reasonable size but dark and dingy, the only light coming from a skylight that like everything else was in need of a good clean. Pauline flicked the light switch near the door and an ancient extractor fan rumbled into life but alas, no light. A grease-stained metal 'coolie' light shade dangled from the centre of the ceiling, hiding the empty light fitting. Pauline made an exclamation of annoyance and the estate agent squirmed uncomfortably.

"Of course," she ventured resolutely, "we'll replace any faulty electrical fittings before the tenancy commences. We've only just had the instruction and hadn't had chance to check it over since you insisted on an immediate viewing."

"Does this work?" Pauline indicated the washing machine that was mottled with rust spots. She pulled open the door and a malodourous stench wafted into the room. She regarded the gas cooker with the same disdain – it was a fifties design with an eye-level grill, and like everything else, it needed a good clean. In the corner stood a tall fridge-freezer, its door propped slightly open.

"That's quite new," exclaimed the estate agent triumphantly. Pauline flicked the switch on the wall and the light came on to reveal a spotless interior. The estate agent heaved an audible sigh of relief.

There was one large bedroom with a window overlooking the street corresponding to the one in the lounge, and another smaller one on the other side of the fireplace wall with a fitted wardrobe and a good sized Velux window. Each was blessed with a similar ancient storage heater to that in the lounge. The bathroom next to the kitchen, sported another small skylight and noisy extractor fan, along with an electric radiant heater high on the wall with a dangling pull switch.

The whole tour of the flat took less than a quarter of an hour, and it soon became apparent that Pauline had made up her mind.

"Come on Netty, I think we've seen enough!" She swept past the agent towards the door.

"I'll take it!" Netty opened her mouth and the words came out. A sudden sense of freedom washed over her. To wake in the morning in her own place; to open the window and let the sunshine in without worrying about letting flies in; to form her own routines and choose her own food. To retire and rise of her own volition without fear of repercussions, and perhaps to make a friend of her son when they were no longer constantly at loggerheads over Pauline's petty rules. "I'll make it nice."

The agent was visibly taken aback. Pauline was speechless for a moment before resuming her customary controlling manner. She turned to Razzy.

"Well Paul? What's your opinion?"

Razzy shrugged and made a gesture with his hands. "Looks ok to me," he said, and flashed his mother a rare grin with, she imagined, a conspiratorial air. He too was exploring the positives of the impending move. He knew full well that his mother was a complete pushover in comparison with his aunt. Pauline drew herself up with an arch look at the agent and said "You two wait downstairs, I'd like to talk to Ms. Pugh alone. Netty and Razzy obediently left the room, and closing the door behind them began to make their way down the stairs. Netty paused halfway down and rubbed again at the dirty window with her tissue and they stood for some minutes side-by-side looking out over their new domicile before descending to the street below, where they sat on a low wall opposite the building and gazed up at the windows of their flat in silence, each of them lost in their own thoughts and emotions. After what seemed like an eternity, the door opened, and Pauline and Helen emerged. They shook hands, and the agent took her leave with a wave of her hand to Netty and Razzy.

"That's sorted then." Pauline appeared well satisfied with the outcome of her lengthy chat with the agent, and the trio set off back down the hill towards the station. "Come on, I'll buy you both a coffee and explain everything."

"Is the flat ours?" Netty asked anxiously. She felt excluded. Pauline would have to let go the reins sooner or later. They turned in to Coffee and Compliments and Razzy headed for a window table where he slumped in his seat and put his earphones back in. Netty and Pauline queued up at the counter and returned to the table with three café lattes and three chocolate brownies. Pauline took a sip of her coffee.

"Well?" Netty was desperate for news.

"Yes and no," replied Pauline. "I've done some negotiating and provided the owner agrees, it will be yours in one month's time. If she doesn't agree, then we'll look elsewhere." She bit into her brownie with relish – Pauline rarely indulged in such frivolous fare.

"But I want it Pauline. I don't want to lose it. What are these negotiations? Shouldn't you have talked it over with me first?"

"Netty, you're just going to have to be patient. I promised to do my best by you and that doesn't end just because it's time for you to be independent. I don't think you'll lose it, because nobody is going to want to rent it in that state. I want a few improvements made so that you can get a good start without spending all your money, especially as it may take some time to find a job, and we haven't really decided what to do with Paul have we?"

"You make him sound like a guinea pig or something," said Netty sulkily.

"Well, he's about as much use as one!" retorted Pauline. "As I see it, we have two choices – we get him into college or he gets off his backside and finds a job; but I'm not sure that you'd be able to make him stick at it." She glanced towards the boy, who was munching his brownie and staring out of the window, earphones in, oblivious.

"When will we know?" Netty asked.

SEVEN: KEN.

It was not much more than a fifteen-minute walk from the market to Lauren's street. The little girl trotted obediently at Lauren's side, her tiny hand enveloped in a vice-like grip, her eyes wide with curiosity as she gazed at the brightly-illuminated shops and cafes bedecked with their Christmas finery, her feet barely touching the pavement and her slight frame offering little resistance, allaying Lauren's concern that she might at some point try to escape. Neither of them spoke, although at first Lauren searched her mind desperately for some point of conversation. Nothing came to her and after a few minutes she recognized the silence as companionable rather than awkward, and relaxed her grip slightly. Remembering the little girl relishing her hot chocolate in the cafe, they made a slight detour into Tesco Metro. Without hesitation, Poppy extracted a wire basket from a neat pile by the door and followed Lauren around the store. Lauren found drinking chocolate, milk, squirty cream in an aerosol can, and a bag of marshmallows and deposited them in the basket. They stood in the queue at the checkout, and Poppy set the basket down and solemnly rearranged the contents in a neat row before turning and rewarding Lauren with a dazzling smile. As they left the store, Lauren saw her granddaughter shiver involuntarily as the now freezing evening air assaulted them. She made a mental note to take her shopping on the morrow for some suitable winter clothes before she, Lauren, was arrested for child neglect.

The newly-lit streetlights along Lauren's cobbled street glowed pinky orange. Suddenly, it occurred to Lauren that she had no idea where her daughter and granddaughter lived, apart from the fact that it was a flat, so presumably not in the countryside. Was it possible that all these years they had, unbeknownst to her, been somewhere close by? Surely their paths would have crossed at some point if that were the case. She would ask Poppy later, she didn't want to risk a very public repeat of her earlier loud distress by mentioning her home now. There were several small towns or large villages within a twenty-mile radius of Chesbury; her home could be in any one of them, and perhaps Ashley deliberately avoided venturing in to the city in case she encountered her parents. Ken lived on the other side of the city, on a modern estate in the suburbs; but his office was less than half a mile away within the shadow of the cathedral, and from its second-floor window you could clearly see the walls of the castle and the chimneys of Castle Row, where Lauren lived. Even though they were no longer together, Lauren took some comfort in his nearness, because she knew she could always call on him in time of need. Not that she ever had, but she could, and she found that strangely reassuring. As she walked along clutching her granddaughter's tiny hand, she wondered how Ken would react to the present situation. He would surely want to meet his granddaughter, but she was pretty sure that was as far as his interest would stretch. She tightened her grip, this time protectively rather than controllingly. *Poor little mite,* she thought. *She hasn't really had much love in her life so far.* She wondered if Poppy had ever had a pet. She guessed not; and yet she seemed so eager to meet Charlie that clearly, she loved animals.

   They reached the house, and Lauren released Poppy's hand whilst she hunted in her handbag for her keys. Poppy sat down on the first step, gazing up at the house and the security light in the form of an owl that Lauren had brought back from a recent trip to London. It had cost an arm and a leg, but was worth it – Lauren didn't want to spoil the period charm of her home with a modern security light, and the old-fashioned street-lights didn't give off enough light to enable her to see to unlock her door.

There was no sign of Charlie.

"He'll be here in a minute, he'll be wanting his tea," Lauren assured a clearly disappointed Poppy. "Now, let's get the fire lit, make us a hot chocolate and get you warm." She smiled down at her granddaughter, who was shivering slightly in her thin cotton dress and shabby cardigan. Lauren drew the curtains and put on the lights. The gas fire leapt into life, and Poppy immediately knelt down in front of it. "Here," said Lauren, and tossed her a large cushion. "Sit on this, you'll be more comfy. I'll be back in two ticks." She glanced back as she left the room. Poppy was gazing into the flickering flames that reflected on her pale face and turned it amber like her hair.

In the kitchen, Charlie pushed his way through the cat flap and leapt onto the draining board, rubbing his head against Lauren's arm as she poured two cupfuls of milk into a small saucepan. She set it on the gas hob, then put three heaped spoonfuls of chocolate powder in each cup and mixed them to a paste with a little cold milk. She stared out of the window at the small patch of garden illuminated by the light from the kitchen window, her mind wandering. It was Sunday tomorrow, and she had planned to run up some prototypes of designs she had been working on, but that would have to wait. She must take Poppy shopping. In addition to the bespoke dress, she would need some decent shoes or boots, some slippers, a warm coat, some underwear and nightwear for a start. The milk rose to the top of the pan and began to spill over the sides with a hiss. She grabbed the pan and poured milk into the cups, mixing furiously. She topped Poppy's up with cold milk then smothered it in swirls of squirty cream, a good sprinkle of chocolate powder, and several marshmallows. She regarded her creation with satisfaction – it was a passable imitation of the one at the Bird in Hand café.

"You can have your tea in a minute Charlie," she said. "There's someone I want you to meet first." She went through to the lounge with Charlie at her heels and her fingers mentally crossed. Poppy turned on her cushion and stared at Charlie, who stopped in his tracks and stared back.

"Hi Charlie," said Poppy in her small tinkly voice, and held out her hand. Charlie marched straight over to her and rubbed against her voluptuously, curling his enormous fluffy tail around her face and kneading her lap with his paws. Poppy giggled delightedly and stroked him gently, heedless of the needle-sharp claws sticking into her legs through the thin cotton dress. Lauren heaved a sigh of relief.

"He likes me!" Poppy exclaimed, her eyes shining.

"He does indeed," agreed Lauren. "Mind he doesn't knock your drink out of your hand." She passed Poppy her hot chocolate. By now Charlie was curled up on Poppy's legs, purring loudly. *How extraordinary!* Lauren thought to herself.

"Can I watch telly?" Poppy asked. Lauren thought for a moment. She wasn't accustomed to daytime television, and usually watched the six o'clock news, and then perhaps a drama or a documentary later. She had a number of DVDs, but none of them suitable for a four-year-old child. If she were honest, she hated the thought of children's programmes and didn't really want to encourage her little guest to indulge in them. However, she had nothing else to offer in the way of entertainment, so she switched it on and found a children's channel. There was some sort of cartoon on, with brash primary colours and loud voices. Poppy seemed happy enough, but Lauren was appalled at this assault on her senses. Whatever happened to Bagpuss and the Flumps that Ashley had watched at this age? She decided to retreat to her workroom and work on her latest project – an elaborate period costume for a charity ball one of her regular clients was attending at New Year. She adjusted the dressmaker's dummy to the client's measurements and holding long dressmakers pins between her teeth, she draped some fine-grade black velvet cloth over it, pulling it down off the shoulders slightly and nipping it in at the waist so that it fell in folds of fullness down to the floor. She chose a deep violet coloured satin and draped it around the hip area, with a ruffle of snowy white lace tucked into the décolletage. The sleeves would be tight, ending in a trumpet-shaped cuff from which the same white lace protruded. A fairly standard Elizabethan-style costume that she had produced many times before with variations of fine detail, fabrics and colour combinations. She worked quickly, folding and pinning until she was happy with the result. She would then fashion a paper pattern based on the loose representation she had just created. She was completely absorbed in her work, and forgot all about the new addition to the household. The sound of the television faded as she sorted through her fabrics and tried different shades of lace and satin, eventually reverting to her original choice. She laid dressmakers tissue paper out on the table and began to measure and mark her design.

    She paused, and glanced at her watch. It was nearly six o'clock, and with a jolt she remembered the little girl who was sitting in her living room watching television. A little girl who must surely be hungry by now, and Lauren hadn't even begun to think about what to give her to eat. Lauren would dine later as always on perhaps a chicken fillet with some salad and a glass of wine. *Goodness! What do four-year-olds eat?* With a sudden rush of panic, she cast her mind through the contents of her kitchen cupboards. Food wasn't generally high on her list of priorities, and she tended to eat simply, choosing to dine out when she fancied something more elaborate. Although a competent cook, she begrudged the time spent away from her work that food preparation involved. *I suppose I had better ask her what she'd like to eat, and take it from there,* she thought. She closed the workroom door and made her way back to the lounge. The news was just starting, and Poppy was fast asleep on the floor, her head resting on the cushion, and Charlie cradled in her arms. On seeing Lauren, Charlie struggled free and headed straight for the kitchen and his food bowl. Poppy didn't stir. *Poor little thing,* thought Lauren, *she must be exhausted from being so upset. Perhaps I should put her straight to bed.* Gently, she gathered her up in her arms and carried her upstairs. She was so small and slight and seemed to weigh barely more than Charlie. She murmured in her sleep but didn't wake as Lauren placed her and Mostly Molly in the bed in the guest room, removed her shoes and decided that everything else could wait. She pulled the duvet up around her and drew the curtains across to shut out the cold, dark evening. She decided to leave the door open. She doubted that Poppy would sleep for long, and when she woke, she may be frightened at being in a strange place. Lauren tiptoed away. Charlie was still sitting by his food bowl. Lauren tore open a sachet of food and emptied it into the dish. She opened the cupboard and cast her eye over its contents, then did the same with the fridge. *What did Ashley used to like at that age?* She cast her mind back, attempting to trawl up the memories. Things were different back then; the role of motherhood had been a natural progression. She had thrown herself into it as she now threw herself into her work. It had been her life and her mission was to do it properly, even though Ashley attempted to thwart her at every turn. However, she had changed completely from the woman she was then and had shaped her life around her own needs with no thought for anyone else with the exception of Charlie, who was easy to please. *Damn!* She should have done some more shopping on the way home; she simply hadn't been thinking straight in Tesco Metro, never getting past the need to please her granddaughter with her favourite beverage. It was too late now; she could hardly go back there and leave Poppy alone in the house.

With this thought, the enormity of her situation hit her. Whilst her granddaughter was with her, she couldn't just come and go as she pleased; couldn't sit and watch the news or listen to music with a glass of wine at six o'clock; couldn't stroll down to Coffee 'n Compliments in the morning to people watch, or to Giorgio's in the evening for a leisurely meal and a bottle of good wine. Her life, albeit temporarily, was about to change beyond all recognition. How long for? Where was Ashley? What if she stayed away for weeks? What if she *never* came back? Panic welled in her breast and threatened to overwhelm her. Poppy was a sweet little thing, but Lauren didn't want to be the mother of a young child again – she was far too old, and far too selfish and set in her ways for that! Tomorrow, she would call Ken, and tell him what had happened. He and Janet would have to share this burden that had been thrust upon her – after all, Poppy was his granddaughter too! She poured herself a glass of wine and sank onto the sofa with a sigh. Should she be drinking? Probably not, she thought wryly. When Ashley was little, she and Ken never drank – even if for no other reason than that they couldn't afford to. Nowadays, she would have two or three glasses of wine every evening, and sometimes more. It helped her to unwind and had no ill effect that she could discern. She had never considered it excessive, and never drank during the day except on the rare occasion that she would meet a friend or a client for lunch. With that thought, she leaped up and returned to the workroom. Switching on the computer, she checked her reminders. She had a meeting with a client scheduled for Wednesday lunchtime to discuss the design of her wedding gown. She had done some preliminary sketches that she was really pleased with – the design was simple and elegant – no frills and flounces, her client had said, and there were none – just a sleek, softly draping crystal satin that fell in glistening folds like a waterfall, draped low at the back and modestly at the front. The sketches, and a swatch of the exquisite and expensive fabric were ready, contained in a cream calfskin folder that Lauren had had made for the purpose. That gave her only three days to find her daughter and make her face up to her responsibilities. She supposed she could leave Poppy with Bessie at the shop for a couple of hours, but that wasn't fair on Bessie and she could hardly be expected to complete her daily assignments with a small child under her feet. *What about school?* Lauren thought now. *Shouldn't Poppy be at school?* She had no idea at what age children started school. She must ask Trisha about that on Monday – *if she turns up that is,* she thought. She returned to her glass of wine, and Leonard Cohen on the stereo, turned down low so that she would hear Poppy if she cried out. Charlie had disappeared, probably outside. He would soon be back in; he didn't like the cold weather – *getting old like me,* thought Lauren. She mulled over the situation in her mind; it seemed pretty hopeless. How was she going to find Ashley if she didn't want to be found? She supposed she could enlist the help of the police; but then they would find out about Poppy, and might involve the social services. She didn't want that to happen, even if Trisha hadn't made a solemn promise to Ashley. First, she needed to find out where Ashley lived, and perhaps gain access to her flat. As her mother she might be granted that, especially when the landlord heard that Ashley had abandoned her daughter. But what if Ashley had left owing rent money? The Landlord might demand that Lauren pay the arrears, and he might report Ashley to social services for abandoning her child. Oh! It was impossible. With each idea she came up against a brick wall. Perhaps Ken would be able to think of something tomorrow; she would just have to be patient. She lay back against the cushions and closed her eyes, allowing her mind to clear – no sense in getting worked up about it all tonight. The room was warm, the fire hissed gently, and Cohen's soporific growl seeped into her mind as she relaxed and let her worries dissipate.

The doorbell shook her from her reverie with its mellow Westminster chime, and she was thankful that she hadn't chosen anything too strident. She paused at the foot of the stairs, but heard no movement. She peered through the wide-angle peephole set into the door, and was surprised to see Ken standing there. He looked strange, drawn and anxious, and he appeared to be alone. She opened the door and put her finger to her lips gesturing him not to make a noise.

"What on earth are you doing here?" she asked in a fierce whisper, and then added, "I mean, it's nearly eight o'clock. Where's Janet?"

"Can I come in Lauren, I need to talk to you." Without waiting for a reply he pushed past her, glancing around as he made his way to the lounge.

"Have you got company or something?" he asked. "Why the finger on lips job?"

"I'll explain in a minute," she replied, "after you've told me why you're here. You look awful! Has something happened?"

"I think you'd better sit down," he said between clenched teeth. Lauren took in his dishevelled appearance and his face that was unusually pale. He was shivering, his teeth visibly chattering. It was certainly cold out; but not that cold. The familiar feeling of foreboding crept over her again. Turning the music down, she sat on the sofa. He perched on the edge of it next to her uncomfortably, and took her hands in his, but without looking at her. She watched him struggle for words with a growing sense of dread.

"What is it? What's wrong Ken? Is it Janet?"

He raised his eyes to hers, and she saw in them pain and anguish. The words were barely more than a whisper. "It's Ashley," he said, and to her horror, tears welled in his eyes and began to trickle slowly down his face. His grip on her hands intensified. "Ashley's dead," he said, his voice broken and barely audible.

"No!" she heard herself cry out, the sound echoing through her head in a disembodied wail. "No Ken! She can't be! There must be some mistake!"

"I'm sorry Lauren, there's no mistake. She was found dead yesterday morning. It looks like she's the latest victim of that serial killer. The police tracked me down through work – I gave them my work address when I bailed her. I thought it would be better for you to hear it from me than from them, so here I am."

Lauren stared at him in numb disbelief. Ken was handsome to a degree, only slightly taller than she, quite grey now but not balding, with 'sensible' features and brown eyes that gave him a benign air and that she had rarely seen flash with anger. Now she wondered why she had let him go. Suddenly she needed him to hold her and tell her that this was just a bad dream that she would wake from any minute now. Waves of nausea washed over her and she screwed up her eyes in anguish as she now recalled the details she had read in the papers about the murders; details that she had skipped over, not dwelt on like many other people with their ghoulish tendencies. She had thought, *this is someone's mother, friend, daughter,* and couldn't bear to think what they must be going through. Now it was *her* daughter, and it hurt no less because she hadn't seen her for nine years. Ken reached out a hand and laid it on her arm. "I'm so sorry," he said quietly, "there was no easy way to tell you."

Lauren put her head into her hands and began to weep uncontrollably. The vision of her daughter's face was strong in her mind as she had last seen her. The daughter that she had never really known or understood, but she had always hoped would one day wish to be her friend.

Ken cradled her gently and they wept together, united in their devastation. Lauren leaned against the rough wool of his damp overcoat and breathed in his familiar smell, transported back to a time when nothing mattered except her husband and her child. Now those days were gone; her husband was with someone else, her child was taken from her forever, and she had never felt so completely alone. Through her searing grief, she sought solace in the brief moment of empathy between them that she knew would soon pass.

Suddenly the door swung open and Poppy appeared, barefoot, pale and dishevelled, clutching Mostly Molly to her breast. She stood transfixed by the sight of the two adults sitting together crying. Lauren pulled away, wiping her eyes as she did so.

"What the f…" began Ken, silenced by Lauren's hand across his mouth. She flashed him a warning look and then said slowly and deliberately,

"Poppy, this is your Grandad Ken." She watched Ken closely as she spoke the words, and saw his sharp intake of breath as he realised the implications of her words. He quickly pulled himself together however, and she could only imagine the turmoil in his mind as he said,

"Hello…er…Poppy. Where did you come from?"

"I want my mummy," whispered Poppy, looking from one to the other of these people whom she didn't know and who were acting so strangely. They exchanged agonised glances, and Lauren's heart went out to this little girl whose world was about to fall apart. How were they going to explain to her that her mummy was never coming back? How, and when? Well, certainly not right now, Lauren decided.

"Are you hungry?" she asked. Poppy shook her head, her gaze fixed steadily on Ken.

"Why is the man crying?" she asked Lauren.

"He's had some bad news, but he'll be alright in a minute," she said with forced cheerfulness. "Even grown-ups cry sometimes you know."

"Only ladies," stated Poppy decisively, then walked over to Ken. "Don't worry," she told him solemnly, placing a hand on his arm. "It will be better tomorrow. You just have to be brave my mummy says." On a sudden impulse, she thrust Mostly Molly into his arms, turned, and fled from the room back up the stairs whence she came. Lauren followed, her eyes once more brimming with tears. This was no ordinary child, she thought, and now their lives were inexorably bound together, and she must find some way to make it up to her for her life so far. She sat on the edge of the bed. Poppy had drawn the duvet up over her face, and lay on her side with her knees drawn up, barely visible in the enormous bed.

"Are you alright Poppy?" asked Lauren gently, reaching out to touch the strands of pale amber hair on the pillow. The little girl turned her head towards her.

"Where's Charlie?" she whispered.

"He'll be in shortly I expect, and I'll bring him up to you," Lauren replied. Right on cue, Charlie appeared from nowhere and leaped onto the bed, purring loudly and rubbing his head against first Lauren, then Poppy. Poppy reached out and pulled him under the duvet beside her, and Charlie made no objection, but allowed himself to be cuddled, still purring.

"Goodnight then you two," Lauren said, and planted the lightest of kisses on the top of her granddaughter's head. "Sleep well." She left the door ajar, and made her way back downstairs to Ken. He was leaning forward, holding Mostly Molly in his hands and studying her intently. Lauren sat beside him.

"Tell me about Poppy," he said. "How long have you known?" The tone was both accusing and resigned.

"I found out yesterday," Lauren replied, "and we met today for the first time." She recanted the story of Trisha's letter, their meeting at the Bird in Hand, and the subsequent arrangement that she was to care for Poppy until Ashley's return.

"Only now she won't be returning," observed Ken wryly, "so what do you intend doing with her?"

"Doing with her? For God's sake Ken, what on earth do you think I intend doing with her? She's four years old; she's my granddaughter, and yours, and now she's all alone. Do I have any choice in the matter? I don't think so. I don't quite know how, but I'm going to have to care for her from now on, and you are going to have to help me. We owe that to her, and we owe it to Ashley." Suddenly Lauren was overcome with guilt and remorse. Where did she go wrong with Ashley that she turned out so dysfunctional and wild? Could she have done things differently? Tried harder, and not given up and left her to her fate – a fate Lauren could never have predicted, but could possibly have prevented. No, whatever the cost to herself, her priorities now lay with her granddaughter; she was no way going to make the same mistakes twice.

"I was going to ring you tomorrow and ask for your help. Well, you've spared me the phone call, so now we must discuss Poppy's future and decide how best to help her."

"And I was going to ring you tomorrow," answered Ken wearily. "Janet's pregnant. My priorities have shifted too, and I need to think about my position regarding Poppy. You do understand, don't you Lauren?"

"Oh yes! I understand alright. Your timing is impeccable Ken! So, Poppy has to take a back seat in your life, because you are going to be a father again. Well, I hope you do a better job of it this time, because I'm not going to shoulder all the blame for what happened with Ashley – she was your daughter too remember. You'd better go. Get back to your nice tidy life. Don't worry about us, me and Poppy; we'll work something out. I don't want her to have to accept any grudging offer of love made out of a sense of duty; she deserves so much better." Lauren rose and opened the lounge door, standing aside to allow Ken to pass through. He paused by the front door and took a step back towards her, his eyes full of emotion that she couldn't read. She waved him away with her hand, and had already turned away from him before the door closed behind him. She returned to the lounge, where Mostly Molly lay on the floor in front of the sofa. She picked her up, and spoke to her. "Well Molly, it's you and me and Pops now – oh, and Charlie of course." Sinking down onto the sofa, she clutched the rag doll to her breast as though it might prevent her heart from breaking.

EIGHT: ASHLEY.

Ashley huddled on the seat by the window of the bus, her knees drawn up under her chin, her arms wrapped around them. The seat was cold, unforgiving and slippery. Outside, a steady misty drizzle enveloped the winter landscape in a gossamer blanket and deposited droplets on the window obliterating the view. Ashley didn't care, the weather and the comfort, or lack of it, was the least of her concerns. Anxiously, she checked her phone, but there was no message from Trisha. Perhaps she hadn't seen Ashley's latest message telling her she was sorry for the delay, but she was now on her way home. Perhaps she didn't open it, seeing a number she didn't recognise.

The trip to Amsterdam had ended badly. Jerzy had made it sound great, but it was soon obvious that he didn't care about anything except getting his next fix. Thank God she hadn't given in to his attempts to persuade her to join him in a 'line'. She didn't mind smoking weed, even the strong stuff, but thoughts of Poppy made her resist all his efforts to make her indulge in anything else. They stayed in a house with Jerzy's so-called friends – all drug addicts, drifting in and out aimlessly. She slept like a cat, with one eye open, because some of them seemed to think she was fair game, and Jerzy couldn't care less because by the third day he was injecting himself with the stuff. At the end of the seemingly interminable week, she was relieved that they were going home. In her mind's eye, she saw Poppy, tears pouring down her face as Trisha tried to comfort her. "Mummy…" It was the last thing she'd seen as they drove away.

Jerzy was sleeping soundly, fully clothed, and when she tried to wake him he just groaned and turned over. The ferry was leaving in a couple of hours, and they must be on it. She had told Trisha she would only be gone a week, and anyway, she was missing her daughter. At last, with less than an hour to go, Jerzy woke.

"Come on! We have to go," Ashley urged him, but he merely sat up, rolled himself a spliff and glared at her.

"What's the matter bitch?" he growled, giving her a look of contempt. "Don't you like it here?"

She knew she had to tread carefully "Of course I do, but I have to get back to Poppy. C'mon Jerzy, we'll miss the ferry!"

"We'll leave when I say we will, d'you get that?" he snarled "An' I say we stay a bit longer – maybe a lot longer. I say maybe we don't go back at all."

Ashley felt sick. "Jerzy please…" He leaped up and lunged at her with his fist. The blow knocked her sideways, and she tasted blood as her teeth bit into her cheek and her lip.

"Shut up bitch! We go when I say, and not before."

Ashley reached for her phone, but he snatched it from her hand. She watched in horror as he took out her sim card and ground them both underfoot with the heel of his boot. Then he took a key from his pocket, and locked the door.

After that, she became a prisoner in that dreadful place. She was no longer allowed to go shopping for food, and as most of the drug fuelled occupants ate little, she found herself going hungry most of the time. She had no money, no passport, and now she had no phone. She was trapped, and she had no way of contacting Trisha to ask her for help, or to explain the situation. She knew Jerzy had money, he had a wad of notes that he kept in his pocket at all times along with their passports. She had no idea where it came from, but knew better than to ask questions. She bided her time, trying to be inconspicuous. She would think of something – but it seemed hopeless. Jerzy ignored her most of the time, and she slept alone in a corner of the room.

There was only one other female in the house, a girl named Amber who came and went sporadically, and who now brought with her the meagre supplies of food. She was very young, about twenty, and quietly spoken with wistful grey eyes and blonde hair. She would smile at Ashley in passing, but only when no one was looking. She didn't seem attached to anyone there, and Ashley wondered how she'd ended up there, and supposed that she was otherwise homeless. When they first arrived there, she had spoken to Ashley and Ashley had told her about Poppy, showing her the picture she carried in her purse, but since then they had done no more than exchange an occasional brief greeting. Nevertheless, it was a comfort to Ashley to know that she had a potential ally in the camp.

However, two weeks into their extended stay, Ashley woke to the unmistakable sound of someone having sex close by. She strained her eyes in the darkness, and realised to her dismay that it was Jerzy and Amber. Tears stung her eyes and she longed to be back home with Poppy. "I'm so sorry Pops," she whispered, "I promise I'll never leave you again." Then, realising that the chances of ever being able to get home were almost nil, she crept back into her corner, curled up with her hands over her ears, and cried herself to sleep.

Amber slept with Jerzy for the next three nights, and Ashley remained in her corner, burning with humiliation. On the fourth night, in the early hours of the morning, she was woken by someone gently shaking her shoulder. She started, then saw that it was Amber, kneeling beside her, her finger on her lips.

"Shhhhh!" she whispered "Don't make a sound, just follow me."

Ashley looked over to where Jerzy slept.

"Don't worry about him, he's dead to the world, I made sure of that. Just don't wake anyone else."

Ashley rose, put on her jacket, and crept after Amber carrying her boots and her canvas backpack. Amber took a key from her pocket and very carefully unlocked the door. They slipped silently out onto the landing, and Ashley watched transfixed as Amber locked the door behind them, her finger on her lips again.

They crept swiftly down the stairs and out of the house. Everywhere was quiet. Amber led her along the front of the house, and then they turned into a narrow street from where anyone looking out couldn't see them.

"Here," said Amber, and thrust something into Ashley's hand. It was a wad of notes, and her passport. "Now go! Get as far away from here as you can, start running, then get a taxi. Go to the end of this street, then turn right, left and right again. There you'll find a taxi rank. You have plenty of money. There's a ferry at 6.30am, you should catch it if you're lucky. Now I've got to get back before I'm missed. When Jerzy wakes up he'll think you robbed him. He may suspect I helped you and I'll get it in the neck, but I'll bluff my way out of it somehow. Good luck Ashley, I can handle Jerzy, don't worry. You look after that little angel of yours and don't do what I did. I lost my Roxy, and I'll never get her back," and before Ashley could speak, Amber was gone.

Ashley ran, trying to remember Amber's directions. She needed to put some distance between her and that house. The wad of notes nestled in her jeans pocket. She hadn't had chance to count it, but it felt like a lot. Was that why Amber had slept with Jerzy? Was it just a ploy to enable her to steal his stash of money? She wished now that she'd got to know her better, and she hoped that there wouldn't be grave consequences for her part in Ashley's escape.

'Right, left, right' she chanted to herself as she ran through the deserted streets, glancing fearfully over her shoulder at intervals, or pausing in a doorway to check that she wasn't being followed. Her breath came in short gasps, and her chest ached. At last the taxi rank came into sight. It was 4.30am, and she would have plenty of time to catch that ferry. As she climbed into the taxi, her knees turned to jelly and tears began to stream down her cheeks.

"Where to Luv?" The middle-aged taxi driver gave her a kindly look. His accent was British – from somewhere near the Bow Bells.

"The ferry terminal please" and she attempted to smile through her tears.

"What time's your boat?" he asked.

"6.30."

"Awww! Plenty of time. You just dry your eyes and chill a bit Luv, get your breath back. We'll get you back to old Blighty soon enough!"

"Oh, thank you! I have to get home to my Poppy – my little girl. She's four years old."

"You been away long?" he asked. She searched his face in the rearview mirror for signs of disapproval, but saw only kindly interest.

"Two and a half weeks," she replied "Two and a half weeks too long. I left her with my best friend, but I wish I'd never come!"

"Well never mind Luv, you'll be back with her soon enough, and she'll be right happy to see her mummy I'm guessing. I've got a little granddaughter that age. She lives over here, so I came here to be near her. One day I'll take her home to London and show her the sights."

Ashley leaned back in her seat, and closed her eyes, relief and gratitude flooding through her veins.

Safely on the ferry two hours later, she wondered how Amber had fared when Jerzy realised he had been fleeced. She dipped into her wad of euros and bought a mobile phone, a sim card, and after some thought, a bottle of perfume for Trisha. She would buy Poppy something when she got home. They would go shopping together and she would buy her anything she wanted. She messaged Trisha, and told her she'd be home in the next couple of days. After changing some of the euros to keep in her purse, she decided to keep her passport and the remaining cash in her jeans rather than the backpack, and the phone in her jacket pocket, so that there was less chance of them being stolen.

Now, huddled on the bus, she was racked with regret. How could she have been so stupid and selfish? How could she have left Poppy in order to go away with that horrible man? She would make it up to her, and to Trisha. Trisha was a good friend, and had tried to make her see sense, but she had thought she knew better. She'd had a lucky escape, and from now on things would be different. She'd get a job, a proper job, and Poppy would have a decent life. She thought about her parents, and once again was filled with remorse. Perhaps she would go and see her mum. Suddenly, she couldn't wait to get home. Christmas was less than three weeks away, and this year she would celebrate it with Poppy, with a Christmas tree and presents and a proper Christmas dinner. She felt the wad of notes in her pocket, and smiled to herself. Now she had money, thanks to Amber. This year would be different; the start of a new life for her and Poppy, and she would even make it up with her parents. *It's never too late!* she told herself.

Trisha's flat was down a narrow side street above a greengrocer's shop in the small market town of Osterley, about 20 miles from Chesbury. Ashley had a similar place above a hairdresser's, but Trisha's was only a studio flat, whereas Ashley had a proper bedroom and a separate lounge cum kitchen. Ashley entered through the side door and hurried up the stairs. Her heart leaped at the thought of seeing Poppy again. She knocked on the door, but there was no answer. She lifted the letterbox flap and peered through. There was no sign of anyone, although there were signs of someone having eaten a meal recently, with empty plates and cups on the coffee table. She would have to go home and come back later. Disappointment flooded her mind, and she bit back feelings of annoyance towards Trisha, who must not have seen her messages.

Ten minutes later, she pushed open the door to her flat, to find a note on the floor.

"Hi Ashley," the note read. *"If ur reading this u must b home. I got a new job so I rote to ur mum an Im goin 2 Chesbury 2 drop it off 2day an im gonna ask if I can take Poppy 2 her on Satday. Sorry but I dint no wot els 2 do. Luv n hugs, Trisha X."*

Ashley sunk onto her sofa bed, her heart pounding. Oh no! This was a disaster! She had spent the last decade avoiding her parents. She didn't even know where they lived anymore, only that they had moved, because when she was expecting Poppy, Trisha had tried to persuade her to go and see them. She had got as far as her old home, then found it occupied by strangers. She had decided it wasn't meant to be. Shortly afterwards, she saw an article in the local paper about her mother's shop, Trendy Tots, in Chesbury market, about what a success she had made of it. She was trading under her maiden name, so Ashley realised that her parents must have split up. Now she wanted to make contact with her mother again, but not like this – dumping Poppy on her when she didn't even know she existed. This was not good, and not at all how she had planned it. She must go to Chesbury and find her before Trisha's letter got to her, and explain what happened, convince her she hadn't meant to leave Poppy for so long. However, the thought of facing her at work was repugnant. Too public by far! Maybe her mother wouldn't want anything to do with her after last time. What if she had already seen the letter and called social services, or the police – was Ashley about to be arrested for child abandonment? She needed to talk to her in private, so she needed to find out where she lived. She thought long and hard. What about her grandparents? She hadn't seen them since she was about fifteen, but she used to get on with them, and they might help smooth the way for her. They would certainly know where her mum was living. She made up her mind to start with them.

The bus to Chesbury seemed to take forever to reach its destination. Ashley got off on the outskirts of the town and made her way along a long straight road to the housing estate where her grandparents lived. It was over a decade since she had last seen them, and she had no idea what sort of reception she would get, but they had always been kindly and slow to judge, so there was hope. She turned the corner into Stapeley Crescent, a long sweeping arc of houses interspersed by pollarded cherry trees, and counted down the houses until she came to the one she remembered as theirs. It looked familiar, and she braced herself as she approached the door, hoping she had remembered correctly. She pressed the doorbell and waited with bated breath. After some minutes, when she was debating whether to press again, the door opened slowly to reveal a middle-aged woman whom she had certainly never seen before.

"Excuse me," she said. "I'm looking for Frank and Barbara Woods," she said. "Do they still live here?"

The woman gave her an appraising stare, taking in her dishevelled appearance and tangled hair, the pale face with dark-circled eyes, the rather bedraggled fur jacket and grubby canvas backpack. She wrinkled her nose slightly, and Ashley felt the heat of embarrassment washing over her – what must she look and smell like? Now she wished she had had a shower and a change of clothes before leaving her flat.

"Who's asking?" The woman regarded Ashley with distaste.

"I'm their granddaughter Ashley. I need to find my mother, it's urgent." Ashley spread her hands in a gesture of pleading.

"They're not here," the woman replied. "We bought this house when your grandparents moved to France two years ago." She began to close the door, then changed her mind, seeing the look of anguish on Ashley's face. The girl looked half-starved and pretty desperate. "Your mother lives in the town behind the Castle somewhere, but I'm not sure exactly where. If you ask in the market, they all know her there. Now if you'll excuse me, I must get back to my ironing," and with that, she averted her eyes, and closed the door firmly behind her.

There was nothing else for it, Ashley realized. She would have to go to the market and face her mother.

It was a long walk into town, and it gave Ashley time to think about how she was going to approach her mother. She was glad that she didn't have to face both her parents. Suddenly, she saw her mother in a different light. Her distress at being parted from Poppy against her will made her realise the heartache she must have put her through when she had tried to offer an olive branch nine years ago only to be betrayed again. Could this be Ashley's chance to reconcile with her, to try and make up for lost time, to present her with a granddaughter who would grow to love her and be loved. Heaven knew, Poppy could only benefit from the family she had never had.

The market was almost deserted by the time she reached it. It was Thursday, and many of the stalls had remained closed. There was a notice on the door reminding the stallholders about the Christmas party that evening. Ashley wandered around between the stalls and along the edge of the market where the retail units were mostly locked up. Almost at the end of the row she found the shop named Trendy Tots. The window was hung with fairy lights, and there were photographs of children of varying ages wearing unusual, but warm, practical clothing in bright primary colours. On the door was an advertisement for Creative Couture, with a collage of snapshots of exotic looking costumes and wedding dresses. There was an email address and a telephone number, but to Ashley's frustration, no address.

The nearby Bird in Hand café was closed, but a woman wearing jeans and a polo shirt with a logo of an outstretched hand with an exotic looking bird perched on it was busy mopping the floor. Ashley approached her.

"Excuse me, do you know the lady who owns that shop?"

The woman followed Ashley's extended finger, and nodded, smiling.

"I certainly do. That's Lauren Woods' shop," she replied. "She'll be open tomorrow morning at nine."

"Do you know where she lives? I need to see her urgently." Ashley said.

"Well...I'm not sure if I should say..." The woman regarded Ashley with suspicion, then suddenly did a double take.

"Why! You could almost be her double!" she exclaimed.

"I'm her daughter Ashley, and I really need to find her." Ashley gazed imploringly at the woman.

"Well, I can't doubt that you're who you say you are," said the woman. "You're the living image of her, but she's never mentioned you."

Ashley's heart sank. It had been such a long time. Perhaps she was simply too late to make amends.

"Please," she begged. "I won't tell her who told me, if that helps."

"Ok, in that case I'll tell you. You need to go out of here and turn left. Keep straight on to the top of the hill past Tesco Express, then turn right. There's a memorial garden at the end of the street. Turn left there, and left again into Castle Row, and your mum's house is near the bottom of that street, it's the one with the owl over the door."

"Thank you so much," Ashley beamed at her, and turned to go.

"Good luck Pet, I've a feeling you'll need it!" The woman gave a shrug, and returned to mopping the floor. *Funny that Lauren had never even mentioned having a daughter.*

By now it was almost dark. Ashley followed the woman's directions. She was tired and very hungry. She went into Tesco Express at the top of the hill and bought herself a takeaway coffee and a warm pasty. When she reached the memorial garden, she huddled in a corner of a wooden shelter and ate her makeshift meal. When she had finished, overcome by tiredness, she leaned her head against her backpack and closed her eyes...

Ashley woke with a start. Somewhere a clock was chiming. She counted the strokes – eight! She had been asleep for almost two hours! The town was coming to life, with people moving around between the restaurants and pubs, already full of Christmas spirit even though there were still over two weeks to go. She brushed the crumbs from her clothes and steeled herself for the encounter with her mother. She was stiff and cold, and still tired even after her long nap. She hesitated briefly, then plucking up courage she set off, following the woman's directions down a short, narrow street ahead of her, then turning left onto a cobbled street lined with red brick houses. The sign on the end house said 'Castle Row'. She had a vague idea that she'd been here before, but the memory eluded her. *Didn't Gandy used to live down here somewhere? she thought.* A vague recollection of a small dark living room crammed with furniture, but with a roaring log fire on which she used to make toast on the end of a long brass toasting fork came to mind. She wondered if her great grandmother was still alive. She must have been well into her eighties last time she saw her, and that was a few years ago, so she supposed it was unlikely. Near the end of the street, she found what she was looking for. The owl above the door flooded her with light and she recoiled instinctively, then determinedly reached up and pressed the doorbell. A mellow Westminster chime rang out inside the house, and she waited with baited breath. It was now or never! However, there was no response, no approaching footsteps, and the door remained closed, an insurmountable barrier between her and her hopes. Crestfallen, she turned away and made her way back into town. Opposite the entrance to the market was a somewhat dilapidated pub called The Ragged Staff. It was busy, but she bought a pint of cider and found a corner seat where she could sit and gather her thoughts. Of course! Her mother was probably out at the Christmas party. She racked her brains. Where was it being held? She wished she had paid more attention to the notice. She hurried out and crossed the road. The market was all locked up, folding concertina gates drawn across its entrance lobby, and you couldn't see the inner door from the street well enough to read the sign. It was hopeless! She returned to the pub, her pint of cider had gone. She would have to stay here until late, and then try again and hope to find her mother at home when the party had finished. There was a darts match in progress. She ordered another pint of cider and a shot and settled down to watch. At least it would pass the time, she was warm, and she could have a few drinks to give her some Dutch courage.

The pub finally closed at one am. The tall coloured man behind the bar draped the bar cloths over the pumps and dimmed the lights. The few stragglers, including Ashley, drained their glasses and left the warmth of the pub. It was raining now, and Ashley huddled into her fur jacket and began to retrace her steps to her mother's house. She walked slowly, anxiety and doubt crowding her mind, and the drink clouding it. The pubs were emptying rapidly now and people thronged the pavements, jostling and laughing, full of the joys of Christmas. She had never felt so alone. As she turned the corner from the memorial garden, silence descended. There were no more pubs or restaurants, just the row of elegant Victorian houses interspersed by deep gated alleyways on one side of the street, and on the other side, tall dark brick walls and open alleyways that backed on to businesses. She stood across the street from her mother's house. A soft light leaked through a tiny gap in the curtains upstairs. She was home! Ashley pictured her, perhaps sitting up in bed reading. How would she react to being disturbed from her bed so late at night? Where were Trisha and Poppy? Perhaps she should have waited for Trisha to come home, and explained to her why she had stayed away so long. Perhaps the letter had not yet reached Lauren, and she could intercept it somehow. Perhaps, and she knew it was likely, her mother would want nothing to do with her. Had she come here to find her only to be turned away? So many questions, and so few answers. She shivered, and blinked away a tear. This was not the way to go about it. She must lie low until morning at least; she couldn't just go barging back into her mother's life at this late hour. What on earth had she been thinking? She turned away dejectedly, and began to walk in the direction of the river. She felt damp and disheartened, but she must find somewhere to shelter for the night, perhaps in the bus station at the bottom of the hill, or the multi-storey car park next to it. In the morning she would go home and speak to Trisha. She longed to see Poppy. She would never let her out of her sight again, and she would make things right with her mother so that they could be a family again. Things would work out, it was never too late.

Feeling a sudden urgent need to pee, she ducked into an alley between two big grey wheelie bins. She never noticed the big silver car pulling up silently near the entrance to the alley. She never saw the man who crept up behind her and grabbed her by her shoulders. She lashed out instinctively, and felt his hands close around her throat...

NINE: TONY.

Tony was a self-made man, and proud of it. When you hit rock bottom, you can go one of two ways. You can lie there and wallow in self-pity for the rest of your miserable life, or you can drag yourself up out of the mire, and turn things around. Tony was only nineteen when he made the biggest mistake of his life, but his sworn mission thereafter was to put it all behind him and move on, and to be a better person.

He hadn't meant to harm the girl. He'd had a skinful, and a couple of spliffs, and she really seemed up for it. She danced close to him all night, abandoning the girlfriends she'd arrived with. Petite, vivacious and very pretty, her mop of shining auburn curls fell over her face as she danced, so that she tossed them back provocatively, laughing up at him. She had the most amazing green eyes that sparkled with the sheer joy of living.

When it was time to leave, her friends were nowhere to be seen, so Tony offered her a lift home. He had 'borrowed' his dad's Ford Consul. His dad had left for London on the train that morning to support his beloved Arsenal in a big London Derby match against Chelsea. He would not be back until Sunday evening, and by then the car would be back in the garage and he would be none the wiser. Tony was in his last term at college where he was studying electrical engineering. On Friday and Saturday nights, he worked in a bar in the city centre, but tonight he had decided to make the most of his dad's absence and had called in sick. He knew he shouldn't be drinking and driving, but he didn't care. He'd be careful and nobody would ever know.

The girl, who said her name was Annette, seemed well impressed by the sleek shining car with the front bench seat and chrome trim that was his father's pride and joy. She snuggled up to him happily as they drove out of the car park towards her home in nearby Perry Barr. After a few minutes, however, she seemed less comfortable and slid away from him, clinging to the edge of the dashboard.

"Tony, slow down" she pleaded, her green eyes wide and fearful. Tony laughed. Elated and reckless, and loving the feeling of power in the face of her abject terror, he pushed his foot to the floor. Fifteen minutes later they reached Perry Bar, and the girl asked him to stop just before a tree-lined avenue of modern semis.

"This is my estate, but I don't want you to stop by my house, my sister won't approve," she told him. Fine by him. He parked up at the end of the quiet, deserted road overhung by trees before it joined the lamplit estate. He pulled her towards him and felt her immediate recoil. *What the fuck?* She'd been coming on to him all night, and he was aroused by the adrenalin rush of the drive. Besides, it was a long way out of his way and she owed him! Ignoring her struggles and impassioned pleas to stop, he forced himself on her. It was quick and brutal, and after her initial desperate attempts to repel him, she lay there limp and unresponsive, her eyes shut tight, as though she had transported herself elsewhere. When he had finished she cowered into the corner as far away from him as she could, her knickers and tights around her ankles, her hair a tangled mess, her face smeared with mascara and tears. She looked like a frightened child, and Tony sobered up with a jolt, shame flooding over him as she hastily made herself decent and fled. He drove slowly home, his head pounding, his heart filled with remorse and fear. Would she report him? He would be easy to find, although she only knew his first name. There were plenty of black boys around, but not so many with two-foot-long dreadlocks. He was just starting out in life. In a few months he would finish college and get himself a decent job with money and prospects.

Many years ago, just before his seventh birthday, his father had taken him to say goodbye to his mother who was dying from cancer. He hadn't seen her for nearly three months, and he barely recognised the frail, almost transparent woman who lay in the hospital bed, her breath laboured, her skin like brown parchment, and her dark eyes sunken, the whites yellow, the light in them fading. She touched his hand and tried to smile, but her face had collapsed in on itself and all he saw was a strange and terrifying grimace.

"Give your mama a kiss Tony," said his father. He steeled himself and leaned over to kiss her paper cheek, careful not to touch any other part of her lest he should hurt her. Her breath was foetid, her lips parched and blistered.

"Goodbye my precious boy," she whispered. "I'm not leaving you, not really. You be a good boy for your daddy, and remember, I'll be watching over you, always."

His father was a broken man, and he had no comfort left in him to offer his son. In between working and sleeping, he fed and clothed him and took him to school, but at night Tony climbed the stairs to bed alone with a heavy heart, remembering his mother's bedtime stories, and the way she used to tuck him in and kiss him goodnight. His birthday came and went unmarked, just like any other day, and he knew life would be empty from now on. Six months after he lost his mother, his father, unable to live with the painful memories, sold their terraced house in Islington and they moved to Erdington near Birmingham. Tony felt his world collapsing as he left his friends and all his familiar territory behind and was forced to, as it were, begin his life again from the beginning.

Mum, I'm so sorry! He sunk his head into his hands now and wept. Sometime later, his anguish spent and his mind made up, he locked the car up in the garage and went into the house. He climbed the stairs to the bathroom, where he proceeded to cut off the dreadlocks, one by one, and then to shave his head. He barely recognised the young man in the mirror – he'd be a lot harder to find now! He would put this night behind him and never think about it again. *It'll be alright mum, I'll make it up to you,* he whispered. No, he wasn't going to let it ruin his life; the girl would soon get over it. Downstairs, he whistled tunelessly through his teeth as he made himself a fry-up.

   Tony was as good as his word to himself. The rape of Netty and his subsequent remorse probably shaped his life into something infinitely better than it might otherwise have been. He left college with a first class electrical engineering qualification, and managed to get a job with a local firm, one of the few that were willing to take on coloureds. He worked hard, and was good at his job, and when he met and fell in love with his boss's daughter Carol, there was no objection from her parents to their marriage, and they even paid the deposit on their new home, a three bedroomed semi on a newly built estate in Great Barr.

  A year later, he set up his own business, mainly repairing and re-wiring for local people. The one fly in the ointment was that, despite their many enthusiastic attempts, they failed to conceive and after nearly ten years of trying they resigned themselves to the inevitable and bought a dog. The absence of any children was a bitter blow to Tony. He had planned to add *'and son'* to the side of his van, and had dreamed of the teamwork and companionship between them. There was a void that could never be filled. Carol wanted to adopt, but Tony had no interest in raising some other man's child and refused to even consider such a thing. They grew apart, continuing to occupy the same house, but without any real closeness or love between them.

The years went by with no respite from the monotony of a life unfulfilled. Sometimes Tony wondered seriously why he bothered, and he suspected Carol felt the same, although as she grew older, she spent more time with her friends and less with him. He never bothered to ask where they went, or what they did.

Shortly after his fifty-fifth birthday, he got a callout to a house in Perry Barr. On the phone, the lady sounded officious and overbearing, and he contemplated turning down the work. It was too good to pass up though, a possible complete rewiring, so on a cold afternoon in mid January, he rang the doorbell of the unassuming semi with a white front door and extravagant lace curtains at the windows. The door was opened by a smart elderly woman wearing a tweed skirt, a blue twinset, and a pearl necklace. Her grey hair was wound into a tight bun at her nape, and she wore gold-rimmed glasses on the end of her nose. She looked him up and down with distinct disapproval, and a slight but discernible wrinkling of her nose. For a minute, he thought she would send him packing, but after a long pause, she finally ushered him in,

"Take your shoes off." She instructed him imperiously. They discussed her requirements at the kitchen table. She contradicted his every suggestion, and he began to doubt the wisdom of taking on this job. She repeatedly emphasised that she wanted no disruption and no mess, despite his assurances that he would minimise both, but that there was bound to be a degree of each involved in such work.

The phone rang in the lounge, and she excused herself. Tony looked about him. There was an old-fashioned sideboard against the wall adjacent to the table. His eye was drawn to small clusters of faded photographs arranged along its length. Suddenly, he froze. He stood slowly and approached the sideboard for a closer look. There it was, a photograph that transported him back through the years; A photograph of a young girl with luxuriant auburn locks and laughing green eyes. There were several, and Tony immediately recognised the girl who, all those years ago, he had raped in his car at the bottom of the road. He had not recognised the road. The trees were gone, and more houses had been built in their place. There was no privacy now, with the road overlooked by neatly manicured lawns sloping away from an array of front-room windows. He glanced through the snapshots, and then felt his heart lurch. There she was again – Annette. Only in this photo, she was cradling a baby that looked to be less than a year old. The baby had thick curly black hair, and skin the colour of ripe acorns. He picked the photo up and stared closely at it. It was definitely her, and the child was definitely half-caste, and that could mean only one thing, since he was pretty sure that she wasn't the sort of girl to repeat her experience with him. He pulled himself together as Pauline Proctor re-entered the room.

"That's my sister Annette," she said, almost snatching the photo from his hand, and carefully replacing it exactly where it had stood. "A long time ago mind. She was very pretty, wasn't she?" she said proudly, as though she were personally responsible for her sister's comely appearance.

"She certainly was,' agreed Tony

"And that's her son Paul. He's just a year old in that photo." Pauline launched into the practised tale of the young man taken too soon on an oil rig in the North Sea leaving a grieving widow in his wake. Tony listened, fascinated, but with a seed of anger germinating in his brain. *How dare they! This was his child, his flesh and blood, no matter the circumstances of its conception. He who had been denied a family, but who unbeknownst had had one all along! He had, surely, a right to know of its existence.*

"Those were the good old days," she sighed, with a wave of her hand at the collection. "Things are different nowadays."

"Where are they now?" he asked, glancing around as though hoping they might appear at any moment.

"Oh, they moved away years ago when Paul was sixteen. They're in Chesbury. I haven't seen Paul for years." She narrowed her eyes and looked intently at him, but for some reason failed to make the connection. In her mind all Jamaicans had long hair in braided deadlocks, and were scruffy ne'er do wells, not smart, respectable tradespeople.

A son! All these years he had had a son! Years of needless heartbreak and disappointment flooded his consciousness, threatening to overwhelm and drown him. He had a son, and that son was out there somewhere, living a lie. His life had not been barren after all.

"Well, do you want the job or not?" Pauline began, but Tony had already left without another word by the way he came in, leaving the door open. *What a rude man, and nosey with it,* she thought, absently wiping his fingermarks off the silver photo frame with her sleeve before placing it back in its position again.

"Hey! You forgot your shoes!" She ran out after him, but he was gone, she heard his van roar away down the road, and, closing the door behind her, she picked up his shoes gingerly and dropped them in the kitchen bin.

Tony pushed his foot to the floor and the van careened along through the streets towards his home. Tears of rage flowed down his cheeks, and he thumped the steering wheel in sheer frustration as a howl of anguish escaped his clenched teeth. He screeched to a halt outside his gate. Carol was in the kitchen, about to dish up their evening meal. It smelt delicious, but Tony was oblivious. He slammed the front door behind him and raced up the stairs. Dragging a large holdall down from the top of the wardrobe, he began to stuff clothes into it from various drawers and cupboards, until it would hold no more and the room resembled the aftermath of a burglary.

"Tony, what are you doing? Where are you going?" Carol implored from the doorway, eyeing the scene with dismay. *What on earth had come over him?*

"What I should have done years ago," he muttered, his back turned to her as he stuffed toiletries into the remaining spare corners of the holdall. "I'm leaving you!"

Carol stood, stunned into silence. For more years than she cared to remember, they had jogged along together in this house. No tangible love, no passion, very little communication at all, but no animosity either, just two disillusioned people finding some companionship in their lack of emotion. What could possibly have happened since he left the house this morning to alter and upset that equilibrium so dramatically.

"Tony," she whispered, the tears pricking behind her eyelids. "Why?"

"What's it to you, you barren little bitch?" he spat the words at her, and she recoiled in horror from their vitriol. "I should've done it years ago, but I felt sorry for you and anyway, I didn't know…" he broke off as the sheer irony of the situation hit him anew. He had believed himself to be to blame for their inability to conceive. He had even believed it to be divine retribution for his earlier indiscretion. He had refused to take the tests that might have proved him to be less than a man, and he had been wrong – he had been so, so wrong. He pulled on some boots, snatched up the holdall and pushed roughly past her. "I hate you!" he yelled over his shoulder as he took the stairs two at a time. "I fuckin' hate your guts!" The front door slammed behind him, and she heard the van start up. She ran to the window just as it tore away with a screeching of tyres and disappeared from sight forever.

Tony drove fast, determined to put as much distance between himself and his erstwhile life as he could. *Chesbury*. He had never been there. Come to that, he had never been anywhere much. In the beginning, he and Carol had planned to visit Jamaica one day, to take their children and introduce them to the land and culture of their paternal antecedents. They had saved towards this goal, and had amassed a substantial nest-egg over the years, because his business had grown and spread further afield along with his reputation for reliability and skill. When the longed-for family failed to materialise, they continued to save and sometimes talked about the trip of a lifetime, but their hearts weren't in it, and besides, Tony was reluctant to take a lengthy period off work, because his customers might turn to other sources. Being self-employed, the need to provide for his own pension lay heavy on him, so he had continued to add to the sum weekly as always. They had continued in their comfortable but humdrum life with little zest for adventure.

He punched 'Chesbury' into the satnav and negotiated his way through the suburbs of Birmingham onto the M6, where the build-up of traffic approaching rush hour meant that his progress was slow and monotonous, stop-start, plenty of time to think and work out a plan. He would withdraw their savings, but continue to support Carol from their joint account. Work shouldn't be hard to find, and he would have to find a cheap hotel until he could rent something more permanent. His search for his son Paul would begin immediately, although not knowing his surname would make it more difficult, and if the girl had faked a marriage, she would have assumed a surname other than Proctor. Damn! He should have asked her sister more questions when he had the chance, but he certainly wasn't going back! With a little distance between them, he now felt bad about the way he had spoken to Carol. He would write to her and explain the situation, and he was sure that she would understand. The house was paid for, and would remain her home forever should she so wish, or if not, she could sell it – he didn't care. He leaned back in his seat and cracked his knuckles, then moved into the inside lane as the M54 slip road came into sight.

Chesbury was shrouded in mist when he drove under the railway bridge and along the dimly lit river embankment. Tall houses lined the nearside pavement, three storey buildings with bay windows and tall Shropshire chimneystacks. He followed a sign for the town centre, driving slowly and following the road round a long bend until he saw an illuminated sign that said Premier Inn. Bringing the van to a halt near the main entrance, he sat for a few minutes gathering his thoughts. Suddenly he was overwhelmed with weariness and something akin to despair. How was he to go about finding the needle in this very large haystack of a town? Now he wished he had kept calm and got more information out of the Proctor woman. As he contemplated his predicament, his resentment grew towards the boy's mother. What right had she to keep her son from his father? How could she raise him in the belief that his father was dead, and how had that misinformation affected him, when all along he had a living, loving father who would have given his eye teeth to have been part of his life? He didn't care about the girl, she was nothing, but this Paul was his own flesh and blood – probably the only one he would ever have. His anger and resentment engulfed his mind. He would find them, he would put things right with his son, and then take him from the bitch for what she did to them both. Dragging his holdall out of the boot, he entered the inn, and requested a room for the night. Tomorrow he would begin his search.

His first aim was to familiarise himself with the town of Chesbury. Only by making himself known would he have the opportunity to meet someone who could direct him to his son. The pubs were an obvious source of information, but having no photograph of Annette, he could only keep his eyes and ears open and wait for the name to crop up. His memory of her was of a bright, vivacious girl with striking auburn hair. People don't really change that much, he told himself.

The King's head was full. It was Thursday night, quiz night. The quiz was well under way and there were several teams in play tonight. At ten o'clock, the quizzing ended and the MC called out the winning order. In first place were the Medical Masterminds, a team of six, three men and three women. Amid much enthusiastic cheering, one of the women went up to collect their prize. Tony's pulse raced. The woman was about the right age, perhaps early fifties. Slim, elegant and petite, she was dressed casually in jeans, a green sweater and a multi-coloured silk scarf. Her hair tumbled to her shoulders in rich auburn waves, and her smile was bright, her cheeks flushed and her eyes sparkling. Could this really be Annette? Had he found her so easily – was it fate? She returned to her seat and Tony strained his ears to catch any mention of her name, but it was lost in the hubbub of farewells from their four companions, as her partner helped her into a warm jacket and they headed for the door.

"We'll get our revenge next week," called one of the other women.

"Perhaps; see you then," she replied with a smile as they left.

Following at a safe distance, Tony dogged their steps through the streets and down towards the river, where they entered a tall detached red brick house that stood above the river surrounded by a neat hedged garden. He saw the light go on in the hallway downstairs and then off again. Slowly, he made his way round the side of the house to the back garden, which sloped steeply away towards the river. There was a conservatory, and beyond that he could see light again. Carefully, he skirted the conservatory and saw that the couple were in the kitchen making tea. There were no curtains or blinds at the window and he clearly saw them preparing tea and sitting at the kitchen table to drink it. The kitchen window was slightly raised, and he caught snatches of their voices in conversation. He was mesmerised by the sight of the woman, and comparing her with his memory of that night so long ago, became increasingly convinced that this was Annette. After a short time, they left the kitchen, turning out the light, and a few minutes later a light showed on the next floor, while the rest of the house remained in darkness. Tony made his way back to his hotel.

For hours, he lay on his bed but sleep evaded him, he was buzzing with adrenaline. He needed a plan, and he needed answers. If indeed this was Annette, and his conviction was growing by the hour, then Fate had drawn him to her, and after all, doesn't everything happen for a reason? Their son would now be in his thirties, and almost certainly not living with them. He might be married, with a family who would be Tony's grandkids! However, he would be bound to visit occasionally, perhaps frequently if he lived nearby. Would it be best to wait for a chance to intercept him, or should he confront Annette and demand that she arrange for them to meet? It was, surely, up to her to explain to Paul and put things right. He might not take kindly to being approached by a complete stranger claiming to be his father whom he believed to be dead – or had she by now told him the truth? No, thought Tony, he must tread carefully. He must try to ascertain whether this woman was indeed Annette. If he could get inside the house, he could search for evidence of his son – family photographs perhaps, and there would have to be something, somewhere with her name on it. Yes, that is what he must do. If he found any such evidence, he would then confront her and demand the answers he needed. As dawn broke, he fell into a fitful slumber.

    Just after seven in the morning, he slipped out of bed, dressed quickly and made his way back to the house by the river. He sat on a bench nearby and watched. An hour later, the couple emerged, embraced on the doorstep, and the husband got into a silver Audi parked near the gate, and drove away. The woman glanced around, arms folded over her chest against the cold, before going inside and closing the door behind her. Tony stayed for another hour, hoping that she would go out, but saw no further sign of her. Clearly she didn't work, at least not every day, and it wasn't going to be easy to gain access to the house. Chilled to the bone, Tony returned to the hotel and ordered breakfast, then made his way to an out-of-town car dealer and part-exed his van for a black Vauxhall Astra.

TEN: RAZZY

In the event, it was three months before Netty and Razzy moved into their new home. During this time his behavior improved somewhat and Pauline was filled with misgivings. She would miss her sister, they had never been apart, and she was a little unsure whether Netty would be able to cope alone – or rather with Razzy. She fussed around, making curtains and cushions for the new flat. The landlady, delighted to have long-term tenants, had agreed to have the whole place painted, and the carpets and cooker replaced along with a new washer/dryer. Netty and Pauline went there and cleaned all the windows, including the ones in the communal area where they also scrubbed the paintwork and managed to make it presentable. Netty was thrilled with her bedroom that overlooked the streets and rooftops of Chesbury. Razzy, however, was less than enthusiastic about his room, although it was now light and fairly airy with the now clean large Velux window through which you could see the stars at night.

"Why can't I have the other one?" He complained petulantly.

"You can, when you start paying the rent," retorted Netty. She realised that she was going to have to learn to put her foot down with her son, otherwise he would walk all over her. She enrolled him in Chesbury College on an engineering course, which she figured would stand him in good stead for future employment, and meanwhile she would still get her child benefit until he was eighteen. She found a job in the local indoor market on the Charlie Cheese stall selling dairy produce. It was low paid, but she would manage, and when Razzy finished college, he would get a job too and help with their day to day living expenses. She enjoyed being part of the market community, people were friendly, and at the end of each day she was able to avail herself of cheap produce from Reg the Veg's stall. The market was within easy walking distance of their flat, and Razzy got a free bus pass to get to the college outside of town. Pauline wrote regularly offering advice which Netty rarely heeded, and later texted her on a very simple mobile phone which she obtained for the sole purpose of sending Netty messages, whilst refusing to take calls on anything but her landline. Most of the market closed early on Thursdays, allowing Netty a day off, and most weeks she would take the train to Birmingham to visit her sister, who would bake her a cake and fuss over her like a mother hen. Once a month or so, Pauline would reciprocate. She would inspect the flat, noting every change they had made and voicing her opinion, mainly disapproval. The evening before her visits, Netty would spend the entire evening cleaning and tidying, dusting and polishing as though it were an army inspection. She would hide things that she knew would meet with her sister's disdain, and put out the gifts that Pauline was wont to bestow on her from time to time with no thought for their differing tastes. There was a cupboard in her bedroom assigned to their storage in between visits. She sometimes used to lie awake at night worrying that her sister might someday make an impromptu visit unannounced, but thankfully, in the light of day, she knew this was highly unlikely. Pauline wasn't really a person who acted on impulse.

In spite of all this, Netty was content with her life. She had no desire for anything that others might have seen as better. Relieved that Razzy appeared to be coping with his college course although not actually enjoying it, she dared to hope that their troubles were behind them.

Her life's experiences made her a naturally caring person, and when her friend Sandie, the woman who owned the New Age stall near the cheese counter became unwell, she visited her with home-made soup and sympathy, sat and read to her, and walked her little dog for her before and after work each day. Razzy was unimpressed because it meant that he had to get his own tea when he got home from college, but she would always make sure there was something in the fridge for him to warm up. Sandie didn't improve despite all Netty's ministrations, although her condition baffled the doctors. Her daughter Sue came to stay from Liverpool, and after a week announced that she was taking Sandie back to stay with her for a while.

"But what about the stall?" Netty asked. "Well," said Sandie, "I was hoping you might take it over until I'm well enough to come home. I'll pay you a bit extra if you can keep it going for me and it'd be a load off my mind. I'll talk you through the ordering and stuff, but it's all pretty straightforward I think you'll find." Netty thought for a moment. The prospect of running Sandie's stall excited her, but she would have to quit her present job, and what would then happen when Sandie returned?

"I'm not sure, I'll have to think about it," she told Sandie, an idea germinating in her mind. When she got home, she dug out the paperwork relating to Paul Stockton's inheritance. She had been saving it for a rainy day as Pauline had advised. It was a substantial amount of money – nearly thirty thousand pounds. Surely that day had arrived. She thought about the stall, with its candles and joss-sticks, tarot cards, crystals, aromatherapy oils and gemstone jewellery. She had always loved browsing there chatting to Sandie, and had occasionally splashed out on something indulgent – notably her beautiful glass oil burner that stood in the centre of the little shrine in her bedroom. She imagined spending her days handling such treasures and chatting to customers about them, instead of serving cheese and eggs the day long. It was a no-brainer. She thought about Razzy, who was halfway through his college course with no real enthusiasm, ambition or drive. He could work with her on the stall where she could keep an eye on him. He could take some responsibility for the stock, and with his head for numbers he could keep the accounts for her. She'd buy him that new stereo system he'd been going on about as an incentive, and she would pay him a decent wage – as long as he pulled his weight. She would be able to take time off when she needed to go and see Pauline, and she and Razzy would be a team, instead of constantly at odds with one another. Her mind made up, she returned to Sandie and put her proposal to her.

"Sell the stall to me Sandie," she pleaded. "I promise I'll make a go of it, and you won't have to worry about it, you can relax knowing it's in good hands. It'll be a lifeline for me and Razzy, and I won't have to worry about the day I have to hand it back to you."

Sandie was somewhat taken aback.

"Gosh! I hadn't thought of *selling* it," she said hesitantly. Netty leaned forward on her chair encouragingly. "I realise that, but don't you think it would be better all round? What if I quit my job, and then in a few months you wanted to come back? I'd be stuffed, or you'd have to keep me on. I don't think a ship sails well with two captains, and with us both being pretty strong willed, I'm afraid that we'd end up falling out over how things should be done. Please Sandie, at least think about it, otherwise I really think I'm going to have to turn down your offer because I need security for me and Razzy, and Charlie Cheese gives me that if nothing else. I'm going to leave you to think about it. You can name your price and I'll try to match it – I have some money put by and I can't think of a better use for it." Netty stood, dropped a kiss on her friend's forehead, and headed for the door.

"Netty, wait!" She stopped in her tracks. "Yes! The answer's yes! It's a great idea! You've been so good to me, and I want to do something for you in return. The stall is yours if you want it; we'll discuss the price when I've spoken to Sue. She wants to build me a granny flat so she can care for me and I can still have my independence, because it looks as though I'm not going to be getting better any day soon. This way I can give her the money to do it. There's no denying it'll be a wrench to part with the stall, but I can't think of anyone I'd rather have take my place there and I know you and Razzy will make great marketeers!"

Netty was overjoyed. This was the best thing ever to happen to her. She hugged her friend, and almost ran home to tell Razzy the great news.

Razzy, however, did not welcome the news.

"What? You want me to quit college, after all your fucking whining about how I must stick at it? You want me to quit halfway through my course and come and be your lackey on a stupid fucking market stall? No way *Mother*! I've had it up to here with you and Aunty Pauline trying to run my life as if I'm some little kid! I'm eighteen, I'm a man for fuck's sake!" He pushed her aside and disappeared into his room, locking the door behind him. Netty headed for the sofa wearily, tears in her eyes. It was so unfair. Aside from making him go to college, she pretty much left him to his own devices. She never entered his room without knocking, and even then only to retrieve his dirty laundry, or empty mugs and plates. The all-pervading smell of cannabis was on his clothes, but clearly, he didn't smoke it at home, so she turned a blind eye – at least he was trying to abide by her wishes. He came and went as he pleased, and sometimes stayed out all night. She never questioned him, and as long as he kept out of trouble she was ok with it. She decided that teenagers are naturally secretive, but she hoped that he trusted her enough to turn to her if he were ever in trouble. On Saturdays he worked in the Bird in Hand café in the market, a job that Netty found for him. He was a good worker, he seemed to enjoy the banter with customers and was popular with the girls. After work he would go out for the evening and she wouldn't wait up. She was aware that he brought girls home and they would spend the night in his room although he never bothered to introduce them. The fact that he already worked on the market had filled her with confidence that he would be happy to be on the stall, and he could still keep his Saturday job if he wished. Although money was tight, she had never told him about her inheritance from Paul; he would have constantly nagged her to spend it on things they didn't really need, like that stereo! He hadn't given her chance to tell him about that! Well, now he would bloody well have to wait. If he came round and apologised, she would tell him then. Netty had a strict policy of not rewarding bad behaviour. He probably assumed that they would be renting the stall. She wondered if she could complete the sale without him ever knowing – it might be safer. She chided herself for her lack of trust, but Razzy was, always had been, volatile and unpredictable, and so she must act accordingly. She decided not to tell Pauline either; she wasn't sure what she would have to say about it. It was, after all, her money to do with as she wished, and she could have frittered it on clothes and holidays and stuff like that. Instead, it had sat there untouched until something came along worth spending it on. Had Razzy known about it, he would have wanted driving lessons, a car or a motorbike, heaven knows what else. They lived in a city; there were buses and trains and she didn't need the extra worry of her unpredictable son having his own transport. She sighed. It was hard being a single mother, having to make all the decisions, all the sacrifices, and having to take all the flack! She and she alone must secure their future, and the stall was the way to go. Satisfied that she was not the one being unreasonable, she had an early night.

The next morning Netty decided to act normally and let Razzy make the next move. She cooked him some bacon, wrinkling her nose up at the smell, and cut two thick slices from the lovely crusty loaf she had bought from the bakery stall the day before, buttering it generously and spreading on some ketchup. She knocked on his bedroom door.

"What?"

"I've made you some breakfast," she called through the door. He opened it a little and reached for the plate in her hand. Through the gap in the door, she saw his rucksack on the bed, its contents bulging it at the seams. "Razzy, where are you going?" she asked, anxiety welling up inside her and filling her eyes.

"I've had it with you," he replied sullenly, taking a large bite of his sandwich. "I'm going to look for my dad!"

"Your dad?" Netty gawped at him. "How on earth are you going to do that?"

"I'll hitchhike up to Scotland, and I'll ask around about those bloody oil rigs until I find the right one. I want to know how he died, and I want to know how he lived, who his friends were, whether he talked to them about me, whether he was proud of me, because you never fuckin' have been!"

Netty felt a storm raging inside her, a deluge of emotions that threatened to overwhelm her. She felt dizzy and nauseous. This was the moment she had dreaded all his life, and had desperately hoped to avoid. Now she must tell Razzy the truth about his father.

"Razzy, you need to stop right there!" she screamed at him in fury. "There are things you need to know about your father. You will sit down and you will bloody well listen to me before you go haring off on a wild goose chase!"

Razzy had never seen her angry like this. She was trembling, a scarlet flush had spread across her neck and chest, and the tears trickled slowly down her cheeks. She was only thirty-six, but suddenly, she looked all of fifty. He threw himself down onto the bed, and Netty sat beside him, pushing the rucksack to the floor.

The tale was long in the telling. She told it without flinching, the truth, the whole truth, and nothing but the truth. She averted her gaze the whole time, only sensing his reaction through slight movements he made, and the occasional sharp intake of breath. When she had finished, they both sat and stared wordlessly at the floor for what seemed like an eternity. Eventually, Razzy broke the silence. In a low voice, he said,

"So, my father was a fucking rapist, not a hero who died supporting his family. Why did you keep me? You must have hated me because I ruined your life. Why did Aunty Pauline let you keep me? She's so strict, and yet she helped you to make up all those lies so you could keep your half cast bastard. I don't understand."

"I don't really expect you to, and that's why I never told you before – never would have told you, but you forced my hand. Oh! Believe you me, there were many, many times I wanted to tell you, when you used to go on about your precious father and how you wanted to be just like him and I hoped to God that you'd be nothing like him! And for the record, I have never hated you, and I never could. You're my son, and I love you the more for not having to share you."

There was a long silence whilst Razzy digested the information. When he finally raised his eyes to hers, his voice was subdued, almost a whisper.

"I guess I owe you Mum, you and Aunty Pauline. I guess I won't be needing this after all." He gave the rucksack a kick.

"I'm sorry Razzy, for all the deception. It seems that once you make a story up, it's the hardest thing to un-tell it. I don't know where your father is, or what he has become, and frankly it has never even occurred to me to wonder, as long as he never comes near us. It was a mistake, a happy night out that went sadly wrong. He said I deserved it, but I don't think I did. All I ask of you Razzy is that you always respect girls, and make sure they are aware of what's expected of them. I think things are a bit different nowadays and girls are not so naive, but I'm sure there are still many young girls who don't realise the effect they're having on a man, don't realise that they are setting something in motion that they never bargained for, and don't know how to stop it except by saying no. They're not playing hard to get or being coy, you can take it that if they say no, it doesn't matter what led up to it, they mean no."

"Maybe I should find the bastard, even more so now that I know the truth. He got away with it didn't he, and he got to live his life but you didn't."

"Rubbish! Of course my life would have been different, but not necessarily any better. Once we had our story straight, I was proud of being a mum, and proud of coping with it unlike my own mother, although I couldn't have done it without your Aunty Pauline."

"So now I understand why you let her be so bossy! I guess we both owe her, but I'm sorry, I'll never be her number one fan!"

One week later Netty signed the lease that made her the new owner of the 'Enigma' stall in the market. She handed over twenty thousand pounds in cash to Sandie, which was what they had agreed. She had withdrawn it at her bank from her savings account, and nervously carried it through the town in a bag on her shoulder. If Pauline could have seen her, she would have had a fit! This way, nobody would know except her and Sandie. The deal included all the stock, and she was happy that she had got herself a bargain. Ground rents were low in the market, and leases were for life, so no need to renew. As long as the rent was paid regularly, there was nothing to worry about. Many of the traders had been there for generations, and Netty was comforted to know that her son now had a job for life – even if he didn't appreciate it yet. Sandie had only had her stall since her husband died a few years ago and her daughter had a career of her own, so it had been different for her, and she was happy to hand it over to a friend, rather than a complete stranger. That night, Netty knelt at her shrine, and thanked the man who had made this possible.

ELEVEN: MURDER. (January 20th 2005)

For the following six days, Tony continued his vigil parked up within sight of the house. The weekend saw the couple both at home, and on Saturday night they were joined by another couple - one of the two from the quiz night. Monday to Thursday saw the husband leave for work again, but not the woman, who never seemed to go anywhere. On Thursday afternoon a supermarket van drew up outside and the driver took several boxes of groceries into the house, which explained why the woman didn't need to go shopping. There would be one more opportunity. Tonight was quiz night.

By six he was positioned in his car to watch for their departure to the pub for quiz night. He would then have several hours to accomplish his plan. He put a CD in the car stereo and settled down to wait.

He came to with a start. The silver Audi was pulling away from the kerb, the lights dazzling him. Damn! He had fallen asleep. It was nearly 7.30p.m, and it appeared that they had just left for quiz night. The house was in darkness. He decided he'd better wait a while in case they came back. He knew that the quiz started at 8.30, so if they weren't back by then he would be safe, and would still have plenty of time for what he had to do. His tools were in the boot, and he selected one or two that might be used to break in, then settled back to wait again.

At 8.45, he left his car, pulled on a pair of leather gloves and pushed the implements and a small torch into his coat pockets. He made his way cautiously around the side of the house. It was shrouded in darkness. There was a hard frost tonight, and the ground was firm beneath his feet as he skirted the conservatory and stood before the kitchen window. He shone the torch, shielding it with his hand. His heart sank – the window was closed. However, when he tried to raise it, he realised that it wasn't locked. He wondered at people who go out for the night leaving their home empty and unsecured, as he carefully lifted it high enough to climb through. It wasn't easy, there were plants in pots on the windowsill, and he had to reach in and move them over before he could manoeuvre his body through the space onto the draining board, dropping silently from there to the floor. The kitchen was warm and smelled of coffee, and was dominated by an enormous scrubbed pine table and chairs. There was a large pine dresser adorned with ceramics, vintage kitchenalia and a group of several candlesticks dripping with wax. There was a letter rack stuffed with various envelopes, bills and leaflets. A quick flick through them revealed that most of them were addressed to Mr. & Mrs. G. Gibson. Then he found one that caused the blood to thunder in his ears. It was some sort of circular, addressed to Mrs. A Gibson! A for Annette! Surely he had hit the jackpot. He needed more evidence, however, and continued his search. A door led off the kitchen to a hallway, and from there to the conservatory, a drawing room, a formal dining room and a small study lined with books.

The torch revealed nothing of interest to Tony. There were numerous paintings and drawings on the walls, but no family photographs. With mounting feelings of frustration, Tony climbed the stairs, still treading silently – somehow it didn't seem right to make any noise in the darkened house that seemed to be watching and listening, and was making him feel very jumpy. The doors along the landing were all closed. He chose one at random. It swung open to reveal a neat, sparsely furnished room that looked unlived-in, and was clearly a guest room, with no photographs. The next door yielded another study area. The torch revealed a desk in front of the window on which stood an iMac desktop and keyboard. The desk was littered with writing materials and notebooks, and there, at last, a photograph frame. However, disappointingly, it contained only a picture of the woman holding a large black cat. Tony stifled an exclamation of annoyance. Then he spotted a stack of novels on a shelf near the desk. He picked one off the top. They were all identical. 'The Decider' by Alison Gibson, proclaimed the cover. He turned it over. There was a thumbnail shot of the woman he had thought to be Annette. Her name was Alison!

Well, that was that. All the anticipation, all the hope, drained from his mind, to be replaced by rage and disappointment. This had been a complete waste of time. He threw the book down on the desk and stormed out of the room, all thought of caution banished from his mind. He began to retrace his steps along the landing, when suddenly one of the bedroom doors opened and there she stood, her face pale in the torchlight, her hair streaming over her shoulders and her white nightgown. Her mouth opened in a desperate scream, and Tony dropped his torch and lunged towards her, his hands reaching for her throat instinctively in an effort to stifle the sound. He pushed her backwards onto the bed and tightened his grip. Rage at his abortive mission welled up in him and seemed to endow him with superhuman strength. She struggled frantically, kicking out at him with her feet, her hands trying desperately to claw his fingers away from her throat, flailing at his head and attempting to gouge his eyes. He held on grimly until she was still; he had no choice. He slid to the floor, drained and fearful. This was not meant to happen. There was supposed to be nobody home. He was reminded graphically of that night all those years ago when he had committed a terrible crime, only this time it was worse; it was far worse. In that moment, he wondered what would have happened if the girl Annette had screamed instead of just caving in, and somewhere deep down the chilling answer echoed in his mind. Pulling himself to a standstill he retrieved his torch and shone it on the dead woman's face. She stared back at him with glazed eyes, wide open and accusing. They swam before him, their glassy green gradually turning to brown – his mother's eyes! She was watching him; she had seen everything, just as she had promised! In sheer desperation, he took the screwdriver from his pocket and attacked the terrible eyes, gouging them from their sockets so that he could be seen no longer. He threw the lifeless body back onto the bed, face down, then, hastily wrapping the eyes in a wad of tissues from the bedside table, he thrust them into his pocket and fled down the stairs and out through the front door.

He didn't know how long he lay on his bed in the hotel, semi-conscious, suspended between reality and a growing fantasy that was creeping insidiously into his mind. Yes, he wanted to find his son, but that wouldn't give him back all the lost years. Who knows, the boy who was now a man might want nothing to do with him – his mother was sure to have poisoned his mind with the tale of her brutal treatment at the hands of his father. He supposed she would have painted herself as an injured innocent, not as the provocative, coquettish and seemingly willing party he remembered. Why else had he never made the effort to find his father. He could surely have got enough information out of her and that sister of hers to make a reasonable attempt at tracing him, and after all, Tony had remained in the same area most of his life.

No, he decided. The bitch must pay for what she did. First he would find his son, and then he would destroy

Annette as she had destroyed him. He remembered the feel of his hands around that woman's throat – the softly yielding flesh, the almost tangible moment her life left her body, and the strange retrospective satisfaction he got now from the memory of gouging out those eyes that were staring at him – his mother's eyes; the mother who had abandoned him at the age of six to a father who didn't know how to love him, the mother who said she would be watching him always. What right had she? He had had to find his own way through life, and he owed her nothing. From now on, he would make sure she saw nothing. He didn't want to hear her last words in his head, and he didn't want to see those eyes again.

After a shower and a change of clothes, Tony set off on a mission to find somewhere to live. Outside the hotel, he pushed the wad of tissues containing his gruesome trophies far down into the depths of a nearby litter bin as he passed.

On the hill approaching the station was an estate agent with a lettings board in the window. There were one or two houses which Tony didn't feel he could afford, and an interesting looking flat on the first floor of a double-fronted house a little way up from the river. It was only a studio, and therefore well within his means without his having to find a job immediately, and it was equipped with the basic requirements of a sofa bed, a microwave, a refrigerator and a gas fire. There were no laundry facilities, but there was a modern shower room and toilet, and Tony knew there was a launderette a couple of streets away. Best of all, there was private parking at the back of the house. Anything else he needed could easily be found in one of several second-hand shops in the town.

Tony was pleased with his find. It meant he needn't worry about getting a job for a while, and he could concentrate on his search for his son, and the woman who had kept him from him.

He decided not to return to the King's Head. He didn't want to attract any attention and must widen his search.

Weeks passed, and as Spring turned to summer, Tony was no nearer to finding his son. He spent his days walking the streets and shopping centres of Chesbury, eyes and ears open and alert. He sat in cafes and pubs, and ambled through the park, and the grounds of the castle, a picture in his mind of the middle-aged woman Annette would have become.

It was quite by chance that at last he came across her. On a balmy July afternoon, he sat in Coffee and Compliments by the station, and saw her walking past, her bright auburn hair falling in waves to her shoulders. She was about the right age, right height, and although she had begun to succumb to middle-aged spread, she was still an attractive woman. She stopped to greet another woman near the doorway.

"Annette! How lovely to see you!' The other woman embraced her, beaming with pleasure. Tony strained every fibre to hear what passed between them, but only caught snatches of their brief conversation.

"See you later", the other woman said, and waved as they went their separate ways. The woman named Annette headed across the busy road past the bus station, and along the riverbank towards the outskirts of town. Tony abandoned his coffee and followed, strolling casually, hands in pockets. To all outside appearances he was calm and relaxed, enjoying a walk with no particular purpose. Inside, however, a maelstrom of emotions was burning him up, his heart racing in anticipation. She walked away from the town past the King's Head and up a slight incline with small terraced houses on either side of the road, eventually turning right into a side street of tall double fronted terraces set back off the main road in a street lined with trees. Steep steps led directly from the street to their rather grand front doors flanked by tall windows adorned with colourful window boxes on their broad sills. Lace curtains or venetian blinds shielded them from the street below. The street was quiet, the only sound at that time of day the chattering of sparrows in the trees. Several cars were parked between the trees, but none in the space reserved for No 7. The woman pushed a key into the lock and stepped inside, closing the door behind her. Tony stood staring at the elegant green panelled door with its gleaming brass fittings. He had rehearsed this moment in his mind a thousand times, yet now that it was here, he hesitated. Suddenly, his mind made up, he climbed the steps and pressed his finger on the doorbell – glancing around as he did so at the seemingly deserted street. The door opened, and she stood there with a slight smile and an enquiring glance.

"Annette?" It was more of a statement than a question.

"That's right," she nodded acquiescence. "Do I know you?" A look of suspicion crossed her face and she pulled the door behind her, leaning out to glance along the street.

"Remember me?" he asked. "Tony."

"I'm sorry, I think you have the wrong house, I don't know anyone named Tony." A look of alarm crossed her face, and as she took a step backwards, he sprang forward, pushing her inside and slamming the door shut behind him. Adrenaline ran through him; this was his moment.

"Where is he?" He leaned towards her, his breath hot in her face. She shrank back against the wall in the hallway and he grasped her arm and half marched, half dragged her into the lounge on the right. She struggled, and whimpered in terror.

"Wh...where's who? I don't know what you're talking about!" Tears and terror welled in her eyes.

"You know who! Paul! My son Paul, that's who!' Tony's eyes glittered and white foam formed at the corners of his mouth. He shook her roughly.

"Y...your son? I don't know anyone named Paul, and I only have a daughter. Please, leave me alone. I don't know you, and I don't know anything about your son." She covered her face with her hands "Dear God" she whispered "Help me!"

Tony glanced wildly around the room, his eyes alighting on a large photo of a family group. He recognised the woman, her head resting on the shoulder of a grey-haired, slightly rotund man. In front of them stood a blonde woman perhaps in her thirties, with her arms around two young children, a boy and a girl, also blonde. All were smiling and happy. Annette followed his gaze, her hands dropping from her face.

"That's my husband Brian, my daughter Sarah and my two grandchildren Tom and Sally. Sarah's husband Phil is taking the photo." She gazed at him imploringly. "Now do you believe me?" she whispered. "Perhaps you should leave."

Tony looked into her eyes gazing back at him beseechingly, pools of turbulent emerald green, and as he did so, they swam before him, distorting and morphing into his mother's brown eyes. His mind was in turmoil. What now? This was all going horribly wrong, and he had made another terrible mistake!

He could have just run and kept running, but she had seen him now, and she knew, and she would tell. It was too late to run, too late to change his mind as his hands automatically reached for the woman's throat, fastened around it and squeezed until she stopped fighting and tearing at his hands, and slumped against the wall, sliding slowly to the floor where she lay in a still, crumpled heap. Those eyes, those terrible all-seeing eyes wavered before him, morphing in waves from green to brown….and he took his penknife from his pocket and dealt with them, after which he fled. The street was still deserted and a minute later he was sauntering back the way he had come, his outward appearance once again belying the turmoil inside. However, when he reached his apartment, he threw himself on the sofa, hands clenched over his head, racked with the agony of shame and regret. What had he become? What had that girl turned him into? If her aim was to punish him for a stupid mistake he made more than thirty years ago, she was doing a good job. He hated the monster he had become, but he hated her more, he hated her so much that it made his blood boil, because it was all her fault! She was responsible for the deaths of two innocent women, and for that he would make her pay!

TWELVE: RACHEL.

Rachel stood and stared out of the window, a strand from the sleeve of her jumper twisted in her hand. It was torn and frayed from being worried, and had begun to unravel in a ragged and haphazard manner. Her fingers worked it constantly, twisting and turning, pulling it into the palm of her hand then releasing it and repeating the process. Outside, the rain swept like a quilt across the meadows that fell away beyond the cottage, and the wind whipped the trees into a frenzied dance like a scene from a gothic rendition of Swan Lake. In the paddock, Sparky grazed calmly, oblivious to the wind and rain beneath his cosy rug. Soon after four, he would make his way up the paddock to his stable, and Rachel would rub him down, feed and water him and bed him down for the night. She had done this every day since Mickey died.

The pony was getting on in years now and was no longer required to do anything but eat his head off and remind her of her beautiful, carefree daughter who had loved him so. His burnished chestnut coat still gleamed in the summer sun, and he still became excitable whenever other horses passed nearby, running to the gate and whinnying to them. Rachel felt guilty sometimes that after Mr. Pickles died, they hadn't found Sparky a new companion; but he seemed happy enough, and until last year a young girl from the village used to come and ride him during the summer months, until she outgrew him at sixteen, just as Mickey would have done.

Crow Lane End was a distant memory now, relegated to the back of her mind. The gracious old house that she had once loved was now a stranger occupied by strangers. She and Michael lived there alone for a year after Mickey's death, haunted with pain and remorse, each blaming the other, or themselves, for what had happened. Eventually, realising that all the 'if onlys' in the world would never bring their children back, Michael decided to sell up, and they moved to Honeysuckle cottage, seven miles away, midway between Farnley and Chesbury, and well away from the sultry river that had carried Mickey's corpse, followed shortly afterwards by that of Rachel's son Danny, down its course to come to rest against the old sandstone bridge.

Danny! The beautiful boy she had abandoned as a tiny baby, setting in motion the chain of events that would ultimately seek to destroy her life and end his.

Their marriage was floundering, and neither of them felt able to speak about it, yet still they clung together in the night when the nightmares became too much to bear, only to become virtual strangers again when the cold dawn broke.

Just after Rachel's fortieth birthday, she realised that she may be pregnant. She was filled with horror at the prospect. She had borne three children, and all were dead. How could she even think of going through that again? She made up her mind to abort the child without Michael's knowledge. Her mind in turmoil, she booked herself in to a private clinic where she would be in and out in a day. Michael need never know, must never know.

It wasn't, however, as straightforward as she thought. The clinic insisted on giving her an ultrasound scan. At twelve weeks pregnant, she was forced to watch the image of her baby on the screen – already recognizable for what he or she was. Everything appeared to be normal, she was told. The nurses left her alone to think things over, but they knew, as did she, that she could never go through with it.

She left the clinic in a daze, clutching the photograph of her unborn child. What would Michael say? Now entering his sixties, he may not feel able to cope with fatherhood again. Molly and Kieran had provided him with grandchildren – a pigeon pair apiece, and he was happy with the low level of responsibility that accompanied the role, happy for them to come and stay during the long Christmas break, but also happy when they returned to their homes in Australia and peace reigned once more. The grandchildren had long passed the baby stage and tended to keep one another amused most of the time, as long as one threw them some food at regular intervals. A baby, though, was a very different proposition, especially when they were already struggling to hold onto their failing marriage.

When the time was approaching for her twenty week scan, Rachel knew she could hide it no longer.

"Michael, we need to talk." He raised his head momentarily from the Financial Times and regarded her quizzically. Still handsome, with wings of silver in his thick dark-blonde hair and wistful eyes that were nonetheless still bright, at unexpected moments he still tugged at her heartstrings as much as he ever had, and she was taken aback by the strength of her feelings for this man to whom she barely spoke these days.

"Can't it wait? I've had a trying week," he sighed, but folded the paper and laid it on his knees resignedly.

"I'm...*we're* going to have a baby." There was no easy way to tell it. She watched him take it in, watched his face change from bored indifference, through shock, puzzlement, and then, suddenly, delight.

"*Are you sure?*" His voice was hoarse with emotion. "When?"

"In about four months," she replied, relief washing over her. She had thought he might be angry, but she had been so wrong! "I've got my twenty week scan on Thursday if you want to come."

"Twenty weeks? For God's sake, why didn't you tell me earlier?" His tone was incredulous – *how could she have kept such a momentous event from him for so long?*

"Because I wasn't sure...didn't know...it doesn't matter, I've told you now. I wasn't sure how you'd react, I'm sorry." Suddenly, the strain of keeping her secret and the relief of unburdening herself at last overwhelmed Rachel, and she began to weep silently, the tears trickling slowly down her cheeks. Michael sprung to her side and took her hands in his.

"It's a miracle Rach," he said softly, his eyes also shining with tears. "I love you so much. This child will heal us my darling, and make everything right again." He drew her gently into his arms and rocked her, smoothing down her hair that was still sleek and shiny chestnut brown with barely a trace of grey. "Oh, I hope so," she whispered in reply.

Four months later, Rachel gave birth to a little girl whom they named Annie. Rachel would sit beside her cot and gaze at her sleeping daughter who looked so much like Mickey at that age. "Please God," she cried inwardly, "Don't let anything happen to this one." She didn't know why she appealed to the unseen deity, the same one that took John, Mickey, and Daniel from her. There was no God, she was sure of that, or if there was, he was a cruel God indeed. No, she would protect this child with her own life if necessary.

Annie was a bright, happy child from the start, and easy-going in every way. She was the apple of Michael's eye; an unexpected bonus in the autumn of his years, and he was happy to delegate his responsibilities at the factory and spend more time with his family. They went to the seaside, for picnics, and for walks in the countryside around the cottage. She gave them a new lease of life and filled their world with smiles and sunshine. As she grew, she lost her resemblance to her dead sister, and took on a look and a personality of her own. She had Michael's blonde hair, not Rachel's rich chestnut locks; it grew in luxuriant curls and was almost impossible to brush. She had a warm chubby roundness that Mickey had never had, and dimpled cheeks like rosy apples that it seemed everyone felt compelled to kiss. Annie was a pure delight, and gradually Rachel lost her apprehensions and settled down to enjoy her charming new daughter. The pain of Mickey and Danny's deaths receded, and sometimes she would wake with a sudden rush of guilt because she had forgotten to grieve for a day or two.

A few weeks after Mickey died, when a second girl was raped and strangled on the banks of the sultry river at Farnley, the full enormity of what had happened to her children had hit Rachel like a ten-ton truck. Danny had been guilty of nothing except loving a girl that he had no idea was his sister. Her heart broke for him, knowing that he had been so consumed with grief and anguish that he had seen the river as his only source of comfort. The cold, sly, all-consuming river that was happy to engulf his young life and extinguish it remorselessly, leaving the whole community believing he was guilty of murdering his own sister. Even she had believed it; even Mariana, the woman who had raised him as her own child had believed it. Certainly Michael had believed it, and refused to acknowledge Danny as her son, forcing her to slip away alone to sit and weep beside his modest grave in the peaceful churchyard at Farnley where his half-brother and half-sister lay together in the family grave. Danny lay in a separate plot, marked only with a small cross at Michael's insistence.

A few months later, when Colin Stapleton was arrested and convicted of Mickey's murder, that of another innocent girl, and the attempted murder of an undercover policewoman, Rachel begged Michael to have Danny's body moved, but he refused, saying that it would hardly be appropriate considering his un-natural relationship with his half-sister.

"It wasn't his fault," she pleaded. "He didn't know!"

"He knew she was under-age," Michael responded, and the subject was closed. Rachel resented Michael's stubbornness, and the knowledge that he couldn't forgive Danny drove a wedge between them that had remained ever since.

Now, however, watching him play with little Annie, hearing their laughter and seeing his absolute joy in their beautiful golden cherub, she felt her resentment dissolve. Michael was a good man, a good father, and she was lucky to have him. The old closeness between them gradually returned and one day Rachel woke to the realization that she was actually happy again, and there was no longer a dark shadow hanging over her.

The email, therefore, came as a shock.

'Dear Mrs. Fenton, Rachel,

My name is Glenn Gibson. I hope you don't mind my writing to you, but I believe you may be able to help me. It's a somewhat delicate matter and I have no wish to reopen old wounds for you but I hope you will consider my proposition, and come to a decision that you feel comfortable with.

I run a victim support group for the families of the victims of the Chesbury serial killer. The group is called 'Second Sight', for reasons you will understand if you are familiar with the circumstances of the case. I am supported in my endeavours by my friend and colleague

Simon Bracewell, a gifted psychiatrist. I was motivated to set up the group because my beautiful wife Alison was the killer's first victim.

One of the crucial aims of the group is to demonstrate to the families that there is life after murder, that life goes on and can eventually be worthwhile again, however bleak it may appear. One way to do this is to enlist the help of others who have been through a similar experience and have triumphed over the emotional turmoil and despair that I know only too well results, and been able to move on with their lives in a positive way.

You are a shining example of this not inconsiderable feat. It takes courage and fortitude to put a tragedy such as yours behind you and allow yourself to live and love again without resentment. I was privileged to meet your husband Michael a short while ago and he told me about your daughter Annie and your newfound happiness as a family. He also told me that it had been harder for you, because you had lost two children and not just one as he had. I was aware of the circumstances of your daughter's death and that your son was held responsible until the real killer was exposed. It must have been an almost unbearable loss, but you bore it, and you didn't let it destroy you or your marriage although Michael also told me that he was perhaps not as supportive of you as he ought to have been regarding your son. You, Rachel, are clearly a strong woman who cares deeply for others, and that is why I believe you could be an invaluable addition to our team at Second Sight. I persuaded Michael to give me your email address; I hope you are not angry with either of us.

The latest victim of the Chesbury Strangler was a young woman who had been estranged from her mother for a good many years. The day before learning of her death, her mother Lauren became aware for the first time that her daughter Ashley had a little girl, now four years old, whom she had never met. Ashley had left the child in the care of a friend, and the friend had duly passed her on to Lauren because her mother appeared to have abandoned her. Having agreed to care for her granddaughter until such time as her daughter should return, it came as a devastating shock to Lauren when she learned that her daughter had, in fact, been murdered and would not be returning at all. The death of her estranged daughter in such a gruesome and public manner has been doubly hard for Lauren to bear because she didn't have the opportunity to reconcile with her daughter as she had hoped to do through the child Poppy. Rather like you and Danny, the opportunity was imminent, but was destroyed by the murder and now she has to try and live with the knowledge and the inevitable guilt that she never had the chance to tell her daughter that she was loved. I can't help drawing the parallel and feeling that you will inevitably have some empathy with Lauren's situation.

You will be wondering what is expected of you. All I ask initially is that you attend our meeting later this week and make yourself available to the families so that they can ask you questions and hear your story. Perhaps you would like to meet me for coffee earlier so that I can fill you in on the background of the families. Lauren's case is different from the others, and she is very much on her own as her ex-husband has a new wife and a child on the way. She has no-one; I think she needs a friend, and I think you, Rachel, could be that friend. She's a little older than you but not significantly, and my instinct (which Simon informs me is pretty much unfailing) tells me that you two have a great deal to offer each other.

I hope you can see your way to joining Second Sight. It's purely a voluntary position, although I shall of course reimburse you for your travel expenses and Simon and I will buy you and Michael dinner afterwards. Hopefully the group won't be needed for long enough to become a registered charity and this bloody killer will be caught soon. Please email me with your response, and if you agree to help I shall meet you at Coffee and Compliments near the station in Chesbury at 4.30p.m. on Thursday. The meeting begins at 6, so that'll give us plenty of time to bring you up to speed with the participants, and any recent developments. Simon will join us just after five (unlike me, he still has a job to go to).

I look forward to hearing from you, and hopefully to meeting you.

Kind regards,

Glenn Gibson.

Her initial reaction was mild annoyance. Annoyance at Michael for discussing their personal business with a stranger; and annoyance at the stranger for thinking he could invade her privacy in such a way. Hadn't she been through enough? She was about to delete it, then she noticed the attachment. It was a perfect madonna and child image of a thin, gaunt woman with pale copper hair, haunting features and emerald eyes, holding a fairy-child with apricot coloured hair and a wistful innocence that cut straight to Rachel's heart.

'*Oh bugger!*' thought Rachel. This man knew exactly what he was doing! She put down her iPad, and moved to stand by the window.

The sun was sinking behind the trees that lined the horizon. Sparky would be on his way to his stable, anticipating his evening feed. Annie was asleep, and Michael wouldn't be home for another hour or more. Rachel was alone, alone with her thoughts, her memories, and her conscience that was screaming at her that she must help this woman and her fairy grandchild if she could. She reached for her iPad, logged into her email, and hit reply.

THIRTEEN: SECOND SIGHT

Glenn parked his car in the multi-storey near the station, and made his way to meet his friend. As always, his path through the streets of Chesbury brought back painful memories, and he was thankful that his route took him nowhere near his former home.

The landlord of the King's Head was expecting him as he entered through the lounge.

"Simon's in the bar," he told him. "I'll bring your usual." It was busy for a Tuesday night. News of the murder had got around and everyone was there to discuss it and expound their theories as to what sort of person might have done it. Simon Bracefield was Glenn's long-time friend and colleague, and an excellent psychiatrist. He specialized in post-traumatic stress disorder and was the lynchpin of Glenn's victim support group. Glenn made his way through the throng and spotted Simon leaning against the bar, deep in conversation with a middle-aged man that Glenn vaguely recognized, although he wasn't sure from where.

"Glenn old chap! It's good to see you!" Simon clasped his hand and thumped him on the back enthusiastically. "Shame we hardly ever manage to meet up under happier circumstances these days," he added ruefully. "This is Mark Pullman, a close friend of the victim's mother." The other man shifted uncomfortably on his stool and made room for Glenn to stand between them.

"Well, not exactly close," he said, colouring slightly. "We work in the same place and have the odd drink together. She keeps herself to herself does Lauren most of the time."

"It's a young one this time then?" observed Glenn with a sigh. "The other two were middle-aged, and my wife was the youngest until now," he informed Mark.

"She was twenty-nine," Mark replied. "Lauren hadn't seen her for years and she doesn't know why she was in Chesbury that night. She's got... she had, a four-year-old kid, Poppy's her name. Lauren only found out about her at the end of last week, and now she's looking after her."

"What about the father?" Glenn asked.

"Poppy's father is unknown, and doesn't even know she exists apparently, and her grandfather, Lauren's ex, remarried a while ago and he hadn't seen Ashley for years either. He knew nothing about the kid until he went round to Lauren's to break the news about Ashley's murder and found her staying there. Bit of a mess really; I don't think Lauren really knows what to do with a four-year-old if the truth's known." Glenn thought this man seemed to have a number of opinions where Lauren was concerned and deduced that his interest in her could hardly be described as a passing one. Still, it was important to get as much background on the support group members as possible before the first visit; it saved those awkward blunders that might further damage their already fragile state of mind.

"I spoke to the family liaison officer and she's warned Lauren to expect a visit from us," continued Simon. "I think it's best if we call ahead, people get jumpy after these incidents, and two strange men turning up at her door unannounced may be too much for the poor woman. Also, she may want time to get the child out of the way. There's a woman called Bessie who's been helping out with that. Do you know her Mark?"

"She works for Lauren in her shop in the market. She's ok, got a heart of gold and the kid seems to have taken to her. You probably need to talk to Ashley's friend Trisha too. They shared a flat together until a couple of months ago and had known each other since primary school, so it's been a helluva knock for her."

Glenn made mental notes as they talked. Mother, father, daughter and best friend. The list wasn't too long, but that wasn't always helpful since large families united and propped one another up in these circumstances. He and Simon, it seemed, might have their work cut out here. He wondered whether Mark was covering some stress also – there was something odd about his body language, but then decided that he actually appeared to be enjoying the whole situation. Perhaps he thought he could offer a shoulder to cry on and take advantage of Lauren's vulnerability. He'd met men like Mark before, they couldn't seem to see themselves through the eyes of the women they obsessed about and he would only exacerbate her distress with his unwanted pseudo-sympathetic overtures.

"What about grandparents?" Glenn asked.

"Living over in France I believe," said Mark. "I don't think they've had much to do with Ashley in donkey's years, and Lauren told me she had forbidden them to come rushing over here, it would only be upsetting for them and her father isn't in the best of health. If it were me, I'd take no notice." *I bet you wouldn't,* thought Glenn wryly. *Not the sort of guy to take no for an answer.*

"Well," said Simon, heaving himself off his bar stool. "I think it's time we made tracks. Eleanor will be keeping our supper warm and I don't know about you Glenn, but I'm starving. Nice meeting you Mark, I'm sure we'll be seeing you again sometime." They both shook hands with Mark, and collecting their coats from the coat rack, set off for Simon's home a few streets away. Halfway up the hill, Simon put a hand on Glenn's arm, and said. "This is where the body was discovered – just down that alleyway. One of the local drunks found it when he went down there for a piss. Must've given him the fright of his life I should think!" Glenn glanced down the alleyway. One solitary street lamp dimly lit it about a third of the way down. It backed onto a Chinese takeaway and a fruit and veg shop, and there were two enormous bins and several smaller ones ranged along its right hand side. On the left hand side was a high wall interspersed with wooden gates that led to a terrace of houses. Why would anyone be walking down there late at night?

"Was she killed there, or somewhere else, do they think?" he asked, aware that the previous victims had all been killed in their own homes.

"Here, at least it looks that way. Bit of a departure from his usual MO, granted. Her body was slumped against the wall behind the big grey bin. She had no handbag, but she had a passport and nearly seven hundred euros in her jeans pocket. A bright young copper recognized her from a few years back when she got done for drugs and theft and they had to trace her parents. Seemed nice people he said; shame their daughter turned out a wrong 'un, but no one deserves what happened to her. Also, she's a lot younger than the other victims, and they were all decent respectable women like your Alison, and happily married. Perhaps this one was a mistake of some sort, or perhaps it's a copycat, and we'll soon know if that's the case because the police have been careful to protect the finer details. Perhaps it was a random mugging that went wrong. We don't really know, and the police are half expecting another one in the next few days I reckon." Glenn shuddered involuntarily. Simon must be hardened to these things to be able to discuss them so easily with a detached interest that Glenn felt unable to share. He had enlisted Simon's help with the group because of his degree in psychiatry and because he needed a friend he could bounce ideas off since he really was shooting in the dark. Simon had an easy way about him that people responded to, and he had proved invaluable to the group.

He was happy to work with the police, and had found other localized family members of murder victims who had managed to get their lives back together and were living proof that such things can eventually be overcome. Simon and Glenn's initial approach was on a personal level, with a visit to their potential group members at their homes, after which they were invited to attend meetings with other people who were or had been in the same position. These meetings were usually conducted in one or other of their homes which gave the whole thing a very personal slant. It seemed to be working well so far, with friendships being forged as well as practical help being offered where necessary.

At eleven o'clock the following morning they knocked on Lauren's door. After what seemed an inordinate amount of time, the door opened slowly. There stood a tall, slim, elegant woman of around fifty years old. Her face was pale and drawn, with such a melancholy expression that it was difficult to imagine her ever smiling. Her pale emerald green eyes were calm, however, as she surveyed the two men before her.

"You must be Second Sight." Her voice was unusually low-pitched for a woman, but with a silky-smooth cadence and not a hint of hoarseness. "You'd better come in." She stood aside to allow them to pass into the hallway. "Go through there," she said, "straight ahead." They entered the living room whose window overlooked the street. The curtains were drawn closed and there was a feeling that time was standing still. "Please, sit down," the woman said, gesturing towards one of the two sofas, and Simon settled down on one side, whilst Glenn perched uncomfortably on its edge, feeling out of his depth as the cool green eyes regarded him steadily.

"I'm Lauren Woods," she stated. "But I imagine you already know that. Would you like some coffee, or tea perhaps?"

"Thank you," said Simon. "Some coffee would be nice." She left the room, and moments later they heard the rattle of cups coming from somewhere down the hallway.

"Well?" Simon hissed in a loud whisper. "What d'you make of her then? In denial, or just one of those emotional deserts? She doesn't look as though she's cried a tear!"

"Oh come on Simon! You of all people know that people don't always cry. Doesn't mean they're not in pain. Bloody good psychiatrist you are! I admit though she does seem a cool customer, but if it's a defence mechanism we'll have to break it down before we can help her." Lauren reappeared with a tray holding a cafetiére, three mugs, milk and sugar. Simon spooned three spoonfuls of demerara sugar into his coffee, whilst Glenn had a little milk and no sugar. Lauren had neither, and settled down opposite them, cradling her mug in her hands and tucking her long jeans-clad legs beneath her.

"Nice coffee," Glenn said, taking a sip. This was awkward. They were used to finding people distraught and vulnerable. This woman appeared to be neither, and Glenn couldn't help wondering what they could possibly do for her. "I'm Glenn Gibson, and this is my colleague, Simon Bracefield."

"I know," she replied steadily. "The family liaison officer gave me your names. She was most insistent I write them down lest I forget. I don't know why everyone thinks I have suddenly gone gaga!"

"Is your granddaughter here?" Simon asked.

"No, she isn't. Flo said it might be better to talk to you alone initially. Are there any other children in the group?"

Glenn smiled inwardly at her use of the acronym like a Christian name. "No, there aren't. Our approach is more to help the adults come to terms with what's happened and to give them a chance to meet other people who have been through a similar experience and come out the other side. It's not that simple with children, and often they appear to cope and the effects come to light years later with devastating results. Does Poppy know what has happened?" Lauren shook her head.

"All she knows it that her Mummy isn't coming back. She's four years old for heaven's sake! I told her that Mummy got lost on the way home and has gone to Heaven. Probably the wrong thing to say, because she clearly has no concept of Heaven and is now convinced that Ashley will eventually find her way home from there. There appear to be many gaps in Poppy's formative education and I'm out of my depth with her, I barely know her, and she trusts my seamstress more than she trusts me."

There was a catch in her voice, and for the first time, Glenn sensed a brittleness in Lauren. She wasn't as self-sufficient as she would like them to think. She was struggling, like everyone does, to come to terms with what had happened, to her daughter, and to her world that had suddenly changed beyond all recognition.

"I know you mean well, and I'm grateful, really I am," she was saying now, looking from one to the other of them. "But I can't see why talking to a load of other people whose family members have been murdered is going to help me. Ashley and I were estranged. I hadn't set eyes on her in years, and I knew nothing of Poppy until last Friday. I don't know how to grieve for Ashley, and I don't know how to comfort Poppy." She sat back, her hands folded in her lap, the long tapering fingers intertwined. Then she continued. "My husband – ex-husband I should say, is about to become a father, and he's made it quite clear that Poppy is not his problem. He is refusing to grieve for Ashley, and since he has a new family pending, he doesn't need to. I, on the other hand, have no one, and I need to stay strong for my granddaughter who says she doesn't like me." She selected a lock of hair from her crown, and began to twirl it around her fingers – a nervous habit that belied her apparent composure.

"What about your parents?" Glenn asked gently. "I understand they're living in France."

"Yes, and they can stay there! This is one occasion when 'the more the merrier' doesn't apply. I have sent them a photograph of Poppy and they can come over when my father's health has improved and all this has blown over. It will, you know. Everything does.

Suddenly, silent tears began to course down her cheeks and she put her head between her hands. Glenn heaved a sigh of relief. It's not good to bottle things up, and if they had done nothing else they had enabled her to cry. She wept silently, her hair hiding her face. Glenn wanted to gather her into his arms – she looked frail and vulnerable now. He reached out and touched her arm gently, and her hand came out and clasped his. He and Simon exchanged glances. "I'm sorry," she whispered through her tears.

"Don't be, it's ok to cry." Glenn replied. He made no move to shrug off her hand but sat quietly, waiting for her to regain her composure. He offered her his handkerchief – fortunately pristine and clean, and she dabbed at her eyes and then blew her nose before handing it back. "It's ok, keep it," he said gently.

"Oh, I'm sorry!" she exclaimed, and suddenly a smile spread slowly over her face like a sunbeam breaking through cloud, illuminating the pale shadows of her eyes and causing her mouth to curve upwards suddenly like a fine archery bow. "I'll wash it," she said, and tucked it into her sleeve. "Well, when is this meeting then, and who will be there?" Simon took out his notebook and checked the details of the scheduled meeting.

"It's tomorrow evening," he said, "at Brian Saunders' house. His wife Annette was the second victim. They have a grown-up daughter who may also attend. He's been attending for three months now, and says it helps him focus on the future because of the people we've found who have found a way forward from murder, in particular serial murders, which are always more difficult because they generate so much publicity. Glenn ran away to Wales to escape it, but he returns at least once a month to assist me and always to the post-murder crisis talks. This whole thing was his idea, and is partly the reason he's adjusting so well to life after Alison, because he has found a purpose in helping others in the same boat." Glenn felt himself blushing, acutely aware of Lauren's eyes upon him.

"We will have living proof at tomorrow's meeting that, however terrible and bleak things may seem, there is a way forward, and sometimes closure can bring unexpected rewards," continued Simon.

"Back in 1995, not very far from here, in the village of Farnley, a young girl was murdered on the day before her fifteenth birthday."

"I know Farnley," Lauren said. "I used to take Ashley there to pick strawberries when she was a child. I remember reading about the murder. Wasn't it her half-brother who did it, because they'd been having a relationship?"

"That's what everyone thought at the time. Danny was abandoned at birth by his mother, and the lady who found him decided to raise him as her own. When he and Mickey met, they were inexorably drawn to one another and embarked on a passionate affair even though she was still underage. He was eighteen when Mickey was murdered. After her body was found he drowned himself in the river. It seemed like an open and shut case – until there was another murder a few weeks later, in almost exactly the same spot, although the body was hidden in the reeds and not floated down the river. Even then, the police weren't sure, and although they questioned about a hundred men, they couldn't turn up anything conclusive. The killer, however, had only become a murderer by chance and wasn't the sharpest knife in the block. They set up a re-enactment along the river bank. Meant to jog someone's memory, but instead they netted a big one. Not realising the whole thing was being recorded, the killer grabbed the undercover policewoman who was a lot older and stronger than she looked, and she promptly arrested him. He broke down and made a full confession. He had been eliminated from enquiries twice because of his apparent disability, but his medical records showed that, actually, he had recovered more than enough strength in his damaged arm to be able to overcome and strangle someone, especially a young girl. Once he got a taste for it, there was no stopping him. Thoroughly unpleasant and obnoxious man, but a bit of a simpleton, and not a born serial killer. They're usually far more complex and that's why they're so difficult to catch."

"So who will be coming to the meeting?" asked Lauren.

"The parents of the murdered girl. They went through a rough patch I believe, but they seem solid now. As a race, we're pretty resilient you know, and have an inherent survival instinct. Rachel and Michael now have another child, Annie, who has helped them to move on.

"What happened to the woman who raised the accused boy?" she asked now.

"She didn't cope so well," Glenn replied. "Had some sort of breakdown I believe. If she'd handed the boy over instead of keeping him for herself, none of it would have happened, and she found it impossible to deal with the guilt."

"Oh! Poor woman, it must have been awful for her."

"We all have our cross to bear Lauren. She was right, wasn't she? It was the wrong thing to do."

"I guess so, but she must have had her reasons," said Lauren sadly. "Who are we to say we wouldn't have done the same in her situation?" She smiled at Glenn, a weary smile that unexpectedly tore at his heartstrings. She was right, of course, he thought. Suddenly, Lauren rose from her seat and said, "Now if you don't mind, I have some work to finish before Poppy comes back from her walk. Thank you for calling." Glenn and Simon stood up quickly – clearly, they had just been dismissed.

"Will we see you there tomorrow?" Simon asked as they stood on the step and the door began to swing to behind them.

"I'm not sure, I'll sleep on it," she replied, and was gone, closing the door firmly behind her.

"Well, what d'you make of her?" Simon asked, raising an eyebrow at his friend. "Bit of a cool customer isn't she. Not sure we're going to have anything to offer her really."

Glenn said nothing, remembering the tears, and his instinctive urge to draw her into his arms and comfort her.

FOURTEEN: RAZZY'S CONFESSION

Netty was weary. How much longer could she continue to ignore the monstrous suspicion that was fast becoming a certainty? When the most recent murder occurred, Razzy had been out all that night, and didn't turn up for work the next day, although she had left him a note to ask him to open the stall as she must go to visit Pauline. When he finally came home, he went to his room and stayed there, refusing her offer of food. Casting her mind back, she realised it had been much the same scenario when the other two murders took place. Razzy had always been moody and unpredictable, and she had always harboured a secret fear that he was possessed of the same evil as his father. The fact that the first two dead women had had red hair and had been of similar age to her, and one had even shared the same name, had eaten away at her for months. He had seemed to take it well when she told him the truth about his birth, but she could never be sure that he didn't harbour some deep-seated resentment towards her for bringing him up without a father. Perhaps these women had been a substitute for his true target – his own mother. It was, of course, pure speculation, and she knew she could never tell anyone her fears and suspicions, so she carefully kept all the newspaper cuttings, and wrote all her own observations down in her diary, at least once a week. It was good to get it off her chest, but each time she read it through, the evidence seemed to her to be more damning and irrefutable, and it was becoming increasingly hard to ignore.

In her darkened room, she knelt at her shrine and carefully lit the candles. The flames burned into her retinas, obliterating everything beyond their smoky dark auras except her face reflected in the mirror above the shrine –

pale and drawn beneath a surreal explosion of fiery henna'd halo. Her sunken emerald eyes glistened with unshed tears in the flickering light of the candles and her lips were set in a thin, feathered line of despair. Reaching her hand beneath the table-top, she felt for the catch of her secret drawer. It clicked, and the drawer slid open. She felt inside.

The blood curdled in her veins – it was empty. *"Oh God, Oh God,"* she whispered as her hands flew into every corner, her fingernails scrabbling frantically at the wood as though somehow her secrets must be buried beneath its smooth surface, but there was no escape from the icy realization that someone, somehow, had found her secret stash. She began to weep, dry-eyed, gasping sobs that echoed inside her head and racked her breast. Her hands twisted together, clutching at one another for comfort, but receiving only the pain of her gemstone rings tearing into her palms. Wildly, she began to search her room. Somehow, she must have forgotten to put them away – yes, that must be it! One by one, she emptied her bedside drawers, depositing their contents on the bed; but they yielded nothing but half-empty blister packs of co-codamol, hair slides, receipts and train tickets. She threw back the quilt and tossed her pillows aside, stabbing her fingers deep into the crevice between the mattress and the quilted headboard, knowing in her heart there would be nothing there. She reached up to the top of the wardrobe and began to drag her carpet-bag towards the edge. It was heavy, and from past experience she knew that it would reach a certain point and then come crashing down on her head. She slowly inched it further forward, the effort of concentrating giving her some momentary relief from her blind panic.

"Is this what you're looking for *Mother*?"

Razzy's voice was soft and low, but it resonated on her ears like the chimes of doom. Her hands dropped to her side as she searched frantically in the turmoil of her mind for some plausible explanation to offer her son. Her hands were clammy and a cold sweat stood on her brow and seeped slowly between her sagging crepe-skinned breasts. The newspaper cuttings she could dismiss as morbid curiosity – but the diary! *Oh God, the diary!* It spelled out, in her own handwriting, the innermost secrets of her mind, her darkest, wildest imaginings, her inexplicable, unforgiveable, terrible suspicions. She turned slowly to meet her son's eyes. He stood in the doorway, indistinct in the gloom beyond the candle-light, the damning evidence resting in his outstretched hand.

They stared at one another. The silence was palpable, time stood still and Netty felt a tightening in her chest that was as ominous as it was familiar. Was this what her life was come to? Was this her ultimate punishment for the recklessness of youth that was her only sin? Her son, her Paul, the boy she had nurtured and adored and defended all her adult life, praying that she could eradicate all trace of his sordid beginnings. She had failed, and now she had to face the consequences and because she had given him life, he would certainly take hers. Tears filled her eyes and overflowed down her sallow cheeks that once bloomed like ripe peaches. She braced herself and sunk to the floor. Clasping her head in her hands, she prayed that he would at least be swift and merciful.

She felt his approach, his shadow fell over her. He knelt beside her and gathered her into his arms, rocking her gently, and to her utter amazement she felt great sobs rack his chest.

"I'm sorry Mum," he whispered, "I'm so, so sorry."

"What do you mean Paul? What is it that you're sorry for?" She held her breath, dreading his answer; dreading hearing her suspicions confirmed by his own lips.

"I'm sorry that I made you think I could do this, I'm sorry that you've been torturing yourself with it, and that you couldn't just ask me. I'm sorry that I have never shown you how grateful I am for everything you've done for me, and I'm sorry that things ever got so bad between us and I didn't even notice."

"It...it wasn't you? Are you telling me it wasn't you?" Netty raised her eyes to his. She was overwhelmed with conflicting emotions – suspicion, doubt, hope, and then a tsunami of relief when he slowly shook his head and said, "Oh Mum! Of course it wasn't me, though after reading this" he turned the diary in his hand, 'I can understand how you thought it was. Can we start again? We need to talk – I need to talk, and you need to listen. I'll explain everything so you'll know it's the truth." He stood and replaced the pillows on the bed, then lifting her bodily, he sat her against them and covered her with the quilt. He left the room and returned a few minutes later with mugs of tea. Netty blew on her tea and began to sip it gratefully. She felt suddenly weak and dizzy now that the adrenaline rush had faded.

"First, I have to tell you something you won't like Mum, but it's not as bad as you'll think. I'm an addict, a coke-head, I have been since just after I left school." Netty winced. She had known about the cannabis, had accepted it, but cocaine? How could she not have realised?

"I'm what's called a functioning addict which means I don't take it every day and I can more or less get on with my life and I guess that's thanks to you, because you've put up with my bad days, my mood swings, the days when I couldn't drag myself out of bed."

"We'll get you fixed Paul," Netty entreated, clutching his hands in hers, and smoothing his dreadlocks back from his brow. "You can be fixed, I promise. I'll get you an appointment next week, and I'll do whatever it takes to get you fixed."

"There's something else," Razzy said, his green eyes filled with tears. "I know I should've told you, but I was scared how you would react, scared you wouldn't understand." *Oh God! What now?* Netty thought, her stomach constricting, trapping her very breath.

"I've been seeing my dad." He waited, searching her face.

Netty was stunned, and for a moment or two was incapable of speech. "W...what? Your dad? How? When? Where?"

"A couple of months ago. He found me, I don't know how, he wouldn't tell me. He's been living here in Chesbury for nearly a year. I was in the pub one night and he just came over, and told me he was my dad. He was very upset, and very angry with you. He said he had a right to know me, and you were wrong to keep him in ignorance of my very existence. I guess I thought he had a point. He wanted to know where we lived, but I wouldn't tell him. I told him you must never know he was here, because if you found out, you would go to the police and tell them he was a rapist. I've been careful. I go to his place and I get the bus back so he can't follow me and he won't know how close he has got."

Netty felt a chill run through her. "H-how close is that?" She closed her eyes.

"Maple Avenue" – the answer was barely more than a whisper. *Only a few streets away!* A silent scream escaped Netty and her hands flew to her face in horror. Tony was here in Chesbury, and he was looking for her! This was a nightmare that she had never envisaged even in her darkest moments. She had told and retold the oil rig story until she had eventually come to believe it herself. *Maple Avenue!* That was in the posh area just up from the river off Madison Avenue, its tall double-fronted houses lately divided into executive maisonettes and studios.

"He made good Mum, he really did. He's not how you remember him, he's respectable and he's got money. He doesn't have dreads any more, and he wanted me to get rid of mine, but I knew you would ask questions so I refused. He says I should have his name, and you had no right to just make one up." Netty was now beginning to recover from the shock, and anger and indignation were rapidly replacing her initial fear.

"Which is?" she asked through gritted teeth.

"Ashton. His name is Tony Ashton."

"Well then, I didn't get it so wrong did I? Only the first three letters." Netty observed drily. "Could've been worse; could've been an advert for Wimpeys!"

"Yeah Mum, that's funny!" Razzy acknowledged grudgingly.

They stared at one another, each momentarily lost in their own thoughts. Netty tried to recall to mind the Tony she had known so briefly, but she had long since dismissed his image and had never really seen much physical resemblance between her attacker and his son. She remembered that he was very dark in skin, hair, and eyes, whereas Razzy was sallow skinned, with muddy brown hair, and green eyes like hers, as if he had been put into a food processor and then reconstituted, with only the eyes remaining intact. Razzy tried to imagine her as a seventeen year old girl, vivacious and happy, with burnished copper locks, rosy cheeks – and those green eyes that had never faded and sagged like the rest of her, and could say so much more than the words she sometimes failed to command. Suddenly he felt overwhelmed with anger and disgust at his father, who had taken the sparkle out of them and replaced it with the shine of tears. His father had asked him questions, which he had mostly avoided answering. What did Annette look like now? How did she dress, what were her habits, where did she work? He had never heard anyone except Aunty Pauline call her Annette before, and he had decided not to enlighten him on that score, being uncertain of his intentions although he assured him that he only wanted to meet up with her to make reparation for the wrong he did her all those years ago. There was something in his manner that suggested to Razzy that this may not be the truth, and his loyalty was, would always be, to the woman who had raised him, loved him and cared for him, not to this stranger who claimed to have been 'robbed' of his son. To Razzy, there was more to being a father than mere biological chance, and a man who could so degrade a lovely young girl was never to be trusted, so he answered vaguely and with only a nod to the truth.

"There's…something about him Mum. I don't know, it's just a feeling I get sometimes. It's like he's waiting for something; like he has unfinished business. To be honest, I don't think I matter as much to him as whatever it is he's still looking for."

"What sort of feeling? Good or bad?" asked Netty, puzzled.

"Not good, in fact, weird really. It's like he's two people and they're constantly fighting each other. Sounds a bit crazy, but I can't explain it any better." He sighed and continued.

"Sometimes I'm scared of him, I mean, really scared, and I don't know why. He's so…intense! I know he tries to follow me, and I'm always careful to avoid that, and I'm always careful not to let him know I know. Shouldn't be like that Mum, should it?"

"No son, it shouldn't. Hell, you're scaring *me* now! What d'you think he wants with me?"

"I honestly don't know, and I don't think I want to find out. I've thought of stopping seeing him, but I don't think he'd let it drop – like I said, he's so intense."

They sat in silence for a while, each one deep in their own thoughts. "C'mon Mum, I'll help you put all this back," Razzy said, waving a hand over the disassembled ruin of his mother's possessions. "Thanks for listening, and thanks for not going off on one with me." He grinned disarmingly, and they set to work together.

FIFTEEN: THE MEETING

Lauren stood on the bottom step, looking up at the green door with its brass fittings, her hand resting on the pole of the estate agent's board attached to the hand rail. Doubt flooded her mind. Was this what she wanted? She had always been a private person, not given to public shows of emotion, with a self-sufficiency that bordered on aloofness. Once inside, she would have to sit through whatever schmaltz they came up with, and would be expected to bare her soul to a bunch of complete strangers. Much as she hated feeling vulnerable and wounded, she hated even more the thought of anyone else knowing about it. She would cope, as always, in her own way and in her own time. She was sorry now that she had allowed her composure to slip, and also that she had agreed to this meeting.

In actual fact, things were working out better than expected. Bessie was embracing almost with glee her new role of Aunty. She had closed up early and taken Poppy to the park, and was then taking her to McDonalds for her tea, which clearly Poppy considered the ultimate treat, although Lauren was thankful that she herself wasn't involved. Decked out in her new outfit, the dress Bessie had made her, with matching woollen tights, a warm winter coat, fur-lined boots and a woollen hat, Poppy had skipped along beside her happily. Lauren had watched them to the end of the street, feeling pleased with her progress so far. Over the past week, she had discovered that Bessie had been widowed long ago, had been left childless and never remarried. Poppy had, in fact, filled a great hole in her life. Lauren felt ashamed that she had never thought to ask Bessie about her life and her circumstances, but had really just taken her for granted.

All three had spent the week getting to know each other, each in their own way. For her part, Lauren had continued to act as she normally did, with a few minor adjustments regarding meals and entertainment. Poppy seemed happy to fit in, and made no undue demands. She was content to watch tv with Charlie. Lauren bought some DVD's of Disney films that were preferable to the rubbish on children's tv. They went to Waterstones, where they bought picture books that Poppy took to bed with her. Lauren would pull up the chair and read them to her granddaughter, who would lie against her pillows with the covers pulled up past her chin, and Charlie purring happily on her legs. Within minutes, her eyelids would droop and very soon afterwards Lauren would make her way quietly downstairs to a much-needed glass of wine, followed shortly by Charlie who had done his duty for the day. He was loving the new routines, because he had a constant companion in Poppy, and she was inclined to keep a few Dreamies in her pocket. Lauren was able to work and had almost finished the wedding dress she was working on. The meeting with her client had gone well, thanks largely to Bessie, who seemed more than happy to look after Poppy in the shop whenever Lauren needed her to. She had cleared a space on the work table, and had treated Poppy to some colouring books and pencils from Roy's Toys (not his real name!)

Poppy was quiet and well-behaved. She would eat whatever was put in front of her, and Lauren decided from the start that she would eat the same as her, rather than the junk food that modern children seemed to exist on. They would go shopping together at Tesco Express, Poppy trundling a small plastic trolley behind her dutifully, occasionally pointing to something, her wistful green eyes questioning in a way that was hard to refuse. Her favourite treat was a packet of dolly mixtures, and Lauren wondered if that was mere coincidence, or a conscious reference to the first treat her grandmother had provided.

It was only after Poppy was asleep, and Lauren was alone with her thoughts, that the enormity of what had happened would hit her anew, and she would sit in silence in her own private Hell, glass in hand, the tears coursing silently down her cheeks and her heart filled with anguish and longing for the daughter she would never see again. It was the guilt that was hardest to bear. She should have tried harder, she knew. Perhaps she should have left Ken when Ashley first ran away, and concentrated her efforts into finding her daughter, reconciling with her and providing a home for her with fewer restrictions that she didn't feel the need to escape from. Although kind, Ken had always been inclined to be strict, and not just with Ashley. He had firm ideas about how they should all live their lives, and it was no coincidence that Lauren had made so many changes in her life after the split. She revelled in the freedom that had been denied to her for the past twenty years; freedom to make the most of her creative talents, not to live in anyone's shadow, and to choose where and with whom she spent her time, which, most of the time, turned out to be herself. Only occasionally, usually late in the evening after a glass or two of wine or on returning from a night out, she remembered with nostalgia the companionship of a long-standing relationship, but not enough to want another one!

Her mind made up, she turned and began to retrace her steps.

"Lauren!" Startled, she turned back to face the house. Glenn stood in the open doorway, a look of concern on his face. Lauren felt herself colour with embarrassment. She hadn't meant for anyone to see her sneaking off.

He came down the steps towards her, leaving the door slightly ajar behind him.

"Are you ok?" he asked. "I was looking out for you, and I saw you leaving."

"I'm sorry, I don't think I can do this." Lauren replied. She threw her head back and her look was a mixture of defiance and panic. She knew she was behaving irrationally, but she wished she could just go home, and that everyone would leave her alone – and then she remembered why she was here, and that Poppy would be back in a couple of hours. Solitude was pretty much out of the question these days.

Glenn put a hand on her shoulder, his touch light but firm.

"C'mon," he said gently. "You don't have to stay long, and you don't even have to speak, but I'd really like you to meet Rachel, and she's come quite a long way." He guided her back up the steps. "It's a small gathering," he said. "Just Simon and myself as well as Brian, whose wife Annette was the second victim, his daughter Sarah, and Rachel's husband Michael who has come along to give her some moral support."

The hallway was warm and welcoming, and Lauren could hear the murmur of voices from the lounge on the right-hand side. Glenn opened the lounge door, and gently propelled her through with a hand on her elbow. Five heads turned towards her, and Simon rose from his seat to greet her.

"Lauren!" He exclaimed. "I'm very glad you decided to come."

"I didn't," she replied. 'I was about to escape, but Glenn caught me." She smiled hesitantly, her equilibrium gradually returning.

"Oh! Glenn is part collie," quipped Simon. He helped her off with her coat.

"This is Brian, whose house this is." Brian was short and a little stout, with thinning grey hair. His smile was genuine, however, and his handshake firm.

"Not for much longer," he said. "I've had an offer on it at last, I'm happy to say. I can't live here knowing what happened – in this very room. This is my daughter Sarah, who has been putting up with me over the past few months." He indicated a slim blonde woman, who nodded and smiled at Lauren.

"Hi," she said.

"And this," Simon continued, "Is Rachel Fenton, and her husband Michael." Rachel sat on a chair next to the fireplace and Michael stood behind her. He was tall and exuded confidence. He stepped forward, offering his hand. Rachel by comparison was small and slight. She remained seated and smiled shyly at Lauren.

Introductions over, Brian offered everyone a drink, and Lauren settled for white wine.

"Rachel has kindly agreed to share her experience with you, in an effort to reassure you that life can, eventually, return to normality following such a terrible and tragic event as the murder of a family member," Simon announced. "There are certain parallels, Lauren, with your case I think you will find. When you're ready Rachel."

Rachel shifted self-consciously on her chair, and Michael placed a reassuring hand on her shoulder. She pulled the sleeve of her cardigan into her palm, and began to twist it between her fingers as she talked.

"I don't normally talk about this," she began, "But Glenn persuaded me that by doing so, I might help others, particularly you Lauren, to come to terms with the unthinkable. I hope he's right. I don't really know where to start, and you must feel free to ask me any questions as we come to them, which I shall do my best to answer."

"When my beautiful Mickey was murdered, I lost not one, but two children. There was only one suspect, Daniel Harding. Unbeknownst to anyone, including myself, Danny was also my son." She glanced up at Michael, who smiled gentle encouragement.

Lauren listened, fascinated, as Rachel's tragic story unfolded. A story that spanned two decades and ended with the deaths of her two children. Throughout, the sleeve was pulled and twisted in her palm, and at several points during the narrative, overwhelmed with emotion, she had to pause to compose herself with the aid of a gulp of wine. Finally, she reached the end of the sorry tale.

"Afterwards, Michael and I merely existed, in a sort of limbo. We moved away from where it happened but the memories followed us and we drifted further apart, only seeking comfort from one another in the dead of night. Then, out of the blue, along came Annie."

She told them how she had considered abortion, but couldn't go through with it, and how delighted Michael had been with the news. She told of her apprehension during the pregnancy, how she'd struggled to believe that nothing would go wrong, and how, when everything went smoothly, their sunny little girl brought joy into their lives once more.

"We will never forget Mickey. Michael never knew Danny, and because of that, I have to bear that sadness alone sometimes. Annie is a delight, and bears no resemblance to either of them, which definitely helps. She has a mop of blonde curls, dancing blue eyes, and not a care in the world – it's infectious! Young children leave you no time and very little room for introspection, as I'm sure you are already beginning to find out." She directed her gaze at Lauren, who nodded in assent.

"Thank you all for listening. I hope it has helped you, and I believe it has also helped me. As I said, I don't…can't normally talk about it."

There was a murmur of appreciation from around the room, and a slightly disjointed and hesitant round of applause. Then Rachel addressed Lauren directly.

"As presumably Poppy has no friends that you know of, perhaps you'd like to bring her over to play with Annie sometimes. Annie's a little older, but not much, and she's very outgoing. We'd be delighted to see you both, and you'll find there's plenty for them to do. How about Sunday afternoon?"

Lauren was somewhat taken aback, but immediately thought of an excuse.

"I'm afraid I have no car," she admitted, somewhat sheepishly. She had never felt the need for one, living in the city, and tended to rely on the train or taxis when she wanted to go anywhere. Panic constricted her chest. Perhaps now she would need to invest in some suitable transport. She turned to see Glenn watching her closely. He cleared his throat.

"In that case, allow me to accompany you. I can pick you and Poppy up at, say, 2.30, and I promise to return you at a respectable hour. That's if Michael and Rachel have no objection, of course."

"None whatsoever," rejoined Michael. At least I'll have some reinforcements against all those girls!"

Everyone rose from their seats, thanked Brian for his hospitality and retrieved their coats. Lauren set off on the walk home, having declined Glenn and Simon's offer of a lift. She needed to clear her head, and Poppy would not be home for another half hour at least. Darkness had fallen, punctuated by the soft pools formed by the streetlights. The evening was crisp and cold, the platinum full moon rode high and myriad stars glittered in the clear indigo sky. Lauren walked down the hill towards the river, past the King's Head on the corner, then along its bank before turning away up the hill as she had done a few nights earlier. Somehow, she didn't feel as vulnerable as she had done late at night, perhaps due to the clear skies, the absence of wind, and the presence of a few people returning from late night Christmas shopping with gaily coloured bags. The trees along the riverbank were still, and the water rippled gently, eddying in silver folds among the reeds and inlets. As always, she thought how lucky she was to live in such an attractive town. She wondered what Rachel's home would be like, and she wondered what she and Glenn would have to say to one another on the half hour or so journey there.

Charlie was waiting on the step, and ran ahead of her to his food bowl in the kitchen as soon as she opened the door. She turned on the lights, lit the gas fire, then went upstairs to put Poppy's electric blanket on. She would be tired when she got home, and hot chocolate and bed would be the order of the day.

SIXTEEN: THE VISIT

By Sunday, the cold frosty weather had given way to milder, damp days that started misty and murky, then cleared to allow the gentle winter sunlight to filter through. Lauren rose early in anticipation of the day ahead. She showered, and dressed casually in slim jeans and a soft green cashmere sweater that hung loosely on her slight frame. A long pendant of mauve charoite, matching silver drop earrings, and a light mist of Chanel No.5 completed the look. Satisfied, she made her way downstairs, peeking round the door to see that Poppy was still asleep; she would wake her later.

She lit the gas fire. In spite of the central heating, it was nice to have a visible heat source. She made herself a cup of coffee and curled up on the sofa. Charlie was still asleep also, his tail covering his face, on the opposite sofa. Aware of her presence, a rumbling purr emerged from the midst of the fluff. Sunday had always been a rest day for Lauren. She tried not to leave any unfinished business to spoil her sense of peace and perfect relaxation. In Summer, she would spend all day in the garden, mostly relaxing beneath a sunshade on the paved area at the bottom, but on cooler days weeding, dead-heading and tending to simple tasks. The garden was mostly shrubbery, low maintenance and easy-going, with a hidden carpet of spring flowering bulbs and a small irregular patch of lawn that required mowing in Spring and Summer. It was surrounded by herbaceous borders. There were also a few pots with pelargoniums in, some of which she moved into the shed in Winter. It was generally pretty low maintenance, and not really a major priority for Lauren.

In winter, she would spend the day relaxing by the fire with a good book, although on a day such as this, she would often go for a walk into town and through the park to feed the squirrels in the cathedral grounds. This is what she had planned to do with Poppy today, but instead they were going to Rachel and Michael's house, about a half hour journey in the direction of Farnley. She wondered what she should take with her. In the end, she settled on a bottle of white wine and the home baked iced Christmas biscuits that Bessie had made for Poppy. She fleetingly wished that she could bake and do the domestic goddess thing, but it was too late now to change the habits of a lifetime.

She and Poppy were ready and waiting by 2.30, having lunched on chicken fillet with new potatoes and broccoli. Poppy was wearing dungarees designed by Lauren over an Aran jumper, her red duffel coat, and her fur-lined boots. Lauren wore a sheepskin coat and calf length leather country boots. Poppy clutched a small paper carrier bag with the biscuits in it, and Mostly Molly. Lauren felt nervous, although she was unsure why.

Glenn pulled up to the door only five minutes late. After removing her coat, he buckled Poppy into a child seat in the back. "I borrowed it from a friend," he explained. "That's why I'm a bit late."

Lauren felt a little embarrassed. She hadn't thought about needing such a thing, and made a mental note to purchase one in case any such situation arose again, or in case she decided to invest in some transport. She settled into the passenger seat, relieved that Glenn had some music on the car stereo which would minimize the need for conversation. He was also wearing jeans, an Aran jumper, a navy reefer jacket and Timberland boots.

"Snap," he said to Poppy, laughing, and she extended an arm to compare jumpers. Soon, they were leaving the town behind and driving along the dual carriageway, turning off it after a few miles onto winding country lanes. Lauren relaxed in the comfortable seat and listened to Coldplay.

"Do you know this area?" Glenn asked Lauren, breaking the silence at last, to which she replied that she didn't. They came to a crossroads. The signpost said 'Farnley' to the left, and 'Osterley' straight on. They went straight on, and a mile or so further on, turned into a narrow lane, at the end of which they pulled up in the gateway of Honeysuckle Cottage.

"Here we are," announced Glenn slightly unnecessarily. "Would you mind doing the honours Lauren?"

Lauren jumped out, and opened the gate. It swung inwards, and Glenn drove through and parked up in front of the cottage, next to Michael's 4X4 and Rachel's blue sports car. Lauren secured the gate and caught up as Glenn was lifting Poppy from her car seat.

The cottage was very pretty, whitewashed with a thatched roof and the bare twining stems of a rambler rose over the entrance porch – a quintessential country cottage. Smoke rose from a chimney, filling the still air with the scent of Applewood. At the side of the cottage was a paddock, long and level, surrounded by trees and with a small stable at the top alongside the house. A chestnut pony was grazing near the gate, and lifted his head to gaze at the newcomers with curiosity.

Glenn approached the door, which opened before he reached it. A little girl stood in the doorway, her golden curls framing her face that was beaming in greeting.

"Hello," she said "I'm Annie."

"Come in!" Rachel called from inside the house. Annie took Poppy by the hand and led her inside, followed by Lauren and Glenn. The cottage was bigger than it had looked from outside. The flagstoned hallway contained a large fragrant Christmas tree, festooned with twinkling fairy lights, hung with baubles and an assortment of ornaments and topped with an illuminated star. Lauren felt a pang of guilt. Only seven days to Christmas, and she hadn't even thought about buying a tree! She didn't normally bother, but this year she realised she must, although it would have to be a small one. The hallway opened out into a large modern kitchen, with painted wooden cupboards and granite worktops that had been made to fit its somewhat irregular shape. There were herbs hung to dry from honey coloured beams, and a large bright red Aga cooker from which emanated the delicious spicy aromas of Christmas. A large island was surrounded by tall stools and strewn with colouring books, newspapers, an overturned pot of coloured pencils, a large cafetiere and two mugs. An enormous rustic bowl of fruit stood at its centre. Rachel was bent over the Aga, removing a tray from its depths. She straightened up, brushing a lock of hair back behind her ears, her face flushed and smiling.

"Mince pies," she announced, and pushing aside the colouring books, deposited the tray on the island. "Annie, do you think you could leave some room on here for food occasionally? You're worse than your father!" The admonishment was good natured, however, as she gathered up the scattered remnants of the Sunday Times and the Financial times into a neat sheaf. She relieved them of their coats, thanking Lauren for the wine and setting it down on the island. She disappeared to hang them up and Lauren remembered seeing coat hooks in the entrance porch.

"Have a seat you two, I'll put some fresh coffee on. Michael will be along in a minute, he just had to make a phone call. He's supposed to be winding down and getting a better work life balance, but I'm afraid progress is slow on that front. Annie, take Poppy upstairs and show her your room."

"Can we take these with us?" Annie brandished the bag of biscuits. "Poppy's Aunty Bessie made them."

"Oh! That was kind of her. Of course you can. I'll bring you up some squash shortly." Rachel smiled as the two girls disappeared back into the hallway, still hand in hand.

"I knew they'd get on. Annie can take her out to see Sparky afterwards, he's quite a sociable old boy, and perfectly safe."

"Oh! She'll love that, she's really into animals," Lauren replied.

They seated themselves at the island. Rachel produced fresh coffee and they were persuaded to accompany it with a mince pie.

"Mmmmm! These are delicious Rachel," Lauren had never been a lover of mince pies but meant every word.

"I make my own mincemeat," replied Rachel. It's time consuming but worth the effort. Michael really doesn't like anything shop bought, especially at Christmas!"

Again, Lauren felt pangs of guilt. Perhaps she should try harder, although her kitchen was very small and pretty basic, as it had never been much of a priority. Living alone, she had the option of eating out when she wanted something fancy, and there was, of course, Jonny's when she fancied something in the bakery line.

I'm really going to have to shift my priorities, she thought, for the umpteenth time since Poppy came on the scene. She noticed Glenn watching her intently. He leaned over and covered her hand with his. The gesture made her blush, but she recognised it for what it was, and was grateful.

"Merry Christmas!" Michael bounced into the room. "I smell mince pies!"

He dropped a kiss on Rachel's upturned face, offered Glenn his hand, then gave Lauren a quick squeeze. Pouring himself a mug of coffee, he sat at the head of the island opposite Rachel and surveyed them all, grinning happily.

"I can hear elephants upstairs, or perhaps it's the girls," he quipped. "They clearly hit it off. Annie loves to entertain!"

"Poppy brought biscuits, so that was enough for Annie," Rachel remarked wryly. "She didn't get that delightful chubbiness from nowhere! I really hope she grows out of it. In a couple of years we'll get her a pony, but she needs to have a few proper riding lessons first. Sparky's old now, he's earned his retirement, but he'd probably like a companion."

They settled down to chat, drink coffee and munch mince pies. The room and the atmosphere were warm and relaxing. Lauren compared it with her home, and for the first time the comparison didn't favour The Owl House. The children came racing down the stairs, their faces flushed and beaming.

"Can we go and see Sparky now?" Annie asked, as Poppy jumped up and down with excitement.

"Of course. Take him some carrots – not too big mind, his teeth aren't what they used to be." Annie opened a drawer in the island and withdrew two carrots which she broke in half. "These ok Mum?" Rachel nodded assent, and the two disappeared into the hallway.

"Don't forget your coats!" Rachel called after them. The front door slammed and they were gone.

Glenn and Lauren spent a pleasant afternoon with the Fentons. The children made a den in the hay bales that were stored in a shed next to the stable, using broom handles and stable rugs. They came back in for torches, crisps and colouring books, and the adults were obliged to troop out and inspect their creation before returning to the lounge, where a fire was blazing merrily in the inglenook fireplace. French doors framed by heavy curtains led out from here to the garden, where another Christmas tree hung with bird feeders and more lights stood on the paved patio. All manner of birds crowded onto its branches enjoying the feast. Lauren glimpsed a pond with a fountain, turned off in winter, Michael said, so it wouldn't freeze, and the garden was divided by rose arbours and pergolas. It must look stunning in Summer, and was clearly a labour of love.

It was almost seven o'clock by the time they took their leave. The girls had joined them in the lounge after tucking Sparky up in his stable when it got dark. Poppy promptly fell asleep on a beanbag in front of the fire, where she remained for the rest of the afternoon. Annie then joined in with the conversation, seamlessly transcending from child to adult.

Glenn had refused a second glass of wine. "I'd love to, but I'm driving," he pointed out ruefully. Reluctantly, they rose, and Michael fetched their coats, and scooping Poppy up in his arms, carried her out to the car.

"What are you guys doing for Christmas Day?" he asked as they piled in. Before they could answer, he continued.

"Come and spend it here with us. We've loads of room because the twins aren't coming this year. Poppy can bunk in with Annie, and we've two decent guest rooms, so you'd be more than welcome to stay over and have a few drinks."

"Ooooo yes!" Rachel said "Please do, it'll be fun!"

Lauren was completely taken aback. She glanced at Glenn, uncertain what to think. It was certainly a tempting offer. She could hardly offer Poppy anything like a special Christmas where they were; it was quite beyond her. Her one concern was whether it would be fair on Charlie. She was sure that Bessie would agree to feed him, but it was, after all, his Christmas too, and he had never spent it without her. Glenn, too, was thinking about Merlin, although he knew Bronwyn would be delighted to entertain him over Christmas and he would want for nothing.

"Can we get back to you on that Michael?" said Glenn. "It's a very generous and overwhelmingly tempting offer, but we have pets to sort out. I'll let you know by the end of tomorrow, and thank you so very much."

"Yes, thank you, it's a very kind offer, and I'm sure Poppy would be delighted!" said Lauren. "I'm sure we can work something out."

They waved goodbye and set off back to Chesbury. Glenn dropped them at the door "I won't come in," he said. "Simon is expecting me for dinner, and I'm rather late as it is. Today was good wasn't it?"

"Yes, it was. I really hope we can take them up on their offer."

"Me too. I'll pop round tomorrow before I leave and we'll talk it through. Goodnight Lauren, good night Poppy, I'll see you tomorrow, about lunch time."

He waited until the door was closed before driving away.

The next morning, Lauren was up early again, after a restless night. So much had changed in a matter of days, she just couldn't take it all in. Suddenly she was thrown into motherhood again, with all its attendant responsibility and sacrifice. New routines, new priorities, and all whilst trying to maintain the old ones alongside. Also, there was Glenn. Undeniably, there was some chemistry between them, although they had not yet acted on it in any way. It was there, not acknowledged, but none the less present. She remembered the reassuring touch of his hand when she had felt her inadequacies exposed. He had sensed her discomfiture, and had let her know without words that there was no need for it. He had made her feel safe, protected, and that was a long-forgotten feeling. Was it something she needed, or even wanted? She didn't think so, she valued her independence and the freedom to live her life as she saw fit. She wouldn't welcome a relationship that forced her to compromise, as all relationships tend to do. Glenn was kind and thoughtful. In some ways he reminded her of Ken; they were even similar in looks, and admittedly she sometimes missed the close relationship they had enjoyed for many years before Ashley brought so much conflict into their lives. Glenn seemed to have taken to Poppy, but would she have inherited her mother's wayward streak? There was no sign of it yet, but in the back of her mind, Lauren harboured the fear of history repeating itself, and she wouldn't want to inflict that on Glenn, who had suffered enough.

"Oh Charlie! What am I going to do?" Charlie turned soft amber eyes on her and rubbed his head against her legs, but made no reply.

Monday morning had always begun with coffee and croissants, and Lauren decided that that was one habit she must maintain. Poppy trotted willingly beside her down to the bakery, where Lauren added a pain au chocolat to her usual order. Jonny chatted to Poppy, and gave her a gingerbread man that she put carefully in the pocket of her coat.

"Thanks Jonny, she can have that for her elevenses," said Lauren.

"Thanks Jonny," echoed Poppy in her tinkling little voice, making them both laugh.

"You take care now *Grandma,*" said Jonny with a wink. "Hey! It suits you!"

In Coffee and Compliments, they settled down in a window seat and Lauren had her usual Americano, and treated Poppy to her favourite hot chocolate. They watched the commuters go by, and Poppy asked Lauren questions about them. Rather than disappoint her, Lauren went along with it, and made up names, occupations and destinations, much as she had done inside her head for the past couple of years. Poppy appeared suitably impressed that her grandma knew so much about everyone.

Bessie was already hard at work by the time they got to the shop.

"Morning Ducks," she greeted Poppy, who drew herself up and replied "I'm not a duck, I'm a girl," before hurling herself laughing at Aunty Bessie who enveloped her in a big hug. Lauren looked on smiling, marvelling in the change in Poppy in only ten days. She was still the same rather wan fairy child, but she had really come out of her shell and seemed to be taking her new situation in her stride. She had not mentioned her mother since the night Lauren told her that she wouldn't be coming back. Had she understood? Lauren wasn't sure, and she had seemed to accept that the absence might be a long one, but hadn't believed that it was permanent. Lauren didn't want to upset the apple cart by mentioning Ashley, and she was sure that the little girl would bring the subject up at some juncture and they would discuss it further, but at the moment, she seemed to be enjoying what must have felt like a holiday. Ashley's funeral was scheduled for the Wednesday after Christmas, and Lauren had decided that it was no place for such a young child, so she had arranged for someone to video the ceremony to keep a record of it to give to Poppy sometime in the future. A humanist ceremony, not a religious one, since neither Lauren nor Ken were religious, and she was pretty sure the same could be said of Ashley. There would be few mourners, namely herself, Ken and Janet, and Trisha and her boyfriend Steve. Bessie had offered to look after Poppy for the duration. Ashley would be cremated, and her ashes interred at the crematorium, so that in the future Poppy would be able to visit her memorial. Lauren's parents had decided not to attend, although they were keen to meet Poppy. Perhaps in the Spring, Lauren could take her to France to holiday with her great grandparents.

At mid-day, the three of them had their usual lunch of bread and cheese, after which Lauren made her way home to meet with Glenn. Poppy elected to stay with Aunty Bessie, and settled down with her colouring books happily.

Glenn's car was already parked outside.

"I'm sorry," Lauren said. 'I didn't think. I could have lent you a key."

"No worries, I've only been here about five minutes." Glenn replied. "have you had lunch?"

"Yes, we had our usual in the shop. How about you?"

"Well, I held off in case you wanted to go somewhere for a bite. I'll pick something up on my way home, I'm not really a lunch person and Bronwyn is making me some Cawl which is worth waiting for!"

"What's Cawl?" asked Lauren, unlocking the door. "I've never heard of it."

"Ooooo, you haven't lived! It's Welsh lamb stew, and Bronwyn is particularly good at it. There's really nothing better at this time of year, and I bought a nice sourdough from Jonny's to have with it."

They removed their coats and Glenn went into the lounge whilst Lauren made coffee.

"Can you just turn the gas fire on please Glenn?" she called from the kitchen.

Glenn did as he was asked, and settled down on the sofa. Charlie appeared from nowhere and jumped up beside him, purring and nudging his arm with his head.

"Hello old boy. You must be Charlie." Glenn rubbed him under the chin as he settled down with his front paws on Glenn's knees.

Lauren came in with the coffee. "Aha! I see you've met the problem cat," she said laughingly. She set a tray down on the coffee table, with a cafetiere, two mugs, and some stem ginger biscuits from 'Crumbs' in the market. She sat down opposite Glenn, and Charlie transferred to sit beside her.

"I've been thinking," said Glenn. "Well, more than just thinking actually. I had a word with Michael on the phone this morning. I asked him what he thought about you bringing Charlie along at Christmas. He was all for it – apparently, they just happen to be between cats at present, but they've always had them in the past and were planning to get a kitten for Annie very soon. There's plenty of room, you can keep him indoors if you're worried about him running off."

Lauren let the idea sink in. "I would never have thought of that," she admitted. "It does seem an imposition when I hardly know the Fentons. However, if you're sure they won't mind, I think it's a great idea. Charlie's an old boy now, he's nearly sixteen, and he's very much a home body, and not at all inclined to wander. He adores Poppy and he'll love being the centre of attention which I'm sure those two little girls will make him!"

"My Merlin will be fine where he is, he spends half his time at Bronwyn's anyway! He's taken to exploring the woodland that surrounds our cottages and may be more of a handful, and I've no idea what he thinks about little girls – or other cats for that matter, although he's fine with the three that Bronwyn has, and with Pero the dog. I worried about him when I decided to move, and then again when I first started coming up here, but animals are more resilient than we give them credit for. He knows I'll always be back."

"I think Poppy has the same faith in her mother," Lauren said sadly. "I don't want to shatter her illusions until she's very much older, which is one of the reasons that she will stay with Bessie whilst I attend Ashley's funeral"

"I've been thinking about that too," said Glenn, and suddenly moved to sit beside her, taking her hand in both of his. "I don't want to intrude, but let me come with you for some moral support." His eyes were earnest, and his hands were warm. Lauren felt the tears beginning to prick at her eyelids. She had been dreading it, being the only single person there – Ken with his wife, and even Trisha with her boyfriend. She didn't honestly know how she would get through it, whether she was strong enough without someone to lean on.

"Oh Glenn! Thank you so much," she whispered through her tears. He drew her into his arms and held her tightly until she recovered her composure, gently stroking a lock of her hair back from her face. Once again, she felt safe and protected, and it was a feeling she found that she enjoyed – she, Lauren, the self-sufficient and aloof 'I'm my own woman' guru. It was a strange revelation. Once again, he offered her a clean hanky. She dabbed her eyes delicately and refrained from blowing her nose this time. He was watching her, a smile playing on his lips, and then suddenly those lips were on hers in a long, deep, comforting kiss that left them both breathless. Lauren felt her world shift inexorably.

Glenn drove slowly back to his home in Wales. He reflected on what had just taken place. He thought about Alison, and wondered if what he was doing was wrong. Alison – vibrant, bright and vivacious, versus Lauren – slender, fragile and slightly fey. Both women possessed of wisdom and a quiet dignity, both powerful in their effect. He didn't think Alison would expect him to live the rest of his life in celibacy, but he wasn't sure he was ready for a full-on relationship whilst she was still uppermost in his mind. He recognized his own vulnerability in Lauren, and instinctively wanted to comfort her, but it wasn't really a sexual feeling, and isn't that what adults are supposed to want? He thought about his little cottage, which was just beginning to take shape after months of hard work. It was his personal bolthole, and wouldn't suit everyone, especially a woman like Lauren. The bathroom was still downstairs, he had seen no need to change it. Now, however, it housed a brand new suite with a large walk-in shower in place of the bath. The substantial wash basin was set into a slate-topped oak washstand that he had found in a nearby antiques centre, with a large driftwood framed mirror above it. The other changes he had made were mainly cosmetic – it's amazing what some paint and a lot of elbow grease can do. The window frames had been rotten and he had had new ones made from oak by a local craftsman. They were golden and mellow, and gave the cottage a timeless air. He had painted all the interior walls white and had stripped and waxed the black stained beams. The flagstone floors now gleamed subtly and were scattered with brightly coloured rugs. He had had the chimneys swept and inspected, and now there was an open fire in the right hand downstairs room. The other room was being joined with the tiny kitchen, and he had ordered a solid fuel powered Aga cooker to replace the ancient (and non-repairable) range. The kitchen was a work in progress, and he currently lived out of a microwave, although Bronwyn frequently invited him round to share her evening meal. In return, he provided her with the ingredients of fresh meat, fish and vegetables obtained locally, giving him an excuse to drive the wonderful scenic route to Porthmadog for the fish. The enormous Welsh dresser that came with the cottage would be a focal point in his remodelled kitchen/diner, and the oak chest was now restored and polished and took pride of place in the lounge. Upstairs, the walls were white again, the ancient oak floorboarding had been sanded and waxed, and sported yet more colourful rugs. He had renovated the iron bedsteads with their brass fittings, and purchased deep memory foam mattresses, warm duvets produced locally filled with sheep's wool, and linen bedding. An antique oak Welsh farmhouse chair stood in the corner by the window of his room, but otherwise there was no other furniture as yet. Searching for suitable pieces had become a bit of an obsession with Glenn, and he didn't want haste to spoil the country cottage effect. He had already grown to love his new home, which had nothing in it that reminded him of his former life. His memories – photographs, items that were special to him and Alison, and Alison's novels were stored away in the oak chest where they would remain safely until he felt able to face them.

    He turned into his drive and pulled up in front of the garage, which was now a temporary home to most of the furniture from his former home. He would probably sell it all, but wanted to keep his options open, and the garage would suffice for a while.

    Merlin was waiting on the doorstep. He wound himself sinuously around Glenn's legs, purring loudly.

    "Hello boy. You don't bear me any grudges, do you? I expect Bronwyn has been spoiling you."

The cottage felt very cold. He would light the fire later. The new range was due to be delivered and installed on 29th in time for New Year, and that would certainly tide him over until the central heating could be installed in a couple of weeks. He emptied a sachet into Merlin's bowl. This was regarded with disdain, and Glenn chuckled to himself as the cat, tail held high, sauntered through to the lounge, where he settled down on the chair nearest the fireplace, gazing intently at the empty grate.

"Sorry old boy, you'll have to wait. Perhaps you should eat something instead of sulking. Bronwyn has invited me to supper, but afterwards we'll have a nice fire until bedtime."

He poured himself a whisky from a decanter on the oak chest, and sank down onto the sofa, suddenly weary.

Why does life have to be so complicated? He mused, swirling the amber liquid in his glass and savouring the aroma of a good single malt. He and Alison had been together for so long that they were almost like one person, perfectly in tune, each knowing what was in the other's mind. Alison was his soul mate, his lifetime lover, and above all, his best friend. Suddenly he knew with absolute clarity that that was what he missed the most, and what he had subconsciously sought in Lauren. A close female friend! He had plenty of male friends, although only one close friend in Simon, but the true friendship of a woman was something to be treasured. They bring a different viewpoint to things, different values, they fill the gaps in the male personality. He had long ago resigned himself to the fact that in any disagreement, Alison was inevitably right. Her calm insistence, her unfailing wisdom, female intuition, call it what you like, she had it in spades, and more times than he could count had made him take stock and alter his course from what might otherwise have spelled disaster. He had immediately recognized the same ability in Lauren, her inner strength, her empathy, the wisdom in her eyes. Would she be willing to settle for such a relationship? Did he have the right, or even the courage to suggest it? What was the worst that could happen? He supposed that would be total rejection and having to accept that she wanted nothing more to do with him. However, in view of how strongly he was drawn to her, and clearly, she to him, it was probably worth the risk.

Merlin had finally given up on the fire being lit, and had disappeared into the kitchen in search of sustenance. Glenn downed his whisky in one, and made his way round to Bronwyn's house for his supper.

SEVENTEEN: FATHER & SON.

The town of Chesbury was a tourist magnet, especially in the Summer. The schools and colleges broke up and the streets and green spaces thronged with teenagers regurgitated from the educational system, along with the many tourists who filled the hotels, the bars and the restaurants. Tony was bored with doing nothing, so he got some seasonal work behind the bar of The Ragged Staff in the town centre opposite the market hall. It was popular with the locals, less so with the tourists, so he figured it might be a good place to base himself with a view to finding Annette and Paul.

It was a busy Saturday night near the end of August, and there were three bar staff, so Tony didn't see the tall, lean man with the coffee coloured skin and matching dreadlocks until he was seated in a corner of the bar. He stopped in his tracks, his heart suddenly pounding so loudly he could almost hear it over the music coming out of the juke box on the wall and the chatter of the drinkers. He threw his cloth on the bar and made his way over. The man glanced up at him, sucking on his pint of bitter and pushed a couple of empty glasses towards the edge of the table before averting his gaze towards the pool table where a match was in full swing.

Tony ignored the glasses.

"Excuse me mate," he addressed the man. "Are you Paul?"

The man looked up with a puzzled frown between his brows.

"Who's askin'?" he drawled, staring at the stranger towering over him with an over-eager stance. His demeanour became defensive – was this some drug dealer he owed? He was pretty careful not to get into situations that could be dangerous, and normally he paid for his gear on the nose.

"Are you Paul?" insisted the man.

"Depends...I might be, but then again, I might not. My friends call me Razzy, but then you'd know that if you were a friend." He regarded Tony with his strange, incongruous green eyes.

"My name's Tony, and I believe you may be my son. I've been looking for you for months."

Razzy regarded the man, his mother's words ringing in his ears. Was this the man who stole his mother's life from her before it had begun? In spite of her protestations to the contrary, he knew that having him had complicated her life, and made it very tedious at times, and yet she had never complained. She could have given him away; she might have hated him, taken her frustrations out on him, especially when he was being difficult, which let's face it was most of the time. But she did none of those things and had given him only unconditional love.

"Yeah, right." He drawled, picking up a beer mat and twirling it between his fingers. The man slid onto the seat beside him and Razzy moved away, the movement deliberately exaggerated. The stranger was a big man, not fat, but well-muscled beneath his pristine blue and white striped shirt. He was clean-shaven with a grade 2 buzzcut and a single gold earring from which dangled an opal and a golden crescent moon. He looked like someone who took care of himself. His skin was like polished ebony, his teeth like marble tombstones, and his eyes dark brown fringed by long black lashes. He was handsome and self-assured. Razzy felt a sudden stab of envy, and a frisson of regret that if this was indeed his father he was not more like him. He, with his mousy dreads and sallow skin, his weird green eyes that lacked the sparkle he sometimes saw in his mother's and his sparse frame and rotting teeth ravaged by the drugs that he had been taking for the past twenty years.

"I don't have a dad, just some bastard who raped my mother when she was only seventeen." He studied the beer mat in his hand intensely, and on hearing Tony's sharp intake of breath, a slow grimace spread across his face.

"Is that what she told you?" Tony spoke slowly, quietly.

"Yep," Razzy replied, and raised his eyes "Are you callin' her a liar?"

"Not exactly, but it wasn't like that." Tony replied. "We went out together, but she dumped me because her sister didn't approve. She never even told me about you, I only found out about a year ago by chance. That's the honest truth, I swear!"

Razzy snapped the beer mat in two. He could just imagine what Aunty Pauline would have made of Tony – older than Netty, and as black as the Ace of Spades! Yes, there was a ring of truth, but he was also pretty sure that his mother would never lie to him – except, of course, the original 'your father is dead' lie, and after all, that was really down to Pauline.

"I bet you've never even met my Aunty Pauline," Razzy challenged.

"I bet I have," replied Tony. "Lives in Perry Barr. A right cow, twin-set and pearls, and a lot older than Annette."

Razzy snapped the beer mat again. Yes, that was a pretty accurate description of his Aunty Pauline. But Annette? Nobody, *but nobody* called his mother Annette except his Aunty Pauline. *Why should her boyfriend call her that?* Something wasn't right, but he wasn't as sure as he had been. Maybe the truth was somewhere between the two versions.

Maybe his mother didn't remember the facts as they were. He was intrigued, but he also knew that for some reason, he didn't trust this man, and he would be very careful what he told him.

"Can I get you another one?" Tony indicated Razzy's empty glass. "And a burger if you like."

Razzy considered his options. He could do with another, and the burger sounded good. Besides, he wanted to know more about this man who claimed to be his father.

"Thanks," he acknowledged grudgingly.

A few minutes later, Tony reappeared with the promised victuals and also a drink for himself.

"I'm due a break," he explained as he sat down opposite Razzy.

"Tell me about Annette. How is she? Do you have a stepdad? Where are you living?"

"Whooooaaa! Not so fast!" Razzy took a long pull on his pint and two bites of his burger.

"She's fine. It's been hard for her at times, but she's a fighter and she's always looked after me, and no, I don't have a stepdad – I'm pretty sure she isn't interested in men, you must've put her off for life!"

"I'd like to see her, I'd like to set the record straight with her," Tony said, pasting on what he believed to be an earnest expression. "It was all a misunderstanding, and I'd like to make it up to you both if you'll give me the chance."

"I dunno. I'll have to square it with her first," Razzy replied, and took another bite of his burger. "She may not want to see you, and that's up to her. Come to that, I'm not sure I want to see you either!" The slight grimace crossed his face again. If this man was genuine, he wouldn't mind waiting a little longer surely.

Tony swallowed his frustration. The boy wasn't going to play ball. He must find out more.

"Does she still have red hair?" he asked.

"Fuck yes!" Razzy chuckled. "Couldn't imagine her without it, though these days it mostly comes out of a bottle." He stopped – was that too much information? He must be careful.

"Listen," said Tony. Why don't you come round to mine tomorrow night. I'll make you some supper and we can have a catch up.

"I dunno…" Razzy finished off his burger and washed it down with the rest of his pint. He stood up, retrieving his jacket and pushing one arm into the sleeve. He glanced at Tony, then shrugged his shoulders.

"Ok, I suppose…" Tony took a fresh beer mat and wrote on it with a pencil that he produced from his shirt pocket.

"Here's my address. I'll see you about eight."

Sleep evaded Razzy that night. In the early hours of the morning, he crept from his room and grabbing his jacket, he slipped silently out, closing the door gently behind him. He stood on the landing, and heard his mother snoring softly. Reassured, he trod lightly down the stairs. On the street, the dawn light was touching the trees and the jackdaws were shuffling restlessly on the branches in preparation for a day's foraging. A ginger cat sat on the wall opposite the flats, and Razzy stopped to stroke it, rewarded by a loud rhythmical purring as it rubbed against his hand. Razzy liked animals, but living in a top floor flat made it impossible to own a pet. He strode down the street, turning left at the end and then right again towards the rows of double-fronted Victorian semis that ran at an oblique angle to the tall Georgian ones that lined one side of the river. He glanced at the writing on the beer mat. No 23 was near the end of the street. It was neat, with a mature front garden of shrubs and small trees. There was an illuminated strip of numbered doorbells betraying its division into flats. He glanced at the beer mat again. Flat 2a bore the name Ashton. Razzy glanced up at the window above his head. It mirrored the bay window below in size, and was covered by a slatted wooden blind. At the side of the house, a narrow ginnel led to a parking area at the back that had been created by knocking down a wall and sacrificing the back yard. There were three cars parked there; a bright red Nissan Micra, a pale blue Fiat 500, and a sleek black Vauxhall Astra with tinted glass and a back spoiler. This must be Tony's car, Razzy decided, he couldn't quite imagine him in either of the others. He noted down the registration so that he would recognise the car again. He didn't want to run the risk of being followed home. With a long backward glance at his father's residence, he made his way back into town. He sat on a bench in the cathedral grounds and smoked a spliff while he watched the urban wildlife beginning their new day – squirrels, birds, and even a snuffling hedgehog that seemed oblivious as it passed within inches of his feet. It was going to be a warm day, and in another couple of hours the students and tourists would begin to arrive and claim a spot in either the sun or the shade where they would remain for much of the day. Razzy would be working the stall today with his mother. He hoped they would be busy and he wouldn't have to think too hard about what felt like a betrayal – his evening assignation with that man! A glance at his watch revealed that Coffee and Compliments would be open by the time he had made the fifteen-minute walk there. A coffee would go down well right now, and he would take his mother a cake for her morning break.

So began the deception that lasted nearly four months. Roughly once a week, on Tony's night off, Razzy would make his way there, and they would enjoy a companionable evening together, with a few beers, a pizza and occasionally a spliff or two. Tony was easy company, but Razzy was always aware of an underlying current that he couldn't quite define.

"What did she say when you told her you were seeing me?" Tony asked him for the umpteenth time. Aside from the fact that he hadn't yet told her, Razzy had no intention of being drawn on the subject at all.

"She said if you go near her she'll call the police." He was pretty sure that was close to the truth. "She's not ready to forgive you Dad, so I'd forget it if I were you."

But Tony couldn't forget it, he had to find her, he had to make her pay.

EIGHTEEN: A MISTAKEN IDENTITY.
(December 8th/9th)

Mark drove slowly through the now sleeping streets, aware that he was way over the limit. He wondered what Razzy's agenda had been that evening since clearly he had had something more important on than the Market Christmas do. *How come that ugly bastard can get laid?* he wondered, grinding his teeth in frustration. He turned off the main street towards Lauren's house. He would drive past and make sure everything was quiet.

Suddenly, he stiffened, his hands tightening on the steering wheel, every nerve strained to catch another glimpse. Yes, there she was – it was Lauren, turning off the street into the alleyway that ran along behind the Chinese takeaway, the Greasy Spoon Café, the Oxfam shop and a couple of shabby terraced houses. Hatless, the street light glinting on her unmistakable orange hair, the tall slim figure hurried into the relative darkness of the alleyway. Where the fuck was she going at this time of night? It was getting on for 2am, and more than an hour since he had watched her enter her house, closing the door and then the curtains. Why was she dressed like that? A cheap-looking cropped fake fur jacket, skin tight jeans and over-the-knee boots were a world away from her normal elegant and sophisticated garb.

Drawing to a stop near the entrance to the alleyway, he got out of his car, shutting the door quietly so as not to alert her to his presence. He would follow her, see where she went. His hackles were up – *Miss High and Mighty! Sneaking around in the middle of the night dressed like a common slut!*

The alley was only dimly lit and at first he couldn't see her. Then he spotted her, crouched down beside a large grey wheelie bin, her back towards him, steam rising from the ground beneath her. *What the fuck? She was having a pee!*

He was overcome with rage and disgust. How dare she put on airs and graces! How dare she reject his advances, then behave like some alley cat – a ginger one at that! She was no better than he was, in fact, not even as good. She was just trash dressed up as treasure, a worthless piece of trash, lying, cheating, deceiving…

She was fastening her jeans when he caught up with her and grabbed her shoulders roughly from behind. She turned and swiftly lashed out at him, a smart right hook to his nose, which immediately began to bleed profusely. Through his pain he saw her face float before him – pale, thin, and angry, and not Lauren! The shockwaves coursed through him. "I'm sorry…" he began, but she rounded on him, kicking out and trying to scratch his face. He grabbed her around the throat and shook her in a desperate attempt to stop the onslaught. She attempted to scream, still raining blows on his shins with her feet, her hands tearing at his fingers, trying to loosen his grip, but it came out as just a gurgling sound. He had no choice but to hold on tighter, until after what seemed like an eternity he felt her go limp in his hands and allowed her to slide slowly to the ground where she lay in a heap, staring up at him through unseeing eyes that were the same pale emerald as those of the woman he loved, fading now as the life drained away from them, droplets of rain trickling into them from her soaking wet hair.

Holy fuck! What have I done?" Stone cold sober now, he knelt on the ground beside her, desperately feeling for a pulse, clutching at straws whilst knowing there was no coming back from this. He took a handkerchief from his pocket and wiped the blood from his face where it was congealing around his nostrils.

"Christ, I've murdered her!" His head in his hands, he tried to collect his thoughts. Could he hide the body? Not

here. The bins were full to overflowing; no room in there for a body. He glanced towards the entrance to the alley. Could he manage to get the body to his car, and take it somewhere far away? No, it was too risky, he might be seen, late as it was, and he must get away from here right now! He rose to a stand on trembling legs, about to flee the scene, and then a monstrous idea hit him like a ton of bricks.

Everyone was expecting another strike by the Chesbury serial killer. He must make this woman look like his latest victim. The details of the killer's MO had long been leaked to the press, and he knew only too well what this involved.

He remembered a movie he once watched in which a man's eyes were gouged out by his killer. He had turned away, unable to stomach it, muting the sound to eradicate the screams of agony. Well, at least his victim was already dead, he thought wryly. He cast around for something to aid him in his gruesome task, and spotted her backpack against the wheelie bin where she must have placed it earlier. Rummaging inside, he found a pair of nail scissors, with which he set to work, feeling his way rather than looking at what he was doing. It took a few precious minutes of fumbling and cutting, but the job was done, if a little untidily. He straightened up and nausea hit him in waves. He vomited into a nearby drain. What had never been revealed was what the killer did with the eyes after he removed them. Did he keep them as trophies? Mark knew that serial killers were inclined to do that sort of thing. He sidled along the wall to the entrance of the alley, where he checked the road in both directions. No sign of anyone, and no other cars except his. He wrapped the offending articles in his already bloody handkerchief and put them in the backpack. He was just about to head back to his car when a thought struck him. He patted the pockets of the fur jacket and found what he was looking for – her mobile phone. He left it there, he certainly didn't want to risk taking it with him in the backpack, he knew these things could be tracked. Satisfied that he had left no clues to his identity, he slunk furtively back to his car, his eyes darting in all directions, his heart thumping loudly inside his head. He slung the bag in the passenger footwell and drove away towards home, still scanning the pavements for any late-night stragglers, of which there were none. Stone cold sober now, it was tempting to go fast, to put as much distance between him and his reckless deed as quickly as he could, but instead he drove slowly, carefully, he didn't want to get pulled up at any price!

Arriving home fifteen minutes later he pulled up on his driveway. The neighbouring houses were all in darkness, their curtains and blinds tight shut. The silence rang loudly in his ears as he leaned back in his seat with his eyes closed for a minute or two. Then, retrieving the backpack and his doner wrapper, he entered the house. Closing the door behind him, he felt relief wash over him, and something else – a strange feeling of satisfaction that he had been clever and would never be suspected of the murder of that girl. She was probably a prostitute, he reasoned, covered in tattoos and piercings. She had, in the end, borne only a superficial resemblance to Lauren. How could he have made such a mistake? Must've been the drink! Now all he wanted was to put the whole incident behind him and forget about it. When inevitably the news broke tomorrow he must convince himself that this was the work of someone other than himself. Right now, he needed a drink. He washed his hands and face, took a can of lager from the fridge, and went into the living room. He lay back on the sofa and tried to clear his mind. The lager was cool and soothing, and after the earlier adrenaline rush, he felt lethargy flooding his body, but he knew he had work to do first.

Returning to the kitchen, he deposited the lager can in the bin, reached inside the backpack and retrieved the bloody handkerchief and its contents, placing it on the kitchen floor with a shudder. Reaching in again, he found a large, slightly battered pink purse. He opened it. It contained a bank card in the name of Ashley Stevenson, and a small amount of cash. In another compartment was a photograph of a child, a little girl about three years old, with red-gold hair and rather sad green eyes. *Oh! My God! She's got a kid!* Overcome with remorse, Mark stared at the photo and felt tears begin to well in his eyes – until he remembered that this was not down to him, he had done nothing, it wasn't his problem. He extracted the photo and tore it in half. He would get rid of it along with all the crap in the backpack, sweet wrappers, bus tickets, cigarette papers and makeup. Then he noticed another photograph that had been tucked in behind it. It was old and faded. It showed a young couple, he with his arm around her shoulders, she cradling a baby in her arms. The woman was tall, nearly as tall as the man, and slim, with long red-gold hair that tumbled over her shoulders in waves. She had barely changed, apart from the hairstyle. Unmistakably, this was Lauren!

What the fuck? Mark recoiled in horror as the truth dawned on him. The woman he had just murdered must be Lauren's daughter! He had no idea she even *had* a daughter, much less a granddaughter. She had never mentioned her and he had never seen her before. She had mentioned that she was divorced and her husband had remarried, but other than that she had kept her private life to herself.

Suddenly Mark felt completely exhausted. He just wanted to crawl into bed and sleep, and wake up knowing this whole episode had been a terrible nightmare. How would he face her after this? *But I didn't do anything. It wasn't me,* he admonished himself firmly. He must keep his head and finish what he had to do. He tore the child's photograph into small pieces, and thrust it, along with the blood-soaked handkerchief parcel and all the articles from the backpack into his kitchen pedal bin. It was bin day tomorrow, everything would be taken away to landfill first thing in the morning. He cut up the bank card also, and it joined the rest. There were various bits and pieces in the bottom of the bag – a lipstick, some wet wipes and half a packet of chewing gum. There was also an unopened bottle of perfume, Daisy, by Marc Jacobs, still in its cellophane wrapper. He set this aside, wondering if he could give it to Lauren for Christmas. Finally, he folded the backpack as small as he could and stuffed it in on top of everything else, and then tying the bin liner tightly he took it outside. Removing several similar ones from his wheelie bin, he pushed it in and replaced them on top.

Satisfied with his efforts, Mark stripped himself off, and put everything in the washing machine. He took a long hot shower, letting the stinging water run over his head, washing away the guilt, the fear and the remorse. There was only the photograph of Lauren with her family left to deal with. He just couldn't bring himself to destroy it. He took the photo frame from his bedside cabinet, and removed the backing board, slipping the photograph inside. No one would ever know. Finally, he crawled into bed and fell into a deep, dreamless sleep.

The next morning, he woke early to the sound of the binmen emptying the bins along the street. Relief flooded over him. The evidence would be in the lorry now, being crushed and compressed with all the neighbourhood trash. A glance in the bathroom mirror showed his bruised and battered nose, and several scratches on his face. He had no doubt that he could easily explain it away. He needed to see Lauren as soon as possible, to face her and rid himself of the demons that otherwise threatened to crowd his head and overwhelm him. The sooner he got it out of the way, the easier it would be to forget. He must steel himself and act normally. She must never suspect.

He set off on foot on the long walk that he hoped would clear his head, towards Coffee and Compliments, where he knew she could be found most mornings before work. It was a dry, frosty morning after the rain of the previous night, and in places the pavements were treacherous, forcing him to concentrate on keeping upright rather than letting his attention wander, for which he was grateful. He felt numb and disoriented, and his surroundings appeared unfamiliar and surreal. A council gritter rumbled by, tossing grit that struck his legs as he walked, but he barely noticed it. The ringing in his ears continued mercilessly, as though it were trying to drown out his thoughts, but nothing could dispel the memory of what he had done. He fervently hoped he could convince others of his innocence a little better than he was managing to convince himself. Nearing his destination, he passed Nick's News, a stand selling newspapers and sweets a short way from the station. There it was, in the early edition of The Herald.

"Chesbury Killer strikes again!" In large headlines outlined in red. He picked up a paper and began to read the article. The so-far unidentified body had been found, it said, just after 2am that morning. *Christ! Only minutes after I left!* He thought with a rush of blood to the head. How near he had come to being caught red-handed! He cast his mind back. He had been certain nobody was in sight when he returned to his car. It was a close call though, too bloody close for comfort. However, it appeared that the news hounds had fallen for his cover, hook, line and sinker.

"Oi!" said the vendor. "Are you going to buy that or what?"

Mark replaced the newspaper on the stand. "Sorry mate, no change," he replied, and walked away. Several deep breaths and a few hundred yards later, he joined Lauren in Coffee and Compliments. It was over!

NINETEEN: CHRISTMAS.

Christmas Eve dawned dry and crisp, with the promise of a fine day in the wintry blue sky. Glenn had been invited to spend the evening with Simon and Eleanor, whose two sons plus wives and three grandchildren were all coming over tomorrow for the big day. He had left Merlin curled up in front of Bronwyn's log fire with Pero and the three cats, Guto, Merv and Siani Flewog.

"Don't think I'll get a look in," observed Bronwyn philosophically. "I'm afraid my daughter will shift them all later when she comes though!"

"I'm glad you won't be alone over Christmas Bronwyn," Glenn said.

"Oh! Duw! It wouldn't bother me if I was! The animals are good company. Mind you, they don't help with the cooking, only the eating, and Bethan used to be a chef ers talwm, so I can put my feet up with a gin and enjoy it!"

"Ers talwm?" enquired Glenn.

"A long time ago Glenn, but it's like riding a bicycle you know!"

"Next year, you're going to teach me some Welsh," Glenn said. 'I can't survive on 'diolch' forever!" They laughed, and Glenn enveloped her tiny frame in a gentle hug before making his way down to the car.

On the drive to Chesbury he mused on the events of the past two weeks, and how his life had taken such an unexpected turn. He had resigned himself to spending his first Christmas without Alison in the company of Merlin alone. He had been dreading it more than he cared to admit. Christmas Eve had, for many years, been spent with Simon and Eleanor, who lived within walking distance of Glenn's former home. It had always been he and Alison, however, and not everyone enjoys having a cuckoo in the nest. He had been thrilled by the invitation therefore, and it had then dawned on him that Christmas was going to be hard for them also, so the continuance of the tradition was as important to them as it was to him. Of course, he would spend the night this year, instead of taking the usual moonlit walk home arm in arm with his beautiful wife in the early hours of Christmas morning to the magical sound of the cathedral's bells.

The traffic was heavy as he approached the outskirts of Chesbury. Everyone it seemed was either coming or going for the sake of visiting friends and family for the festive weekend. He wondered how Lauren was enjoying her first Christmas Eve as a grandmother, and smiled to himself at a mental vision of her dressed as Santa Claus, filling a stocking for Poppy before retiring for the night. He knew that Bessie had had a hand in the preparations, and wondered how Lauren would ever have managed without that marvellous woman over the past couple of weeks.

He had promised to call her later that day to finalise their arrangements for the visit to the Fenton's on Christmas Day. His boot was loaded with gifts from Wales – notably Penderyn whisky, Dyfi gin, a crate of assorted Purple Moose beers from Porthmadog, and Snowdonia cheese hampers. Bronwyn had also been the recipient of a bottle of gin and a cheese hamper in thanks for being his willing cat sitter. He had also left her a gift under her Christmas tree – a warm Welsh tapestry blanket from Felinfach. For Lauren, he had bought a large dark brown Rhug Estate sheepskin rug, and for Poppy a bright red stuffed dragon and a Welsh Lady costume.

The town was winding down, but a few last-minute shoppers (mainly men, of course) were hurrying along in a state of blind panic on a desperate mission to salvage some kudos with their wives, girlfriends, mothers, and mothers-in-law. Laden down with shopping bags (receipts safely stashed for future use), they began to join the throngs, also mainly of men or teenagers, spilling out of the jam-packed pubs onto the pavements, glasses in hand. By the time the pubs closed, many of them would be in no fit state to even contemplate the next day's festivities. Glenn was thankful this was not his scene! He braked sharply and swore under his breath as a huddle of young women in sparkly outfits that appeared impossibly skimpy for the winter temperature clattered into the street without even looking. They giggled and clung to one another for support on their tottering heels, one of them raising a hand to him. *Not like I had a choice,* he muttered, but supposed it was better than nothing.

Simon's house looked warm and welcoming, with a large Christmas tree in the lounge window sporting multi-coloured lights – static ones, Glenn observed with relief, *not those dreadful migraine-inducing flashing efforts.* He chided himself on sounding like a grumpy old man, and pressed the doorbell. The door opened immediately.

"We saw you arrive," Eleanor enveloped him in a hug. "Come on in and get warm, and we'll have an aperitif."

After another hug and a backslap from Simon, he settled himself into an armchair, and Eleanor thrust a gin and tonic into his outstretched hand.

"Cheers! Merry Christmas!" They chorused, and the glasses chinked and sparkled in the firelight. It all seemed so normal, but Glenn knew they must all be thinking of the missing note.

"To absent friends," he raised his glass again. "To Alison," Eleanor ventured bravely, and they repeated the process a little less exuberantly, each one lost in a memory.

Meanwhile, Lauren (sans Santa outfit) was just putting the finishing touches to her Christmas tree, with help from Poppy. It stood on the octagonal table in the corner, and the lamp was relegated to the sewing room for the duration of the festive period, which for them would end on Tuesday since Ashley's funeral was on the following day. Bessie had arrived earlier with a box of assorted decorations that she had found in the Cat's Protection shop to add to the lights Lauren had bought from M&S. Poppy was now standing on a chair busily tying them or throwing them onto the tree with gusto. *I'll tidy it up when she's in bed,* thought Lauren rather uncharitably. She reclined on the sofa and watched her granddaughter rearrange the ornaments, turning each time to seek approval. Charlie helped himself to some of the lower ones that dangled within his reach. "Oh! Charlie!" Poppy giggled. "You're a good boy helping, isn't he Grandma?" Lauren smiled and nodded agreement.

"Come along, young lady," she said eventually, rising to her feet. "Let's get you to bed, or Father Christmas won't come."

Poppy's eyes grew wide. "Will he come into my room?" She asked, fearfully.

"No! Silly, he will come in here and leave you something nice under the tree – but only if you've been good mind. Let's hang your stocking up here." They carefully pinned a bright red felt stocking onto the chimney breast. It was, of course, made by Bessie, with 'Poppy' embroidered on it in gold thread. They stood back to admire it.

"How will he get in?" Poppy was not about to be hoodwinked. Lauren thought back to her childhood, when everyone had a chimney. It was necessary to be more inventive nowadays!

"Well, I told you he's magic, and that's how he gets in. Let's take your book up with us, and I'll read it to you again," Lauren reassured her gently. Poppy had had no concept of Father Christmas, and Lauren's heart had gone out to her – what had Ashley been thinking of? She bought her a story book all about Father Christmas, his elves and his reindeer, and Poppy was learning fast, but perhaps Baby Jesus would have to wait until next year when she would be at school. It was all far too complicated for one little girl to take in.

Half an hour later, with Poppy and Charlie tucked up in bed together, Lauren curled up on the sofa once more, with a large glass of red wine. It felt peaceful, with only the flickering firelight and the tree lights, and a CD of King's College Cambridge singing carols on the stereo. She leaned back and savoured the moment, until her eye was drawn to a small parcel on the shelf above the fireplace. She retrieved it. Bessie had brought it with the decorations, she had found it on the work table in the shop.

"I went to make a cuppa, and when I came back, there it was. It has your name on it, but nothing else."

Lauren had thought little about it, it was probably a gift from a grateful client. Now, however, for some reason it was niggling at her, and she decided to open it.

It was beautifully wrapped in expensive looking gold embossed Christmas paper finished with a red satin ribbon and bow. There was a small matching gift tag, with just her name written on it in a hand she didn't recognise. Someone had gone to a great deal of trouble to impress her, she thought.

A sudden shiver went through her, and she had no idea why. It reminded her of Trisha's letter, the same speculation, the same foreboding. *Now who's being silly?* She removed the ribbon, and eased the paper away from the contents, withdrawing a box containing perfume – Daisy, by Marc Jacobs. She removed the cellophane wrapper and opened the box. Pretty bottle, she thought, as she sniffed at the contents, but not really her cup of tea, she preferred something classic like Chanel No.5. or Prada Amber. She was about to screw up the wrapping paper when she saw the note nestled in its midst.

"To Lauren. Have a wonderful Christmas. I hope you like this, and will let me buy you a drink at New Year. Sincere regards, Mark."

"Shit!" The exclamation was involuntary, and she almost dropped the perfume bottle in her hand. Again, that feeling of foreboding swept over her – *what was the matter with her?* She downed her wine, and with shaking hands poured another one, then, her mind made up, she took the perfume, the wrapping paper and the note and pushed them into the swing bin in the kitchen. It seemed to her that Mark had become something of a pest over the past two weeks since Ashley died, as though he sensed her vulnerability and thought he could take advantage of it. She was sick of his unwanted attention and he had become increasingly repugnant to her, although she couldn't really put her finger on why, unless it was his endless speculating about the mind of the serial killer and whether Ashley had been killed by mistake. It seemed there was some doubt that the same man was responsible, but Mark would have none of that.

"Nah! Definitely him! There can't be two psychos like that in a little place like Chesbury," was his indisputable opinion.

Her mobile phone was buzzing. She had set it to silent so as not to disturb Poppy. Her heart leaped when she saw that the caller was Glenn.

"Hey!" He greeted her. "Merry Christmas Eve." There was a pause.

"What's the matter? Are you ok Lauren?"

She answered in a small voice "I think so. It's good to hear you Glenn. Are you at Simon's?"

"I am, yes. But hey! I can tell something's wrong. D'you want me to come round for a while? I don't think dinner's ready yet."

"Oh! Gosh no! There's no need. I'm ok, I've just got the heebie-jeebies," and she told him about the gift from Mark and how it had unsettled her but she didn't really know why.

"There's just something about it. I can't explain it, it was just the weirdest feeling. I've binned it, I don't want it."

Good for you! That man is such a creep! Are you sure you're ok? I'll pick you, Poppy and Charlie up at eleven tomorrow. Just try and relax and enjoy your evening, and forget about the stupid gift. Have you got something nice for dinner? We're having pheasant and it smells delicious!"

"Hmmm! Lucky you. I'm not very hungry, and I'm saving myself for tomorrow, but I've got plenty of wine, some cheese and biscuits and a box of really expensive chocolates that my parents sent me from France. I'll be fine, and I'm looking forward to tomorrow."

"Me too. Christmas isn't easy is it? This is all new to both of us. I have an empty space, and you have a new responsibility. It'll get easier when we can get back to normal."

"I know it will, but I'm dreading Wednesday. I've only ever been to one funeral, and that was my grandmother's, and she was in her nineties so it was only to be expected. It's so final, isn't it? Oh Glenn! I'm so sorry! It must be so much worse for you because the last funeral you went to was Alison's. Thank you for being there for me, but I won't hold you to it."

"Don't be ridiculous! I offered, you didn't ask, and I'm happy to do it, so that's the end of that! I think dinner is ready. Now, be a good girl. Pour yourself some more wine, or a gin and tonic, put a Christmas chick-flick on the tv, scoff chocolates and cheese and forget everything else, and I'll see you tomorrow morning."

"I'll consider myself told! Goodnight Glenn, and have a lovely evening."

She ended the call, a smile playing on her lips. Glenn was such a good man, but she hated chick-flicks. Instead, she put on one of her old favourites, the original version of Far From the Madding Crowd, with Julie Christie, Alan Bates and Terence Stamp.

Meanwhile, Mark was propping up the bar in the King's Head. Ever since Ashley, he had taken to drinking far into the night in an attempt to delay the nightmares that assaulted him as soon as he slept. He would wake in the morning with a crushing headache that left him barely able to think straight. His business was suffering because most days he couldn't even be bothered to dress, much less open his stall or go on buying trips.

This morning he had dragged himself out of the doldrums determined to make a new start. He had headed in to the market, with the Daisy perfume nestled in his pocket. Once there, he availed himself of the Christmas gift wrapping service being offered by an enterprising young lady named Izzie. She wrapped it, beautifully and swiftly, incorporating the note that he had written earlier. He paid her, and made his way to Lauren's shop, only to find that she wasn't there. Of course! She would be spending the day with her granddaughter, he realised. Only Bessie sat at the table working flat out to complete last-minute Christmas orders. Swallowing his disappointment, he decided to await his opportunity and leave the gift in the shop anonymously. He began to browse the shelves of the secondhand bookshop across the way, from where he had a good view of Trendy Tots. He didn't have to wait long before Bessie headed for the back room to make a cup of tea, and he deposited the gift on the end of the work table where she couldn't miss it, then headed back to his stall. Later, he returned to find the shop closed. There was no sign of either Bessie or the gift, so he hoped that she had delivered it to Lauren. He pictured her opening it on Christmas morning and imagined her delight at his thoughtfulness. He might call in later in the day to wish her a merry Christmas in person. The thought warmed his heart, and locking down his stall, he crossed the road to the Ragged Staff and ordered a pint of Guinness and a whisky chaser. He spotted Razzy sitting at a table in the corner, deep in conversation with the black guy from behind the bar. He sat himself down opposite them – Mark never worried about being an unwanted intruder.

"Merry Christmas guys," he announced, raising his pint glass. They responded in kind somewhat unenthusiastically.

"I'll see you later Paul," said Tony, and nodded briefly to Mark as he returned to his post behind the bar.

"Paul?" Mark shot Razzy an enquiring glance.

"Yup, that's my name," replied Razzy, taking a long pull on his pint. "I know him from way back before I was Razzy."

"Oh! I didn't know that," said Mark, stupidly.

"Why would you? I've always been Razzy here, and nobody asked, but I'd have thought it was obvious it's not my real name." Razzy suppressed a chuckle – *How dumb can you be Marky?* He thought, but he didn't want to embarrass the guy so he said nothing more. Nevertheless, Mark shuffled uncomfortably and after downing his drink, took his leave and moved on to his normal haunt, the King's Head, where he remained until the early hours of Christmas morning.

He woke on Christmas morning with a thick head, plus the uncomfortable realisation that there would be nowhere open and he had very little in the house in the way of food. No sitting in Coffee and Compliments nursing his hangover today, and no tucking into a nice Christmas lunch like everyone else either. He cursed himself, he must get a grip. He found a pack of sausages in the freezer and after thawing them in the microwave, he fried them up and made himself a sausage sandwich, slathering the bread with butter, and drizzling copious amounts of ketchup on top of the sausages. Two strong cups of coffee later he felt a little better, and thought he would walk into town to clear his head and get a hair of the dog before going to Lauren's place. Who knew, she might even invite him to share her Christmas meal.

By the time he reached the King's Head, it was almost noon. There were the usual suspects in there, thrown out by their wives whilst they prepared the food in peace. Reg The Veg was there with his usual pint of Guinness.

"Alright Marky?" he greeted him cheerily. "Merry Christmas mate. Who's cooking your dinner then?"

Mark wasn't in the mood for Reg, who was always moaning about his wife, yet was never short of a decent meal on the table when he eventually showed his face.

"I'm off to Lauren's shortly." He said – well, it was sort of true, wasn't it?

"Blimey! How'd you swing that then?"

"Guess it must be my fatal charm," he replied. "And the present I bought her. Women can never resist a bit of pampering."

"Aye!" Agreed Reg. "I bought mine one of those new-fangled grill things she's bin on about. George somebody-or-other. Cost an arm an' a leg! Supposed to be healthy an' help you lose weight, an' she can do with that mind you!" Reg himself was practically skin and bone, and Mark had never seen his wife.

"I like a nice slim woman," Mark agreed, knocking back his whisky chaser, "like Lauren."

"Got a kid now though, hasn't she? Bit of a pain I expect,"

"True, but the kid spends half her time with Bessie in the shop. I don't think Lauren will let her get in the way of a bit of how's your father, do you?" Mark spoke with a confidence he didn't really feel, but it sounded good anyway.

"Anyway, I'd better get going, I don't want to be late." He heaved himself down from the bar stool.

"Well, have a good one, and I'll see you on Wednesday if I don't see you before," Reg said. All this fuss over a couple of days, then it's business as usual."

"Ah! Not for me, I won't be opening on Wednesday. It's Ashley's funeral, and I'll be going along to support Lauren."

"Oh! I see! I thought it was family only," Reg looked slightly non-plussed.

"It is, but being as we're so close, I offered to go along and she was very grateful. I mean, she can't go there alone when her ex-husband will be there with his new woman can she? She'll need someone to lean on of course."

"Well, I hope it all goes well. I'll send her a card. See ya Marky."

Mark made his way along the riverbank and up the hill to Lauren's house. On the way, he passed the alley where, just over two weeks ago, he had encountered Ashley with disastrous consequences. He quickened his step and tried not to dwell on it. Everyone, even the police, thought it was the work of the Chesbury Strangler, and he appeared to have got away with it, so it no longer mattered. In fact, it presented an opportunity to offer Lauren a strong arm to lean on, and he intended to do just that.

He climbed the steps to Lauren's door, and pressed the doorbell. He heard the chimes echoing through the house, but there was no response. *Where could she be?* Ach! She was probably at Bessie's house, wherever that was, he decided. He turned away dejectedly. He probably wouldn't see her now until the funeral. He would make sure he was there on time and he felt sure that his presence would be a comfort to her. Resolutely, he returned to the King's Head. It was almost empty, and there was no sign of Reg.

The strains of carol singing emanated from the cathedral, amplified to the outside for all to enjoy as Glenn set off to collect Lauren and Poppy. Eleanor was already busy with the preparations for the big family meal, and Glenn had refused the proffered cooked breakfast in favour of a couple of slices of toast. He would be back on Wednesday evening after the funeral. He was beginning to feel a bit of a nomad and wondered if and when his life would ever settle down again. He thought about Merlin and realised that he missed him terribly, his absence on Christmas morning intensifying the feeling of longing for his former contented existence.

He found an excited Poppy eager to show him their Christmas tree, and a slightly harassed Lauren trying to gather the essentials for an overnight stay with virtual strangers. He placed his gifts under the tree, and saw that there were several others. They had agreed to get the present opening out of the way before joining the Fentons to lessen the intrusion.

"I'm beginning to wonder if this was such a good idea," said Lauren. "Annie is lovely, but very spoilt and I don't want Poppy to feel left out. I haven't gone overboard with the presents because to be honest, I didn't have a clue what to get her." She made a gesture of despair. Glenn put an arm around her shoulders.

"Look at her Lauren. She's a different little girl from the one I first met two weeks ago! She's not making any comparisons, this is so much more than she has ever been used to, and if I know anything about the Fentons they will do everything to ensure that she feels included. Annie may be spoilt, but she is also friendly, caring, and I'm sure generous. Try not to worry, it'll be fine!"

Lauren produced wine, and hot chocolate for Poppy, and Glenn gave out the presents with cries of "Ho! Ho! Ho!" Poppy squealed delightedly, then carefully opened her gifts, savouring the moment. Charlie put in an appearance and immediately settled down on Lauren's new sheepskin.

"Well! I thought I had forgotten to buy anything for Charlie," laughed Glenn, "But he clearly has other ideas. Sorry Lauren, I think you've been mugged!"

"Perhaps he'll forgive me for subjecting him to the carrier now," said Lauren. "His present was a new blanket to go inside it, but he seemed singularly unimpressed when I tried it out yesterday. I'm guessing that a spot of Christmas dinner might mollify him, so I hope he gets some."

"I'm pretty sure he will," said Glenn. "Well, I think you've lost your rug, so it's a good job I got you something else," he said, and handed her a small package.

She opened it with bated breath, took out the box within, and slowly opened it. Inside was an exquisitely worked golden locket.

"It's Clogau gold from Wales," said Glenn, "Though I think to be honest there's only a small amount of the real stuff in it."

"It's beautiful. Thank you so much Glenn." Lauren carefully prized it open Inside were two photographs – one of Poppy, and one of Charlie.

"When did you do that?" she asked in amazement.

"When you weren't looking over the last week or so. Thank goodness for being able to print them off my phone, it makes such subterfuge a great deal easier." He fastened it around her neck, then said,

"We'd better be going I think."

Poppy appeared, wearing her Welsh Lady costume, having jettisoned her new party dress. Lauren hurried to find a warm pair of tights to match it.

"You look splendid!" said Glenn. "I have one for Annie also, and you can give it to her when we arrive."

They had a memorable Christmas Day with the Fentons. The atmosphere was relaxed and happy, the food was delicious and the accommodation superb. Poppy slept in Annie's room on a pull-out truckle bed. Glenn and Lauren had an en-suite room each, and after an hour of hiding behind the sofa, Charlie decided that he would claim the hot spot on the hearthrug in front of the inglenook.

Rachel refused their offer of help with the dinner, but clearly this was a role that Michael was happy to fulfil whilst chatting to Glenn who sat at the kitchen island. Lauren made herself useful by setting the table in the dining room, a task she had always enjoyed, although, no longer having a dining room, one that she had had to forgo for the past few years. A large sideboard contained everything you could possibly need to prepare a festive table. There was a snowy white linen tablecloth and matching napkins, gold filigree placemats and coasters and an abundance of sparkling cutlery and glassware. A Christmas centrepiece of greenery and tall metallic red candles and a few festive sprinkles finished off the understated elegance perfectly. There were golden Christmas crackers adorned with sprays of berry laden artificial holly, tied on with red silk ribbon. Poppy's high chair (that used to be Annie's) had been decorated with a string of fairy lights wound around the legs, the tray removed so that it could be pushed up to the table next to Annie. The mantlepiece was draped with lights and fresh greenery interspersed by church candles, and a fire burned merrily in the grate fed from an enormous log basket at the side.

"Rachel, you have gone to so much trouble!" exclaimed Lauren.

"It's Christmas," Rachel replied with a smile. "I love it!"

"So do I," admitted Lauren. "For years I've just let it slip, being on my own, but from now on, I'm going to have to make the effort aren't I?" She felt strangely happy at the prospect, and she began to mentally peruse her garden and wonder if there was room to build a workroom, so that she could reclaim her dining room.

After dinner they played old-fashioned parlour games 'I Went to the Shop and Bought...', and 'Guess What', that brought back happy memories to Lauren of her childhood days. Poppy tried her best, and with much prompting from Annie managed the first round of shopping, after which she retreated to curl up on the bean bag in front of the inglenook with Charlie in her arms, where she promptly fell asleep. Annie went on to win both of the games, but Lauren wasn't sure if everyone else let her do so.

At nine, it was bedtime for the children. Annie chose a book, and tucked up in bed, she read to Poppy and Charlie who had snuggled down happily on the truckle bed beside her. Lauren and Rachel stood together in the doorway savouring the moment, and Lauren fought to keep the tears from her eyes. *I must be getting soft in my old-age,* she thought.

The grown-ups then sat and chatted with drinks until just after midnight, when Michael announced that he was off to bed, and wished them all goodnight. Rachel followed suit.

"Help yourselves to a nightcap," she said "I'll see you in the morning," and Glenn and Lauren were left alone with their thoughts and the dying embers of the fire.

Glenn poured a measure of Penderyn into their glasses.

"Are you glad we came Lauren?" he asked.

"It's been wonderful," she replied. "I wouldn't have missed it for the world, and it's all down to you for introducing me to this lovely family."

They chinked glasses, and drank to their new-found friends. Glenn put an arm around her shoulders and she leaned her head against him happily. Her eyes closed, and her glass began to tilt dangerously.

"Come on sleepyhead," laughed Glenn, rescuing it.

"Drink up, I think it's past your bedtime."

Outside Lauren's bedroom door, he took her in his arms and they kissed – a long, deep satisfying kiss filled with promise before bidding one another goodnight.

TWENTY: AN UNWANTED VISITOR:
(December 28th)

Netty toiled up the stairs, a shopping bag in each hand. Every few steps, she paused to rest, her heart pounding but the nagging pain in her bladder spurring her on. Living on the third floor had its one main drawback, but otherwise she loved their little flat, with its views over the roofs and treetops. It was light and airy in Summer, and warm and cosy in Winter, and with nobody living above, quiet too. It was also very secure, since a few years ago a caretaker had been installed in the ground floor flat, and the intercom system that allowed only residents access to the building. She always tried to limit her shopping, generally buying what she needed from the market on a daily basis, with only the occasional foray to Tesco Express to top up the store cupboard, and on those occasions she would normally enlist Razzy's help in carrying everything home. She had hoped to do so today, but he had left the stall early and not returned. She wondered if he had gone to see his father again. She never questioned him about it, and he ventured very little information beyond a brief description of his flat, and the fact that he worked in the Ragged Staff in the evenings, thus ensuring that she gave the place a wide berth. He had gone out on Christmas Eve and stayed out late, but on Christmas day, he had stayed at home with her. She had cooked him a small turkey crown, and had treated herself to a nut loaf from the relatively new market street-food shop that had a wide range of unusual vegetarian and vegan foods. The loaf was spicy, warming and utterly delicious – so much so that Razzy had finished it off on Boxing Day, much to her annoyance. However, she had enjoyed spending the day with him and they had gone for a walk in the afternoon and then watched a silly Christmas movie together with a few drinks and snacks. The downside was that today, Wednesday, she had had to go shopping yet again in Tesco Express.

Opening the door, she dropped the bags on the floor and ran to the toilet. Too late!

Behind her, the door of the flat swung gently closed, her keys still in the lock outside.

Cursing old age, Netty washed herself down, rinsed her knickers and trousers and deposited them in the washing machine. She would put a load on later. Returning to her bedroom she rummaged in her chest of drawers and found some clean clothes. Wearily, she sat on the bed and pulled them on, followed by her slippers. She would put the shopping away, make a cup of tea and settle down in front of the tv to watch a game show with a slice of the carrot cake she had treated herself to in Tesco Express.

The gas fire flared into life, and Netty leaned back against the colourful cushions on her sofa with a contented sigh. The cake was delicious, the tea hot and sweet. Within minutes of finishing them Netty was sound asleep, oblivious to the raucous laughter on Blankety Blank. Oblivious too, to the stealthy turning of her keys in the lock and the door inching open slowly. Oblivious to the soft footsteps approaching her slumbering, snoring form on the sofa, oblivious to the man who now stood leaning against the mantlepiece with one leg crossed over the other, observing her; oblivious to the eyes that glittered with rage and disdain, and the twisted snarl of hatred on his face.

Something, though, must have penetrated her subconscious and she stirred, and opened her eyes. For a moment she thought she must be dreaming, but then the dream morphed into consciousness and she was confronting her worst nightmare. Tony. He stood there before her very eyes, leaning on her mantlepiece with a vicious sneer on his undeniably handsome face.

"How did you...?" Then, in her mind's eye, she saw the keys in the door, and answered her own unspoken question. Wide awake now, the adrenaline coursing through her, she drew herself up to a sitting position, and tried to look confident.

"What are you doing here? I'd like you to leave – now!"

"Oh, don't worry, I'm going," he snarled. "But not until you answer my questions."

Netty stared at him, her mind calculating his strength. There was no way she could hope to escape if he decided to attack her. She must keep her head, and keep him talking whilst she worked out a plan.

"Why did you tell my son that I was dead?" He spoke the words quietly, but with a malevolent force that was unmistakeable. "What right did you have to do that?"

"Huh!" retorted Netty. "What right did *you* have to rape me? Did you even care that I was a virgin? I *begged* you to stop, but you didn't. You treated me like I was worthless. What makes you think you have a right to share in the son that I raised all by myself? Did you ever even think to look for me and make sure I was ok? You knew more or less where I lived, but I knew nothing about you except that you just took what you wanted and left me to deal with the consequences. I made a life, for me and Razzy, and he's *my* son, and nothing to do with you! I didn't steal anything from you, but you stole my innocence, and with it my life, which believe me hasn't been anywhere near as good as it could've been." Netty paused for breath, amazed at her own outspoken eloquence.

"You stole from me the chance to be a father, that's what! You and your prissy sister with her pearls and twinsets and her snotty attitude. Fuck! She even trotted out that ridiculous tale to me, about your husband who died on a fuckin' oil rig. Was that her idea then?"

Missing the significance of his words, Netty retorted,

"Well, what were we supposed to do? I had a black baby for heaven's sake! It would have been bad enough to have an illegitimate white baby, but a *black* one? We would never have lived it down. Pauline took it all in her stride, and Razzy and I have everything to thank her for. She even found us this place, and we're happy here. Just leave us alone Tony. I know Razzy has been seeing you, and I don't mind, but just leave me out of it and let me get on with my life in peace. I don't get what your problem is. You have your son; you don't need me!

"My problem is, *bitch,* that for over thirty years I thought I couldn't have kids, and all the time I could. All the time I had a son, and if I'd known that, I wouldn't have stayed with my pathetic barren wife, I would have found someone who could give me the son I wanted, the son to take my name and work in the family business. I made good, and I wanted to share it, but *you* took all that away from me."

Netty narrowed her eyes. "You would have found someone who could give you…so it isn't Razzy you want at all! What is it you really want Tony? Why are you even here?" Even as she spoke the words, the answer crept insidiously into her consciousness.

"Revenge." He spoke the word quietly, but with a timbre that lent it a deadly emphasis. Netty froze as the implication sunk in, but she needed more answers, and she needed to keep him talking.

"How did you find us?" she asked.

"By chance," he replied. He shifted his position, uncrossing and re-crossing his legs. "Your sister asked me for a quote for re-wiring. I saw your photo, with the baby in your arms. I recognised you and I asked her where you were. She didn't tell me much, but she said you were here in Chesbury, so I came here to find you."

Netty searched her memory. She recalled Pauline saying she was having a complete re-wiring, but she hadn't mentioned Tony, so obviously hadn't made the connection. It was just under a year ago, she remembered, around the time of the first murder. Netty felt her blood run cold. Revenge? What did he mean by that? The murdered women had all had red hair, and one was even called Annette. Was it possible he had mistaken them for her?

"How did you find this place?" she asked. "Did Razzy tell you?"

"Fuck no! He wouldn't. He said you didn't want to see me. I tried following him, but he always managed to give me the slip. Then today I decided to check out the market and I saw you both on that stall of yours. It was a shock! Believe me, I'd never thought you'd turn out so fuckin' ugly, or I wouldn't have touched those women. I was supposed to meet Paul – Razzy, at my place at four, but I waited until you finished and followed you home. He's probably there now, helping himself to my booze, or he might have gone down the Staff to wait for me."

Netty's heart sank. It didn't sound as if Razzy would be home any time soon. She edged along the sofa towards the door, and wondered if she could make a run for it, but she knew it was impossible. *If only she hadn't been so careless*, she thought, inwardly cursing her overactive bladder. *The one time she had gone and left the keys in the door!* She had probably only done that a handful of times in all the years that they had been living there. Was this fate? Had it been wrong of her to lie to Razzy about his birth? Was this retribution from some unseen source for her own misdoings? She thought about her little shrine in the bedroom, the one where she had prayed for forgiveness throughout the years for every vow she had held sacred, and had broken to placate her son whom, if she were honest with herself, she had never quite been able to love completely. Looking at his father now, towering over her a few feet away with murder in his heart, she could understand why. She had been wrong, and now she would pay. What would happen to Razzy when she was gone? Would he carry on as though nothing had happened? He had never had to look after himself, and she doubted that he was capable of the basic organisational skills required to live independently day-to-day. His involvement in the stall was no more than that of any employee, in fact, considerably less so, since he was often absent without any explanation. Netty had hoped he would help out with the ordering, stocktaking and keeping the books, but in the end, it had all fallen to her alone. She doubted that he even knew how much rent they paid on the flat, or any of the other necessary expenses, and his idea of shopping for food was a trip to MacDonald's or the late night doner van. He was, however, a grown man, and would probably survive. Then her thoughts turned to her sister. *Oh! My God! Pauline!* Pauline would be devastated, and now approaching seventy, would be unlikely to survive such a blow. She would blame herself, and rightly so, since the whole thing had been her idea, and Netty had gone along with it, not knowing what else to do. Suddenly resentment against her sister bubbled up in Netty as she realised that all her life she had been shielded, controlled and manipulated. The only decisions she had made for herself (and kept from her sister) had been the best ones, and had brought her more happiness than she had ever previously known. She had refused to turn the flat down, she had known its potential, and would have made it a comfortable home with or without Pauline's interference. The market stall, bought from her friend without her sister's knowledge. She remembered vividly withdrawing the money and carrying it through town in her canvas shoulder bag to hand it over to Sandie. Remembered the wonderful feeling of freedom, and of being in control of her own destiny at last. She had never looked back from that day, in spite of the compulsory visits to her sister that had steadily increased in number over the years, although they were never really pleasurable, but merely a duty to be fulfilled.

In those few minutes under Tony's malevolent stare, Netty's whole life flashed before her and she realised how much better she could have handled it all. *I should never have listened to Pauline! Ah well, it's too late now,* she thought sadly. Then the full implication of his words hit her. *Those women? He must be referring to the murders. It must have been him!*

"Was that you?" it was a mere whisper. She held her breath, fearful of hearing the unthinkable confirmed.

"Not that last one," he replied. His air was nonchalant, as though he were discussing a minor misdemeanour. "That was nothing to do with me."

"But…why?" Netty implored, a sick feeling spreading through her.

"I made a mistake; they weren't you," he replied with a shrug of his shoulders. "I had to shut them up."

"But…the other thing? Why?" Netty shuddered as she remembered the details of the murders.

Suddenly, the sound of a key being turned in the lock brought the exchange to an abrupt end. *He left them in there!* She thought incredulously. Tony had left the keys, and now Razzy was home! He stood in the doorway, transfixed by the tableau before him.

"Mum? *Dad? What the fuck…?"* His eyes flashed from one to the other of his parents. In an instant, he saw his father's aggressive stance, and his mother's terror. In two strides, he reached Netty and gathered her, trembling now, into his arms. She clung to him and wept tears of relief that seemed to wash all the fearful anticipation away as they fell. Razzy tightened his arms around her protectively.

"Get out!" he told his father. "Get the fuck out of here, and don't even think about coming back – *ever!*"

Tony hesitated for only a split second, then strode across the room and out through the door, slamming it shut behind him.

TWENTY-ONE: THE FINAL RECKONING.

Tony had worked the early shift, finishing at three because his son was coming round to his flat at four. They'd have a drink together and probably something to eat. He had over half an hour to kill as he emerged from the pub, and his eye was drawn to the indoor market across the road. He had never been in there, in spite of working opposite it, because he normally worked the late shift and it was closed by then. He decided to check it out, there might be something interesting he could get to offer Paul to eat instead of their usual takeaway. Indeed, delicious aromas assaulted his senses as he entered through the single swing door. He turned to the left, and wandered along past a pet supplies stall, to find the source of the aromas – a street food stall selling bowls of steaming spicy creations that you could eat there, perched at one of the tall round tables, or take away in a polystyrene container to reheat at home. Tony decided to return after he had been around the rest of the market. All around the perimeter there were stalls selling fabrics and knitting yarns, handbags and travel goods, toys and games, and clothes. Down the middle there was a cheese stall, an organic veg stall, a chicken and eggs stall, and one selling home-made cakes and biscuits. The stall holders were cheerful and engaging, drawing in potential customers with their good-humoured banter. Tony spied a café at the far end. It looked very busy and he could smell the coffee from some way off. Passing a New Age stall on his way to the café, he was drawn to the incense burners on display. He rather fancied one for his flat. As he approached the stall, he suddenly froze. The man behind the stall looked familiar, and he realised with a jolt that it was his son, Paul. He was leaning on the counter talking to a customer. Fortunately, his back was turned, and

Tony was able to duck behind the adjacent stall where brightly coloured raincoats provided some cover. He rifled through them feigning interest, but his eyes were glued to the 'Enigma' stall. A woman came around from the other side to join Paul at the counter. Her plump, shapeless form was swathed in a virtual kaleidoscope of colour – voluminous purple trousers, a green tent top, an oversized multi-coloured cardigan. Her hair was bright, vibrant henna red above her pale face with its sagging jowl and neck. She laughed at something Paul said, and for a moment her face lit up and her eyes sparkled with mischief, and Tony was transported back to that fateful night almost thirty-seven years ago. Yes, she was still recognisable, but the radiant young girl was long gone, and only the eyes remained seemingly unchanged in their sunken state, beneath pencilled-in eyebrows. As he watched, Paul gave her a quick hug and left the stall, passing within inches of his father lurking among the raincoats, presumably on his way to Tony's flat. With his heart racing, Tony moved quickly away and skirted the stalls back to the entrance. The notice on the door gave the opening hours as 9-5, and now it was gone four. He crossed the road and sat on a bench outside the pub to wait for Annette to leave for home. She emerged half an hour later, and he followed her up the hill to Tesco Express, where he again found a bench with a view of the door and waited there until she emerged again, carrying two heavy looking carrier bags. She proceeded wearily down the hill towards the station, turning left into a sloping street of tall houses. Tony followed at a safe distance, and watched her climb the steps to one of the houses, and press a button at the side of the door. She spoke into what appeared to be an intercom, whereupon the door opened and she disappeared inside.

Tony hastened across the street. There was the microphone with a call button, above which were tabs with names on, none of which meant anything to him, and the numbers 2 – 5. Tony racked his brains. He would have to improvise. He crossed the street and sat on a wall opposite the building. There were three tall windows with lights on that must have been on the stairwell. The lights remained on for several minutes, and he pictured Annette negotiating the stairs with her heavy bags. At long last, another light came on in one of the topmost windows to the left of the building. A few minutes later, the other window was briefly illuminated, then curtains were drawn across both windows. *So, they live on the top floor,* thought Tony. *Well, knowledge is power!* He waited for another twenty minutes, working out his strategy, then crossed the street and climbed the steps to the door. He pressed the call button and a lazy male voice answered,

"Yeah?"

"I'm here to see Paul," he said.

"Paul?" replied the disembodied voice. There was what seemed like a long silence, then a slight chuckle and "Aw! You mean Razzy? Nobody calls 'im Paul."

"I'm sorry, I'm his teacher from way back, and I've always known him as Paul. I've been looking for him, and someone said he lives here on the top floor with his mum. I don't know what number though." He waited with bated breath whist the person on the other end took in this information.

"Awww! I get ya. It's flat 5, on the left at the top of the stairs. I know his mum's there, she just went up." The door clicked, and swung open to the touch of Tony's hand. He walked swiftly past the ground floor flat which he supposed must be occupied by the keeper of the intercom, and set off up the stairs. As he climbed, he pictured Annette opening the door and seeing him standing there. Would she realise who he was? Would she let him in, or would he have to force his way, yet again?

A few minutes later, he stood outside a bright yellow door, with a brass number 5 on it. To his utter amazement, there was a bunch of keys sitting in the lock. *What a stroke of luck!* He listened, his ear to the door. He could hear the sound of voices, but quickly realised it emanated from a tv, not from actual people. Very carefully, his heart thumping loudly, he turned the key and gently pushed the door. It opened slowly to reveal a comfortable if somewhat shabby lounge. There was a small drop-leaf table against one wall flanked by two chairs and adorned by a slightly wonky and clearly artificial Christmas Tree, festooned with copious amounts of tinsel and brightly coloured baubles, but no lights. A sideboard next to it held some photographs, an old-fashioned stereo, a rack of CDs and a green glass bowl piled high with fruit. Next to the enormous ornate fireplace was a low table on which stood a flat screen tv, showing some sort of game show. It was very loud, a cacophony of laughter and applause, and the room was hot and stuffy thanks to the gas fire that blazed in the fireplace. Opposite that was a large sofa, from which emanated the sound of gentle snoring. An empty mug and plate stood on a low coffee table in front of it, along with the tv remote control. The woman from the stall was recumbent on the sofa against the bright, garish cushions, her head back, her mouth open, a dribble of saliva trickling from the corner of her mouth.

The sight of her lying there, totally relaxed, apparently not a care in the world, made bile rise in his throat. This woman, this great shapeless drooling lump, was responsible for everything bad in his life. He loathed her with every fibre of his being, and he would make her pay. He should finish her now, but he wanted answers, answers that his son couldn't or wouldn't give him. He picked up the remote control and pressed the off button. Silence filled the room, broken only by the hissing of the gas fire and the snoring that now seemed so much louder. Tony leaned against the mantlepiece and waited.

Suddenly he stiffened. She was stirring, her mouth closing as her eyes opened – those heart stopping eyes that were the only vestige of the lovely young girl he remembered. They opened slowly, then flew wide, blazing defiantly like molten emeralds in her pale face as they took in the man standing before them.

She had courage, he gave her that. She ordered him to leave, and he almost felt tempted, because suddenly his lust for revenge was faltering in the face of this determined woman whom admittedly he had wronged. But he needed answers; answers he probably wouldn't get unless she felt a need to bargain with him, to buy time.

She talked, he listened, and then heard himself telling her about his own feelings, the childlessness that blighted his life, the reason for his need for vengeance. She listened, and her eyes reflected every emotion he evoked – surprise, consternation, even sympathy, and then self-doubt as she appeared to wander away on some personal voyage of remembrance. He watched her, and felt all thoughts of revenge drain away from his consciousness. She was a victim, and not just of rape. He remembered her sister's haughty demeanour and realised that she had probably had no choice but to go along with whatever Pauline decided.

When she asked him if he was responsible for the murders, he felt cornered, and the only thing he could think of was to deny the one that hadn't been his work. He immediately realised that he had told her too much, and panic began to well up and chill his blood. He wondered now how he could get out of this, how he could leave without fear of repercussions. Would her story be believed? Would Paul believe her? More to the point, would they go to the police? The panic threatened to overwhelm him as he searched desperately for a way out of this, and realised that he was running out of time. Perhaps after all, he would have to kill her because of what she knew.

He took a step towards her just as the keys turned in the lock and Razzy stood framed in the doorway, a look of total disbelief on his face. Without a moment's hesitation, he rushed to comfort his mother, yelling at his father to get out, and Tony fled.

It took him less than ten minutes to reach his flat. He couldn't believe how close he had been to his goal for all this time. How had this happened? How had he got himself in this mess? He had been totally blindsided by the difference in names – not Annette and Paul, after all, but Netty and Razzy! *Fuck!* They had a stall in the market, and were probably known to practically everyone in Chesbury, if only he'd known who to ask for! *If he had only known!* Those two women – *Christ! What had he done?* For a moment he considered the third one. Whoever did that had tried to pin it on him. *How dare they!*

He dragged his hold-all down from the top of the wardrobe. With no time to form a plan, he would take only what he could fit in, just as he had when he came here. He would trade in his Astra for whatever he could get without further ado, because if Netty and Razzy went to the police, they'd be looking for it. He didn't want to spend the rest of his life in gaol, that would just be the icing on the cake, and besides, he had unfinished business, and right now that was his number one priority. He would leave his bits of furniture, his tv, stereo and most of his clothes. That way they wouldn't be sure that he had left, and his rent was paid up until the end of the month, so he had a few days grace, after which it wouldn't matter.

He returned to the garage where he had traded in his van, and soon afterwards was the not-so-proud owner of a dark blue Ford Fiesta, about as inconspicuous as you could get. The garage owner asked no questions but was, he realised afterwards, a little surprised that Tony didn't haggle over the deal. The Fiesta was a huge comedown after the high spec, handsome black Astra, and he accepted the part-exchange offer without hesitation, much to the garage owner's surprise; but he simply said he needed some cash in a hurry, and the guy probably thought he was dodgy, but didn't care as long as he got rid of the heap of crap and came out of it with a fat profit. He threw in a tank full of petrol, and Tony guessed that was his conscience pricking him.

Thankfully, the traffic was light as he made his way back towards his home town of Birmingham. As he drove, he thought about Carol, and wondered how she was faring since he had left so suddenly eleven months ago. Very soon afterwards she had started divorce proceedings, and the decree absolute would arrive through his letterbox any day now, although now he would not be there to receive it. The urge to drive past his old home was irresistible. He parked up across the road, and allowed the exquisite torture of regret to overwhelm him. If only they had been blessed with children none of this would have happened, and he was sure they would have enjoyed a good, happy marriage. Now there could be no going back to what he now realised had been a decent life in every sense of the word. If only his male pride had allowed him to take a fertility test. They could then have had treatment – the money would not have been a problem. He thumped the steering wheel in frustration, and felt hot tears of anguish coursing down his face as he recalled his last words to her; words he could never now take back, words that would define their relationship in her mind forever. Now, one way or another, his life was over, and perhaps hers was beginning anew. The house looked much the same as when he left, except that the front door had been painted the colour of a summer sky. The garden was neat and there was a new gate, designed, he quickly realised, to contain the golden retriever that stood in the porch, plumy tail waving expectantly, waiting to be let in. He didn't think it would have to wait long, and sure enough, within minutes, the door opened and there she stood. She had changed her hairstyle, it suited her and made her look younger. She was still an attractive woman and his heart gave a jolt. He felt an irresistible urge to get out of the car and approach her, but that was immediately quelled by the appearance of a tall man behind her. He placed an arm across her shoulder and led her back inside the house, the dog following behind them. The door closed, and Tony was alone.

Perry Barr was less than a twenty-minute drive away. Tony drove slowly down Laburnum Avenue, and pulled up outside number 13 – *unlucky for some,* he muttered beneath his breath. His nerves were jangling, his hands gripping the steering wheel so tightly that his wedding ring, which he still wore, cut into the flesh of his finger. He found the house easily, remembering it from his last visit. It was in darkness, the curtains drawn, but he could see a chink of light between them in the bay window that faced out over the front garden that was as neat as a pin, with a low hedge of neatly trimmed privet, a wooden garden gate, and low picket fencing lining the path to the door. Unlike all the neighbouring houses, there were no Christmas lights to be seen. There were lace curtains at all the windows, and the white front door had a polished brass letterbox and doorknocker.

Tony gathered his wits and, opening and closing the gate silently, made his way up the path. There was a doorbell as well as the knocker, and he elected to use that as it wouldn't sound so intimidating. He needed to get over the threshold, and the rest would be easy. He noticed a CCTV camera above the open porchway and wondered if it worked, or was it just there for show as so many are. He stood as far into the porchway as he could, shielded from view of the lounge window, and pressed the doorbell. To his dismay, after a few minutes, he heard a chain being drawn across the door.

"Who's there?" A querulous female voice demanded. Tony wondered how long it was since she had spoken to her nephew, and he guessed it was probably some time, since there was clearly no love lost between them. Remembering how Razzy had referred to her, he took a deep breath, and answered,

"It's me Aunty Pauline, Razzy."

The door opened as far as the chain would allow. Tony stood to one side, away from the opening through which light now flooded. It was dark in the porch, and he wondered why she didn't put on the outside light. Perhaps it hadn't occurred to her, or more likely it wasn't working. In answer, he heard her mutter under her breath, "Bloody thing! Bulb must've gone!" Then the chain was drawn away, and in an instant, Tony was inside.

Pauline didn't scream, that was not her style. She stood in the lounge doorway, barring the way. "I'll thank you to leave," she said, quietly, but none-the-less forcefully. Pauline brooked no dissent in those she considered her inferiors, and that included most people, but especially 'darkies'.

Tony stood his ground. "We need to talk first," he said, "and then I'll leave."
She gave him an arch look, and then he watched as realization dawned on her stern features.

"*You!*" she snorted derisively. "I know who you are. You raped my sister Annette! You are an animal of the lowest order!" She glared at him, her chin held high, her eyes blazing with anger and disdain.

"It was a misunderstanding," Tony replied. "I've spoken with her, and she knows that now." The lie issued from his mouth of its own volition, being a slightly altered form of the truth, and he felt only the briefest pang of guilt. Pauline didn't buy it.

"Huh! I don't think so!" she retorted. "Well, you needn't have any designs on me, I'm not as naive as my sister. She was never the sharpest knife in the block."

Tony stared at her in disbelief. This woman was such a bitch! He shuddered in disgust at the very thought of what she was suggesting. Clearly, she had no respect for her sister either, in fact, he doubted she had any respect for anyone on the planet.

"All I want from you is the truth," he replied quietly. "Was it all your idea? The oil rig, the dead husband, the name Lipton, the fact that neither of you made any attempt to find me and tell me that I had a son?"

"Huh!" she scoffed again. "Well, Annette would never have had the brains that's for certain. I've always looked after her since our mother wasn't capable of it, and I always will. I did what was best for her and that misbegotten son of hers. He was always trouble, right from the start."

"He was always missing a father," Tony said quietly. "Maybe that's why he behaved badly, if indeed he did. Or perhaps it was just that he didn't fit into your outmoded idea of who he should be. You despised him, and you denied him the chance to know his father, and he is what he is because of that, not because of me."

"As I said, I looked after them. I had to face the neighbours, and I had to think of an excuse for my sister having a baby *that* colour. Then when he got too much to handle, I found them a nice flat and helped them get on their feet. Nobody could have done more for them than I did."

'Well, that's right for sure, but in the end it was all for you wasn't it Pauline."

"How dare you call me by my first name. It's Mrs. Proctor to you, young man."

"I'm not a young man *Mrs. Proctor,* so don't patronize me. Is there a Mr. Proctor then? I'm guessing there probably never has been. Who the fuck could put up with a control freak like you? Did you make up that name too then?"

"Proctor is my real name, and Annette's also. I almost married once, but it was not to be." Tony saw a small chink in her armour as she spoke.

"Well, whoever he was, he had a lucky escape, and he's better off without you, wherever he is!" Tony stated with feeling, then staggered backwards as Pauline set about him in a fury, pummelling him with her fists and shouting.

"*You!* You know nothing about me! *How dare you!*" she yelled, tears of rage now filling her eyes. Tony recovered himself, and grabbed her by the wrists.

"Shut up bitch!" he whispered fiercely, his face inches from hers. "Shut up *now* or I'll kill you!"

She stopped shouting, and he let go of her wrists. She turned away and entered the lounge, where she perched on the edge of a chair next to an electric fire that pretended to be a wood burner, her hands clasped before her and an expression of defiance on her face.

"I want you to know," said Tony, sitting himself in the opposite chair. He leaned forward, his arms on his knees, and spoke quietly "What you have done to your sister, who you claim to have cared for. You have controlled and manipulated her just because you could. I've seen her, I've spoken to her, and I know she is a good woman who cares for people, not a selfish arrogant bitch like you. If I had been given the chance, I would have married her, and we would have brought our son up together, and we would have been happy. I regretted what I did to her as soon as I had done it, but I was afraid to come back and try to make amends in case she had gone to the police, so I kept away, and made a good life with a good job. I married someone else – a white woman in case you're wondering, and we had many years together but we failed to have children. I thought it was my punishment for what I did to Annette, and it wasn't until I came here for that rewiring job that I saw the photos and realised the truth. How do you think I felt, finding out that all those years I'd had a son? Finding out that it was my wife who couldn't conceive, not me? What do you think that did to me – or are you such an insensitive bitch that you neither know nor care? I went to Chesbury, and I searched for them. I thought I would recognize Annette, and I thought my son's name was Paul, but it turns out that everyone else calls them Netty and Razzy, which didn't make my task any easier. I had anger in my heart because I thought Annette had done this on purpose, until I talked to her earlier today, and she told me that it was all your idea."

Pauline sat bolt upright, taking it all in. Once or twice, she opened her mouth as though to protest, but Tony raised a finger to silence her. Now she could hold her tongue no longer.

"I did what I thought was right for Annette," she said. "If I'd known what an aberration she was carrying I would have made her get rid of it, believe me. I didn't find out until it was born, and by then it was too late to change our story."

An Aberration! This was too much for Tony. Something snapped inside him and he sprung forward and grasped the wretched woman by her neck, her hands and feet flailing at him as he wrung the life out of her. When she finally went limp, he stood back and surveyed the wreckage of probably the most despicable human being it had ever been his misfortune to encounter. Her eyes were wide open, staring at him, grey and expressionless. He reached down and closed them before sitting her back in her chair. Then he turned off the electric fire and left, but not before he took the photograph of Netty and Razzy, all those years ago, out of its frame, and put it in his pocket.

TWENTY-TWO: A FUNERAL. (December 28th)

The day of Ashley's funeral had arrived, as these things are wont to do, creeping up behind the weekend's celebrations like a dark shadow. For most people it was the first day back to work after the extended Christmas period. For Lauren, it was a day to be got through and then put behind her. It was closure, the final goodbye, although not quite, because there was the small matter of her killer, and that of two other women, still being at large.

Thankfully, the morning dawned dry, and a wan winter sun hung in the sky. It had rained on Lauren's grandmother's funeral, she remembered, serving to make it all the more sombre.

Lauren had kept the arrangements simple and straightforward. It wasn't an occasion to celebrate a life, because that life had really held little worthy of celebration. She didn't want people dressing in pink (she had no idea if Ashley was a 'pink' person but she thought probably not). She didn't want doves, or (heaven forfend) balloons, or any of the other crazy stuff of modern-day funerals. She wanted quiet dignity, and nothing for the media circus to get their teeth into. She knew they would be there, but she hoped they'd keep a low profile, and refused to give them any excuse to do otherwise.

She dressed in black, as she had asked everyone else to do; a simple black dress beneath an ankle length black wool and cashmere coat, and black knee length boots. Her only adornment was a pair of gold stud earrings, and the Clogau locket that Glenn gave her. Trisha had been worried that she didn't have anything suitable to wear, so Lauren had lent her an outfit. She didn't suppose she would ever get it back, but neither did she care. She wanted everyone to look smart in an attempt to dispel the spiteful whispered rumours that her daughter had been a prostitute; rumours that the loyal Trisha absolutely refuted. She had even supplied Trisha's boyfriend Steve with a basic black suit from M&S, and strict instructions that he was to wear it. Poppy had gone to stay with Aunty Bessie the night before, and would return later in the evening none the wiser of the day's proceedings. She had been very excited at the prospect of yet another sleepover, and Lauren was once more indebted to Bessie, although she knew that Bessie was probably even more excited than Poppy at the prospect.

At eleven o'clock, Glenn arrived. He looked as tense and nervous as she felt. He held her to him in a warm embrace,

"It'll soon be over," he whispered gently. Lauren bit back the tears. She must remain strong, especially in the face of Ken and Janet, whom she hadn't laid eyes on over the past three weeks. Ken didn't want his expectant wife to be put in a stressful situation, although Lauren really couldn't see why that had also applied to him. Ashley was, after all, his daughter too.

At eleven-twenty, the small group of mourners gathered outside the crematorium. Situated on the outskirts of town amid green fields and down a tree-lined drive, it was a peaceful place, with well-tended memorial plots surrounded by flower borders and overhung by trees and tall shrubs. Even in the dead of winter birds sang in the branches, and the winter jasmine and witch hazel were in bloom, the magnolias beginning to bud, and thin spears of snowdrop leaves were already pushing their way up out of the ground. The press were already gathered, but Lauren and Glenn walked quickly past them, Glenn waving them away impatiently.

Lauren greeted Ken and Janet with cool politeness. She introduced them to Trisha and Steve (who she was relieved to see had both complied with her dress code, apart from Steve's black trainers, which she supposed would have to do), and then to Glenn. The two men shook hands and Lauren was amused at their body language – Glenn's detached and polite, and Ken giving off the vibes of a circling stag about to attack. *He doesn't like the competition, even though he isn't interested in the prize,* she thought.

The six of them filed inside, leaving the thwarted newshounds outside. The chapel was enormous, the coffin so small and insignificant on its dais at the front. Lauren felt sick as she looked upon the wooden box containing her daughter. It was almost impossible to comprehend that she was actually in there; it felt surreal and she wished with all her heart that it was all a nightmare from which she would wake at any minute. The casket was topped by a single large ivory church candle surrounded by a wreath of greenery, and no flowers as she had requested. They approached it silently in their pairs, reaching out to touch it in a gesture of farewell before returning to their seats.

The ceremony was brief. There was no eulogy, only the reading of a short poem that Lauren had chosen, but had felt unable to recite. The celebrant's voice was clear and resonant.

"I am left with your smile asleep in my memory, and my heart tells me that I will not forget you;
But, being left alone, knowing that I have lost you, perhaps I might begin to love you as I never loved you before."

(anon).

Then, the celebrant said "I shall now give you all a few moments to remember Ashley in silence, each in your own way." They all bowed their heads, lost in their thoughts, some more than others.

A slight shuffling sound from the back of the room caused everyone to look up, and turn to see what or who had made it. There stood Mark Pullman, dressed in black, his head bowed. As they turned to look at him he smiled at Lauren, and raised a hand in greeting. Lauren felt incandescent with rage. *How dare he!* She got to her feet and made her way over to stand before him.

"*Get out!*" she said in a fierce, loud whisper. "*Get out now!*" He held up his hands in protest, then seeing the look on her face, turned away towards the door.

There was a murmur among the gathering, as most of them had no idea who he was. Lauren returned to her seat, trembling, and after a short pause, the celebrant read the words of the committal, and the coffin began its slow journey through the curtains to the poignant tune of 'Daughters', by John Mayer, again chosen by Lauren. Everyone sat silent until the song had finished. Throughout the ceremony, except when Lauren had gone to evict Mark, Glenn had held her hand in his gently, and she wondered how on earth she would have got through this day without him. They began now to file out through the doors at the back of the room.

Outside, there seemed to be a sudden flurry of activity. The newshounds' cameras were working overtime, and to her astonishment, Lauren realised that the object of their interest was Mark Pullman. He stood between two uniformed police officers, handcuffed and protesting loudly. What on earth was happening? Had he created some sort of a disturbance outside, and been arrested for it? It seemed a bit over-zealous, however much she disliked him. She approached the distinguished looking man on the edge of the melee who appeared to be in charge of proceedings, and asked him what was going on.

"DI Matthews. I'm sorry for intruding on your grief, Miss Woods," He said respectfully, lifting his hat. "But we have just arrested this gentleman for the murder of your daughter Ashley."

"I...I don't understand..." Lauren began, whereupon Mark called out to her,

"Tell them they've made a mistake Lauren. Tell them I couldn't have done it. You know that's the truth because you know how much I love you!"

"I'm very sorry ma'am, I didn't know that you and he... but the evidence is overwhelming."

"We're not!" exclaimed Lauren vehemently, and felt Glenn's arm tighten around her shoulders. "This man has been harassing me for weeks, and I wish you would take him away, lock him up, and throw away the key! He had no right to come here in the first place!"

The inspector barked an order to the two policemen restraining Mark, and they dragged him away, and pushed him into a waiting police car, still struggling and protesting his innocence to Lauren.

"Who the fuck is he?" Trisha asked. "Are you ok Mrs. Stevenson?"

"Is he a friend of yours Lauren?" asked Ken, with the emphasis on the word 'friend'.

"Is he the Chesbury Strangler then?" asked Janet.

"I think we should all go home now, the show's over," said Glenn firmly, and began to shepherd Lauren towards the car park, the others following. The newshounds continued their endless snapping, throwing questions at Lauren. She pulled her coat over her head and tried to block them out and as she hurried with Glenn to the car, the tears began to flow. They drove away, the tyres spinning on the gravel of the car park. There hadn't been time for goodbyes, and thanks to Mark, the whole day had turned into a circus in a way Lauren could never have imagined, and all her careful planning to make it dignified had been for nothing.

Back at home, Glenn sat her down with a glass of wine, turned on the fire and drew back the curtains.

"It's over Lauren," he said. "You need to put it out of your mind and move on, for Poppy's sake." She knew he was right, but so many things were puzzling her.

"But *Mark*!" She exclaimed. "I know he's a creep, but a *murderer?* Now that beggars belief! What the hell was he doing at the crem? How did the police know he was there?" So many questions that she may never know the answers to.

"Revisiting the scene of the crime in a way, I guess. He couldn't resist, and perhaps the police suspected that might be the case. They may have been concerned for his state of mind, and wanted to protect you. Well anyway, he's going to be put away for a very long stretch, presuming they have irrefutable evidence against him. I wonder if they fancy him for the others? I doubt it, I think he was probably just trying to pin it on someone else. Perhaps he panicked or something."

"That perfume Glenn. It still bothers me, and I still don't know why."

"Feminine intuition. Hmm… Alison had that too, and she was very rarely wrong, but I really can't imagine what has spooked you so badly about that perfume, except that you knew the guy's a creep and nobody wants gifts from that sort. Can I take you out for dinner Lauren? Poppy won't be back until her bedtime, and we haven't even been out together yet. Let's go to Giorgio's."

Lauren forced a smile. He was right again of course, but her mind wouldn't let her move on. However, she nodded consent. Glenn would be going back to Simon's tonight, and then home to Wales tomorrow, and she didn't know when she would see him again, if ever.

Giorgio's was quiet and they managed to bag a window table. They dined on delicious Italian food and copious amounts of wine.

"I'll leave my car at yours, and pick it up in the morning, and we can discuss New Year. A New Year Lauren, and a new beginning." They chinked glasses.

'There's still a serial killer at large Glenn. I can't believe that Mark is responsible for the others. I wonder if they're anywhere near to catching him?"

On the walk back to Lauren's, they linked arms companionably. As they turned up past the memorial garden, Glenn suddenly stopped. He took her in his arms and kissed her. It seemed a long time since their last kiss on the landing at the Fenton's, and she responded fervently.It felt good, it felt right, and suddenly she knew that, given time, life would be good again.

The next morning Glenn arrived just after nine to collect his car.

"I came via Jonny's," he said, placing a brown paper bag on the kitchen counter from which emanated the delicious aroma of croissants. I also picked this up at Nick's News. He placed a newspaper next to the croissants and awaited her reaction. The early edition of the Herald bore the unmissable front page headline.

THE CHESBURY STRANGLER IS DEAD!
AT DAWN THIS MORNING, WEST MIDLANDS POLICE
RELEASED THE FOLLOWING STATEMENT:

Late last night the body of a man was discovered in woods outside Erdington, near Birmingham, by a man walking his dog. He was identified as Tony Ashton, formerly of Great Barr, but currently resident in Chesbury. The cause of death is believed to be asphyxiation by hanging. Police are not looking for anyone else in connection with the death of the man believed to be the notorious Chesbury Strangler. Last night, at about the time of the discovery, his son Paul informed Chesbury police that Ashton had earlier that day confessed to he and his mother Annette to the murders of Alison Gibson and Annette Saunders. This brings to a conclusion the investigation into the Chesbury Strangler. It is also believed that Ashton may have been responsible for the murder of his son's aunt, Pauline Proctor, in Great Barr earlier yesterday evening, although this has yet to be proven. Our sympathies are extended to the families of the murdered women.

"Thank God!" Lauren whispered. "I mean, we can all breathe easy now. But poor Netty! She and her sister were very close. I don't quite understand – he was Razzy's dad? I thought he died years ago, at least that's what they told everybody. You never really know people do you?"

The doorbell interrupted them, and Lauren went to answer it. The family liaison officer, Sinead, who had been assigned to her after Ashley was killed, stood there with a bag in her hand. She smiled hesitantly at Lauren, and thrust the bag towards her.

"The boss asked me to return these to you Lauren. It's Ashley's personal effects." Lauren took it and thanked her.

In the lounge, Glenn watched as she took out each item and laid them on the sofa. The skinny jeans, the fake fur jacket and over the knee boots. All that was left of her wayward daughter. There was a small ziplock bag containing her underwear, her passport, and a wad of folded euros. Lauren unfolded them, and a receipt fell out from their midst. It was from the DFDS ferry duty free shop. It was for a bottle of Daisy by Marc Jacobs. She turned to Glenn, a look of great sadness mingled with horror on her face.

"Oh my God Glenn! He stole it from her, and gave it to me for Christmas!"

They sat in stunned silence for several minutes, then he folded his arms around her, rocking her gently and stroking her hair.

"Like I said, feminine intuition Lauren. You were right to have those feelings. You're amazing Lauren Woods! Why don't you and Poppy, and Charlie of course, come and spend New Year with me in Wales? You can leave all this behind you for a while. I can't promise you luxury, but I have all the basics, including some heating hopefully by the end of today, and most importantly, complete peace and quiet. We can go for walks along the Mawddach Trail, or on the beach at Barmouth which will be almost deserted at this time of year. There's a few decent pubs within easy reach too. I'm sure Bronwyn will make a fuss of you all, and you might even get a Welshcake or two."

Lauren hesitated, but only for a moment. It sounded wonderful!

"I'd love to," she said, "and I'm sure Poppy would too. As for Charlie, he'll probably make *his* feelings known all the way there, so I hope you can deal with that!"

Remembering the constant racket he had kept up on the way to the Fenton's, Glenn grimaced. "Guess I'll have to take the rough with the smooth," he said with a rueful grin.

"Now I have to go, I need to be there to supervise the new Aga, I don't want to get home and find they've installed it in the bathroom! I'll pick you up on Saturday at about eleven. You can stay as long as you like, but we'll aim for Tuesday at least. I'm sure Bessie will keep the shop ticking over for you once the weekend's over. She's a national treasure, that woman!"

As Glenn drove back to Wales, he reflected again on the events of the past few days, and the deepening of his relationship with Lauren. They were certainly friends, and he believed they would soon be lovers, but he also knew that neither would wish to give up the life they had, so they would always have separate homes. He decided that, ultimately, that was probably the best of both worlds, and he was content.

TWENTY-THREE: CLOSURE. (December 29th)

"Thank you," said Netty with a smile, as the customer put the oil burner she had just purchased into her bag. "I hope you enjoy it." *Good start,* she thought. The oil burners were expensive, and she didn't sell many in a week.

She turned, and saw two men in suits and overcoats approaching the stall. They didn't look like her usual customers, in fact, they looked like detectives. Netty frowned in consternation. What had Razzy done now? They both took id cards out and held them up for Netty to inspect.

"DI Matthews and DS Taylor. Is there somewhere we can talk?" The elder man asked.

Netty lifted the hinged hatch in the counter and invited them in to the inner sanctum where she kept her cash, her books and her teasmade (bought from Mark's stall some time ago). There was only one stool, and the men declined to sit, but indicated her to do so. Her anxiety mounted and she wondered where Razzy was. He had been very quiet since the encounter with his father yesterday. He had wanted to turn him in immediately, but Netty, not wanting to rattle Tony's cage, had persuaded him to let it lie for a few days until they knew of his further intentions. Razzy had checked out his flat later, but there was no sign of life and his car wasn't there.

"Perhaps e's slung 'is hook," said Razzy when he arrived back later. "Good job too! Let's hope that's the last we ever see of 'im Mum."

She jerked herself back to the present. The younger of the two men was now speaking.

"Are you Annette Lipton, formerly Proctor?" he asked. "Do you have a sister named Pauline?"

"I am, and I do" replied Netty. "Why? What's happened? Is Pauline alright?" Her eyes were wide with anxiety, and a knot had formed in her stomach. Pauline had only just returned from her holiday the previous day. Netty had heard nothing from her and had assumed that she was exhausted from her journey, so left her alone. She planned to pay her a surprise visit on New Year's Eve. Now, her mind conjured up all manner of reasons why she might not have returned, or how she might be in hospital due to some foreign disease she had succumbed to. Yet, in her heart she knew that these men wouldn't have come calling because of either of those scenarios.

"I'm very sorry, Mrs. Lipton, but I'm afraid we have some bad news for you," the elder one now spoke. Netty's blood ran cold, and a clammy sweat broke out on her forehead. She braced herself for whatever was to come.

"Your sister, Pauline, was found dead in her home late last night. I'm afraid she has been murdered."

Netty was stunned. This couldn't be true; there must be some mistake. Suddenly she felt faint, and swayed on her stool. The younger man reached out to steady her.

"I'm sorry for your loss," he said.

Netty recovered herself a little. "Wh...what happened...how?" she asked.

"She was strangled in her lounge. The neighbour heard some shouting earlier, and went around to check on her. The front door was open, and she was sitting in her chair. Whoever killed her must've put her there. A thorough search was made of the house, but there was no apparent motive, and nothing appeared to have been taken except a photograph from one of the silver frames on the sideboard."

"A *photograph?* Why would anyone do that?" Netty cast her mind back to the photographs on Pauline's sideboard. They were mostly old ones of her, with one or two of her and Razzy when he was a baby. Suddenly, the penny dropped.

"Did he…did the…person… do anything else?" she whispered, hardly daring to ask.

"No ma'am. There was no sign of any…interference."

"I didn't mean that," whispered Netty, suppressing her disgust at the very idea. I meant, did he…mutilate her?"

"Oh! I see what you're asking! No, it was a straightforward strangulation. It appeared there had been a bit of an argument between them. We have no real evidence linking this incident to the Chesbury Strangler."

Relief of a kind washed over Netty. She didn't think she could have borne the alternative. All the same, Tony's words came back to her. Should she now tell these police officers about his visit yesterday? He was the only person she could think of who might have reason to steal that photograph. She felt weak and nauseous. She realised they were preparing to leave, and decided she would keep shtum and talk to Razzy about it first.

"Is there anyone you would like us to contact ma'am?" The elder man was speaking again.

"No. Thank you. My son will be here any minute now, and I'll be ok until then." Netty spoke with a lot more conviction than she felt. "Will I be informed if they catch the person that did this?" She asked.

"I promise you will be among the first to know," the elder man reassured her.

What a day, thought Netty as she watched them disappear from sight, *and it's only just begun!*
She decided to close up and go home, and hoped Razzy would be there. The market was already buzzing with the news that yesterday, Mark Pullman had been arrested for

Ashley's Stevenson's murder. It sent shockwaves through the stallholders and speculation was rife. Was he also responsible for the other two murders? Netty thought not, she was pretty sure that was Tony, and that it was also he who had killed Pauline. *Oh My God! Pauline!* It was incomprehensible!

Back in her flat, she knelt before her little shrine and poured out her grief. She wept until her eyes were sore, and her chest hurt from sobbing. Images of her sister floated into her mind and she deeply regretted her uncharitable thoughts towards her; she had always tried to do right by Netty, even if sometimes her actions had been misguided. Pauline had never been a demonstrative person, but Netty had never doubted that she was loved, and had loved her in return, even if she didn't always agree with her. Now she was gone, and a great empty chasm had opened in Netty's life. *Tony!* It must have been him, it was too much of a coincidence. Perhaps if Razzy hadn't turned up when he did, he would have killed her instead, or perhaps he would have killed them both. Razzy had been all for going to the police there and then, but cowardice had made Netty persuade him not to. "I don't think he'll be back," she had said, "and now he knows who I am, there won't be any point in killing anyone else. "Let's just see if he goes away."

So Razzy went out later that night to check on Tony's flat and see if he was still there. He was gone some time, and said that he had also checked the pub in case he was at work. He had seemed a little cagey, but Netty put it down to nerves. Where was he now? she wondered, just as the door to the flat opened, and she heard him go to the fridge, then open a can of beer, so he probably hadn't realised she was home. After a few minutes, she rose stiffly to her feet and went to join him. He was lying on the sofa with his eyes closed and a faint smile on his face, a can of lager in his hand. On the coffee table was a copy of this morning's Herald, the front page headline proclaimed…

THE CHESBURY STRANGLER IS DEAD!

Netty picked up the paper with trembling hands, and read the article. As she read, she realised that Razzy must, after all, have gone to the police the night before. She should have let him go earlier, and then perhaps Pauline would not have died. She had been a coward. Pauline would never have let things lie, she would have marched down to the police station and made her presence felt in no uncertain terms. 'A bit of an argument' – Netty could imagine that Pauline would not have succumbed without having her say. She had been a force to be reckoned with, and in the end, she had caused Tony to take his own life. Something in her demeanour must have stopped him mutilating her as he had his other victims. Even in her grief, she felt proud of her sister.

    She looked at Razzy, sleeping now, still with the smile on his face. She gently prized the beer can from his hand. Life would never be the same, but she had her son, and he had protected her. She had her business, the means to support them both, and, she admitted to herself with a pang of guilt, she now had her freedom.

THE END

Thank you for reading The Blindside.
I hope you enjoyed it.

I now have to begin work on the next offering.

As always, I welcome your feedback.
annie27965@gmail.com

Printed in Great Britain
by Amazon